SAVAGE NIGHT

Allan Guthrie

First published in Great Britain in 2008
by Polygon, an imprint of Birlinn Ltd

West Newington House
10 Newington Road
Edinburgh
EH9 1QS

9 8 7 6 5 4 3 2 1

www.birlinn.co.uk

ISBN 10: 1 84697 019 9
ISBN 13: 978 1 84697 019 1

British Library Cataloguing-in-Publication Data
A catalogue record for this book is available
on request from the British Library.

Typeset by Hewer Text UK Ltd, Edinburgh.
Printed and bound by
Clays Ltd, St Ives plc

PRAISE FOR ALLAN GUTHRIE

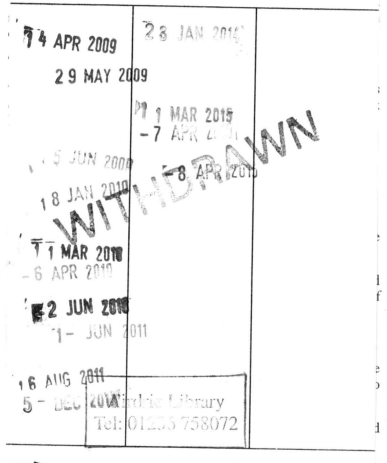

For Leblanc

SAVAGE NIGHT
10.30 P.M.
FRASER'S

WHEN HE OPENED his sitting room door, the last thing Fraser Savage expected to see was a corpse. Stuffed inside a stainless steel bathtub on a plastic sheet in the middle of the floor, the body was naked and clearly male, even though it was face down.

'Who the fuck is that?' Effie said.

Fraser shook his head slowly. The corpse had pale skin. Hairy buttocks. It was plump round the middle.

Holy fucking Christ, it couldn't be . . .

Fraser's toes and fingers started to prickle and his stomach cramped. The two pints he'd had earlier in the evening suddenly seemed like a lot more. And those three – or was it four? – lines of coke hadn't helped. Sweat rolled down his back. His nose was running too. He dabbed at his nostrils with the back of his hand.

'I think it might be Uncle Phil,' he said.

'Does he have any identifying features?' Effie asked. 'Tattoos? Scars?'

'I don't think so.'

He shivered. Not that he was cold. Felt like he'd puked his guts out and there was nothing left. Another shiver rippled through him.

Was it his uncle? Same waxy pale skin that ginger people have, same overall body shape.

But he'd never seen Uncle Phil naked. He might have identified him by his hair, that permanent ginger bed-head, but that wasn't an option. Maybe the corpse had ginger pubes. Although even that didn't mean it was Uncle Phil. There were plenty of other poor bastards with ginger pubes. Maybe the skin was excessively pale because of the blood loss and he wasn't ginger at all.

Fraser could turn him over, find out.

Yeah, right. He wasn't wrestling with that.

There was a good reason for the tub. There was a good reason Fraser felt sick. There was a good reason Fraser didn't want to turn him over.

Somebody had cut the poor bastard's head off.

And it was nowhere to be seen.

'DRINK THIS.'

He took the glass of vodka from Effie, the liquid sloshing around as his hand shook. Steadied it with his other hand and knocked it back. It burned his throat nicely. He gave her back the glass and she poured him another. He took it, drank it. Felt warmer now, less shivery, hands not so shaky.

Effie didn't appear fazed by the situation at all. Almost as if she was used to stumbling over corpses in her boyfriends' homes.

Not that he was her boyfriend, exactly. But they'd been getting along well and maybe something would have happened tonight. It certainly wouldn't now. A headless corpse was a major turn-off.

Jesus, he had to grow up.

Maturity, that's what it was. Fraser was twenty-five. Effie'd have to be around the thirty mark. He hadn't asked her, didn't want to risk screwing things up. Anyway, she'd had more experience than him, which is why she was so much more composed.

Although it was unlikely, however old she was, that she'd seen a naked, headless corpse before.

And yet, Fraser couldn't help but think of the way Effie had introduced herself when they first met. Wearing a two-tone orange blouse, open at the back, checked headscarf, sandals, almost a hippy thing going on. Said the cold didn't bother her, although her nipples suggested otherwise.

That was less than a week ago.

'Effie,' Fraser had said, shaking her hand, feeling her cool palm in his. 'Nice name. And what do you do?'

Her grin brought out tiny wrinkles round her eyes. 'I kill people,' she'd said.

Fraser grabbed her hand tighter, laughing. Played along with her. 'Like a mercenary or something?'

Effie squeezed his fingers hard, then slid hers out of his grip.

You just had to take one look at her to know she didn't have what it took to be a paid killer. She was no more than an inch over five foot.

But, Fraser wondered now, staring at the tub in his sitting room, what if it *was* true?

Shock. Had to be. Starting to suspect Effie was plain fucking crazy. She'd been at the pub with Fraser, so she couldn't have done it. Even if she was some kind of psychokiller. What the hell was he thinking? He should concentrate on more important questions.

Like, where the fuck was the head? And why would anybody want to run away with it? Jesus, maybe it was lying around somewhere. Under one of the chairs, or beneath a cushion or behind the curtain. Christ's sake.

Fraser didn't feel too good.

He was glad Simone wasn't here. She'd probably order him to get down on his hands and knees and start hunting for it.

'Want to take a closer look?' Effie said.

She was as bad as Simone.

Fraser found himself stepping towards the tub. Swaying as he walked, as if he was drunk. Hadn't had much, though. Just those pints and the neat vodkas Effie'd given him.

The plastic sheet scraped underfoot. He bent over the body, peered down at the neck. Ragged skin and gristle. He looked away. Straight at the inch or so of dark liquid clotting in the bottom of the tub. A bloodbath – yep, that's exactly what it was.

And the smell: sharp and raw. His stomach muscles tightened, cheeks puffed, but somehow he held his dinner down. Amazing he could smell anything, the way his nose was streaming. He wiped it with the back of his hand, beyond caring what Effie would think.

He stepped back from the tub shaky, a bit fuzzy headed, but okay. Shit, yeah.

The corpse's legs were bent at the knee, flopped sideways. Fraser couldn't remember seeing the soles of Uncle Phil's feet before. They were white and tender looking. It felt wrong that they were exposed like this. He shouldn't be staring at them.

Effie said, 'Recognise that?'

Fraser followed her gaze towards the corpse's hand, twisted behind his back. He wasn't sure what she meant.

'The ring,' she said.

Of course. If Fraser got a close-up of that ugly monstrosity, he could be sure, right enough. But he couldn't tell with the hand lying palm-up like that.

'Go on,' Effie said. 'Take a good look.'

Fraser didn't move.

Effie strode over to the tub, grabbed the hand, turned it over, held it out. She bent the ring finger towards Fraser.

No doubt about it. Uncle Phil's silver Viking longboat ring.

Effie raised her eyebrows.

Fraser tried to speak. Nodded instead.

Effie dropped Uncle Phil's hand and said, 'I'll call the police.'

FRASER WATCHED HER step over to the table, pick up the phone, dial. Calm in a crisis. Every bit as capable as Simone. Fraser didn't feel calm or capable.

If he'd been alone, he'd be shouting fit to rip the lining from his throat by now. If he could summon up the energy. That's what he wanted to do. Open his mouth and yell and yell and yell. And throw up and throw up and throw up. Then probably yell some more, throw up some more. Or just fall asleep.

Anything, as long as this would all go away.

Another line of coke might do the trick.

He stuck his hand in his pocket, but took it out again when Effie said, 'Police.'

He thought she was warning him, but she was speaking into the phone. Made him think, though. Probably not the best time for him to indulge in any dodgy habits. He listened as she explained what had happened. Gave the cops the address.

Impressive. Memory like a bank vault.

She'd only been here once before. All over him when they'd arrived – clinging to him as he punched in the alarm code – but she'd grown more distant as the night went on. Not that it went on that long. Called herself a taxi after a couple of drinks. Fraser was probably coming on too strong.

But she wouldn't be here now if there wasn't some hope. Thing was, he fancied the pants off her, but he liked her a lot, too. Anyway, he suspected he was creating a bad impression right now, one that wasn't hugely attractive, forgetting Uncle Phil for a minute. Right now, he'd settle for not throwing up or pissing himself.

He wiped his nose again, breathed deeply through his mouth, and immediately wished he hadn't. He wasn't ready for the taste that clung to his tongue, his lips, his teeth. Like he'd just sucked a penny. He glanced over at Effie, who shrugged, spoke into the phone again.

Fraser felt like crying. Not that he felt sad, exactly. Come to think of it, he could just as easily break into a fit of giggles. Really fucking odd. Like he'd taken a fistful of pills and was buzzing and sloppy drunk at the same time. Could be the coke, but it was a feeling he didn't recognise.

He was glowing under his skin.

What he really wanted was for Effie to hold him, stroke his hair while he fell asleep. That'd be nice.

THE NIGHT HE met Effie, Fraser had been doped to the eyeballs – so much so that all the beer he'd drunk wasn't having any effect – but even straight, Effie would have made him laugh his balls off. She had something about her. An air, a friendly face, a charm, a genuine smile. And that dark humour you either loved or hated.

Fraser loved it.

At first he decided to use Effie to make Simone jealous. Simone was Fraser's on/off girlfriend. She was also Worm's wife. Fraser had never slept with a married woman before, and it was fun, and a little dangerous. Anyway, his plan wasn't working. Simone didn't pay them any attention and before long Fraser was having a good time chatting to Effie and didn't care if Simone noticed.

'Come with me,' Fraser had said an hour or so later, grabbing Effie's arm. 'I want to show you something.'

He steered her towards the back door of the house, weaving through the throng along the way, careful not to spill his beer. Through the lobby. Into the kitchen.

'How do you know Worm and Simone?' he asked Effie.

'I don't,' she said. 'I gate-crashed. How about you?'

'Friends of my Uncle Phil. I'd introduce you but he'd embarrass me.'

'He's here?'

'The fat, ginger guy sinking beers like there's no tomorrow.'

'Maybe there isn't,' she said, shrugging. 'I can see the family resemblance.'

'Thanks.' He grinned.

'My pleasure.'

'What *do* you do?' Fraser asked as they jostled past a stoned couple all tangled up in each other in the doorway. 'You never told me.'

'I did.'

'That's right.' She killed people. Fraser laughed. Laughed till his eyelids were heavy with tears. It wasn't that funny, but he'd started and couldn't stop.

Effie moved off.

He followed, wiping his eyes. 'Oops,' he said as he tripped. She caught him. Lightning reflexes. A killer's reflexes.

He laughed again but managed to control himself before it turned into another fit of giggles. Didn't want to get hysterical. Anyway, if it came to a square go, he could take her easy.

'What's so funny?' she asked.

'I love your . . . style.' He smiled. Her eyes widened and she smiled too. He chinked his beer bottle against hers. 'I like you, Effie,' he said.

'I like you too,' she said. 'What did you want to show me?'

He wrapped his arm round her waist and dragged her to the end of the garden. There was a shed at the back. An ordinary shed. A common shed. A common or garden shed. Ha! 'Whoo.' His legs nearly gave out there. Stumble bumble. Maybe the drink was having an effect after all. About bloody time.

'Here.' He stopped. The shed was padlocked. He rattled the lock.

He handed his beer to her, raised a forefinger. Then dipped his hand into his pocket and rummaged around. Found his keys. Ran his fingers through them, found the little brass fucker.

Effie said, 'I won't ask why you have a key for Worm's shed.'

Fraser nodded, put his fingers to his lips, licked them. They tasted of beer. Put the key in the slot. Or tried to. Wasn't as easy as it looked. It was dark and the slot was tiny and he was pissed as a fart.

Effie placed the beer on the ground, took the key from him. Opened the padlock. And then pressed her palm against the door.

'After you,' Fraser said.

'After you,' Effie said.

And she wouldn't budge. So he didn't budge either.

'You're a bumshite, Fraser,' she said. 'What do you want me to see?'

'Just step inside.'

'I don't think so.'

'Okay,' he said. 'If you're scared of the dark, I'll go first.' He stepped inside the shed, switched on the light. Nice touch, the outside electricity. He'd been impressed when Simone had shown him. 'That better?'

Effie moved into the doorway, keeping the door open.

Fraser said, 'Well?' cause her face was a blank.

'What am I looking at?'

These hippy-killer-types, you had to spell everything out. 'These,' he said, pointing at the rows of swords hanging on the walls. All sorts. He was no expert, and neither was Simone, but there were a couple of dozen types on display, from the medieval to the modern. Some decorative, some kept razor-sharp by Worm. Simone said it gave him something to do when he couldn't sleep at night.

Fraser reached up, took one off the wall. 'This,' he said, unsheathing it, 'is Japanese.' He held it, two-handed, between himself and Effie. Nice weight. Beautiful curved blade. 'Run your finger over that, you'll cut it off.' Made his stomach flutter just thinking of the damage this baby could do.

Effie looked but didn't react.

'Well?'

'Looks very nice,' she said. 'Does Worm fence or something?'

'Nope. He just collects them. A real fucking waste.'

What he didn't tell her was that he'd mentioned to Uncle Phil that he was thinking of stealing them, selling them on eBay, imagining that Phil would be up for making a quick buck, but Phil had clipped him round the ear and told him not to be a cunt.

'We better go, then,' Fraser said, slotting the sword back in its sheath, carefully hanging it on the wall. He noticed a gap a couple of rows along. Either Worm had a sword in the house, or Uncle Phil had pulled a fast one without telling Fraser. He'd keep an eye on the new eBay listings. 'Sure you don't want one?' he asked Effie. 'We could smuggle one out. Killer like you is always going to need another weapon, right?'

'A killer like me,' Effie said, 'likes to use something that can't be traced. You want to steal me something, a length of clothesline would be just fine.'

FRASER STARED AT the headless body in the tub. Hard as he tried, he couldn't drag his eyes away from it.

A human without a head. Triggered some kind of primeval fear of your brain being separated from the rest of your body.

Or was it that having no head made you appear to be more dead than you would otherwise?

He was having a hard time seeing that thing as Uncle Phil. Come to think of it, he was having a hard time seeing. His eyelids didn't want to stay open.

'Why do you –?' Fraser said, before the rest of his sentence was choked off.

Felt at first like his collar was buttoned too tight. But he was wearing a t-shirt, so it couldn't be that. Then a sudden jerk and a shout from Effie and something crushing his windpipe. It was like the time when he was a kid, messing around with his pal, Ian. Playing at strangling each other. Seeing how far they could go.

His hands flew to his neck, feeling for the thing that was digging into his throat.

Effie said, 'Relax,' and grunted in a very unlady-like manner.

What the fuck was she doing? Trying to get this thing off him?

Oh, he knew.

He had always known.

Oh, fuck, no he hadn't. He just wanted to be right, even now. It was fine to be right after the event, but he hadn't fucking known, otherwise he wouldn't have let the bitch within spitting distance.

She was strangling him. And it wasn't going to be like Ian. No chance she'd let go, finally, say, 'Nearly killed you. Na na na-na na.'

Still, she was only a woman. A small one, at that.

Fraser swiped behind his back with his hand. Smacked something. But there was no power in it. Like he was moving underwater. Resulted only in the cord – or whatever it was – tightening round his neck.

A fucking clothesline. She'd told him that's what she'd use.

His head felt like somebody'd blocked up his nose and mouth and was pumping air through a hole in the top of his skull.

He wheezed.

Eyes back to the tub. To the body. Fraser didn't want to admit it to himself, but there was every chance he'd be joining Uncle Phil soon.

Fraser's cheeks puffed out. Behind his eyes, blood pounded and surged and bubbled against the inside of his skin. He tried again to dig his fingers into the clothesline, but it had sunk in too deep. And he was too weak to prise Effie's fingers off the cord.

Why the fuck was she doing this?

Fraser's remaining strength drained out of him. He wasn't going to hold out. She had been playing him all along.

He made a last attempt to breathe. Sucked in nothing. Couldn't even make a noise.

A figure appeared in the kitchen doorway, wearing only a pair of disposable yellow gloves, clutching a carrier bag in one hand, a lit cigarette and a hacksaw in the other. Smudges of red tangled the hairs on his bare thighs, spattered his clear plastic booties.

The stranger's eyes widened as if he hadn't expected to see Fraser staring at him. His head tilted to the side. Hands covered his crotch.

Careful with the hacksaw, pal.

Fuck that. This was the fucker who'd killed Uncle Phil. Not that Fraser could do anything about it now.

Fraser's eyes closed. He struggled to open them, finally raising his lids enough to see that the naked murderer had gone.

Tears burned tracks down Fraser's cheeks. He wasn't going to see Dad again. Off on some trip, hadn't seen him in ages. Never see his arsehole little brother again either. Never see his granny again.

Ringing in his ears. Metallic taste in his mouth. He licked his lip, spat. His nose was bleeding. Fucking brilliant.

Had to be Worm who was behind this. The bastard must have found out that Fraser had been sleeping with Simone. She was a great fuck but she wasn't worth dying for. Still, Fraser hoped she was okay, that Worm wasn't planning some kind of fucked-up revenge for her too. Was somebody strangling her this very minute? Was Worm doing it himself? Would he cut her head off too?

But why would Worm want Uncle Phil dead?

Fraser's vision blackened at the edges. In the middle, spots and bars of colours hovered and drifted: livid purple and burnt orange and tangerine and scorched brown and lime green.

His eyes closed once more and this time he knew they'd never open again.

PRELUDE TO A SAVAGE NIGHT: THE SAVAGES

ST ANDREW'S BUS station. Pretty small for a city the size of Edinburgh. Which was a good thing. A dozen or so lanes, or stances as they were called. Appropriate, really, since a stance was what you adopted when you were about to fight, and Tommy Savage was in a fighting mood.

It wasn't going to be a physical battle, though. No fists, or knives. Tommy didn't approve of that. No, this was a battle of minds. Just so long as Phil kept his eyes peeled and didn't get drunk and fall asleep or something equally stupid, then Tommy's plan should work.

Tommy closed the locker door, pocketed the key. He was going to follow the instructions to the letter.

He turned towards the exit. After a couple of steps, the key felt strangely loose in his pocket. He imagined the consequences of losing it, and dug it out of his pocket and clasped it in his hand. Held it tight enough for his palm to hurt as he strode past the seat where Phil was perched, pretending to read a magazine. Or maybe he was actually reading it. Riveted by the cartoons, no doubt. At least he was awake. And sober, although he was swigging from a can of lager.

Tommy ought to swipe it from him to make sure he *stayed* awake, but he walked past, spotting three more cans on the seat as he did so. Phil kept his colourful head buried in his paper. Tommy was glad those genes had bypassed *him*, although it'd look a lot better if Phil got it cut properly, or put a comb through it occasionally.

Anyway, everything was as it should be. No eye contact, no sign that they knew each other. If anybody was watching, they'd believe Tommy was alone.

Nothing for it. He'd had to place his trust in Phil. Tommy was hard on him sometimes, but only because he'd turned into a slob. But if you couldn't trust your own brother, that said a lot about the kind of person you were.

Tommy's instructions were to grab a taxi and head for an address in the west of the city.

Onwards and upwards, then. Up the escalator and out of the station.

The outside air hit him hard. It had grown chilly in the last hour. Felt like icy hands clasping his cheeks. He pulled his coat tighter around him. He ought to do up the zip but he didn't like wearing a zipped-up coat. It was like wearing a bag over your left shoulder. Plain wrong. But try explaining that to somebody (and he had), and you got nothing but strange looks. He kept his coat open, stuffed his hands in the pockets cause that's how he liked it.

Could feel his stomach rumbling through the lining. He hadn't been able to eat all day. Any stress and his stomach was always the first thing to go.

In Amsterdam, last month, for a few days, business trip – got a nice sale, too – Tommy'd been unable to eat a thing for twenty-four hours. Made him wonder how he hadn't succumbed to stomach ulcers over the years. Although, maybe he had. Maybe it was the ulcers that were burning in his stomach right now.

He'd had a financially comfortable existence for a long time. Prospered in a dangerous business for a few years without getting hurt and then got out of it as soon as he'd made enough to invest. He'd been lucky. Dad always said you couldn't go wrong if you bought property. Not that Dad had ever owned so much as a single brick himself, but that's where Tommy'd ploughed all his cash. And made a fucking packet.

But his existence wasn't comfortable any longer.

Not since the arrival of Mr Smith.

A TELEPHONE CALL had kicked it off. Tommy was at home in his office, which was where he preferred to work. He picked up the phone, already annoyed at being disturbed, and heard: 'Is that Tommy Savage?'

'Yeah. What do you want, I'm busy?'

'Now that would be telling.'

'So tell.'

'Well, Tommy. I want your arse.'

'Huh?' Tommy wondered if he'd heard right. 'You want what?'

'Your arse. It's mine.'

Little fucking creep. Tommy didn't know how he could tell that the guy on the other end of the phone was little. But he heard the voice and pictured a little man.

Whatever the creep's size, Tommy'd had a good day up to that point. Taken Jordan to school in the morning, did a couple of hours work, then popped out for coffee and got talking to an Italian divorcee called Bella. She was in her late thirties, from *Napoli*, no kids, living in Edinburgh. She liked Blues music, wine, walking and football. He liked her accent, her smile, the way her sweater curved.

They'd exchanged phone numbers. Which was promising. He hadn't had a girlfriend since Hannah and caution was now a habit. Tommy didn't want somebody else 'falling out of love' with him. Fraser was grown up when Tommy and his mother split, but Jordan was only nine at the time. She wanted to take him to South Africa with her. With her and her new boyfriend, Russell.

Dirty divorce, filthy custody battle. But Tommy'd won. She couldn't prove any of her allegations, and he could. She wasn't exactly stable and medical records showed just how fucked up she was. It helped that Jordan didn't want to leave Edinburgh. And that he hated Russell.

But right up to the day she'd got on the flight, Tommy didn't think Hannah would leave.

Anyway, whether it was Bella from Napoli or because the sun was shining, he was in a good mood so he didn't hang up, or swear when the caller said he wanted Tommy's arse.

Instead, he made a joke of it. 'Sorry, I'm spoken for.'

'Witty.' Same little voice. 'I want you to pay.'

Tommy wasn't entirely sure how to reply to that. 'Pay what?'

'You mean, pay *for* what?'

'I do?'

'You will pay for what you've done.'

Very dramatic. The guy sounded like he was reading the words from a script. 'Oh, I see,' Tommy said. 'And how will I pay?'

'With money.'

This guy was thick as mince. Made Phil seem like a brain surgeon, and that took some doing. 'So I'll pay by paying,' Tommy said. 'Is that right?'

'Don't be fucking smart. You know you have to pay.'

He had no idea what the fuck the creep was talking about. He said so. Then added, 'Who are you?'

'You can call me Mr Smith,' the guy said. 'You'll be hearing from me again.' He hung up.

It had to be a crank call. Tommy put it out of his mind. Mostly.

For a couple of days, life went back to normal. And he'd pretty much forgotten about Mr Smith. But sure enough, the bastard called again.

'I was thinking about how best to start the ball rolling,' he said.

No introduction, but Tommy recognised the voice immediately. 'Fuck, no, not you again.'

'Fuck, yes, me again. We should meet.'

Tommy walked over to the door of his office, closed it. 'Why should we do that?'

'Cause I want to show you how serious I am.'

'About what?'

'Making you pay.'

'Christ's sake. For what?'

Smith laughed.

Tommy sat down at his desk and stared at the computer screen, randomly clicking on various properties he'd been looking at on the ESPC website. Smith carried on laughing. After an age, he stopped and Tommy closed his web browser and said, 'You finished? Listen to me. I don't want to meet you. I have nothing to say to you.'

'But I have quite a bit to say to you,' Smith said.

A FRENCH CAFÉ off Princes Street. Tommy breathed in the smell of coffee and steamed mussels while he waited for Smith.

Tommy ordered an *espresso*, wanted to be wide awake. Smith was going to get his full attention.

A diner arrived, a small bald guy. Maybe this was his lunch guest. Or host. Although he doubted they'd be eating much, let alone squabbling over who was going to pay the bill. But the bald guy waved to a woman at a nearby table and went to join her.

Smith arrived ten minutes late. He didn't look at all like Tommy had imagined. The man who gangled towards

Tommy's table, slight swagger to his walk, was as tall as Tommy, maybe had an inch on him, which made him well over six foot. Skinny, clothes hanging off him. But the thing that made him stand out was that he was wearing a black ski mask. He'd caused a visible tremor as he walked through the restaurant. Diners stopped eating to stare. A couple of waiters paused to look at him.

Tommy wondered what the protocol was for dealing with a patron in a ski mask. Especially one who wasn't armed, or causing any trouble. At least, no trouble as yet.

Wasn't against the law to wear a ski mask, was it?

Smith shoved his tongue out through the mouthhole, let it stay there as he stared down at Tommy. He wasn't being rude, just seemed to be his habit to stick his tongue out while he was thinking. Couple of seconds later, he held out his hand, uncovering a bracelet of barbed wire tattooed on his wrist. Looked like a prison job.

Tommy ignored the outstretched hand, noticed that in the other one Smith clutched a large Poundstretcher carrier bag.

'Glad you could make it,' Smith said, his tongue finally sliding back home and his tattooed hand tucking back into his pocket.

Tommy tilted his head.

Smith said, 'Nobody eating rare steak, is there?'

Tommy said, 'I beg your pardon?'

'Look around. Tell me if anybody's eating rare steak.'

Tommy did as requested. Faced Smith again. Shook his head.

'Okay, then.' Smith sat down opposite Tommy, bent to take something out of his carrier bag. A book. A large one. He shunted a sturdy green-and-white-dotted vase housing a single dried flower out of the way, and dumped the book on the table hard enough to make Tommy's teaspoon rattle.

A waiter approached the table. A couple of other waiters stood behind their colleague, a few feet away. The waiter looked at Tommy. Tommy gave him nothing. 'Sir,' the waiter said to Smith.

Smith said, 'Give me a minute.'

The waiter didn't move. He cleared his throat. 'Sir.'

'I said, give me a minute. I'm not ready to order.'

The waiter said, 'Can I ask you to remove your . . . hat?'

'You can ask,' Smith said, dark brown eyes staring at Tommy through the peepholes in the ski mask. 'But if I did, you wouldn't like what you'd see.'

'I'm sure, sir, it'll be fine.'

'I'm sure,' Smith said, 'that it won't. Come here.' He beckoned the waiter closer. Whispered something in his ear.

The waiter chewed his lower lip, then said, 'Certainly, sir. I understand.'

'And, son,' Smith said. 'Anybody orders a rare steak, let me know.'

The waiter looked at him, nodded.

Smith reached into his pocket, gave the waiter a couple of coins.

'Thank you, sir,' the waiter said. He walked off, indicating by a subtle blend of gestures and whispers to his colleagues that they should get back to work, leave Smith alone, he was harmless. Tommy wondered why the fuck Smith was so interested in steak.

One by one, the other guests returned to their food, occasionally sneaking glances over at Smith and Tommy. But now they seemed reassured that Smith didn't carry a threat. The waiter had checked him out. The new arrival was an eccentric, a man who felt the cold more than most. Tommy didn't know what they were thinking, but that's what was going through his head.

'What did you say to the waiter?' he asked Smith.

'Never you fucking mind.' Smith tapped the book on the table. 'To business.'

Tommy said, 'A phone book. Very kind of you to bring me a present. I'm afraid I don't have one for you.'

'I really hate mouthy cunts like you.' Smith flicked through the book. Opened it. He turned the book round to face Tommy. 'Fifth name from the bottom,' Smith gestured with an outstretched palm. 'Go on. Look at it.'

Tommy played along. 'Which page?'

Smith swivelled the book round. Looked at it. Swivelled it back again. 'Left.'

Tommy let his gaze travel up from the bottom. Counted five lines. Mr E McCracken. 'Never heard of him.'

'You will.' Smith reached into his bag. Produced a pen. A pink marker. 'Mark it.' He handed Tommy the pen.

Tommy looked at the phone book. Looked at the pen. Looked at Smith. And drew a line through the name and address in Sleigh Gardens. The pen wasn't a marker, it was a highlighter.

'All the way along,' Smith said.

Tommy shrugged. Whatever made the fool happy. He rubbed the nib over the rest of the line, highlighting the phone number too.

Smith fished around in his bag again, tongue poking through the ski mask as he concentrated, and surfaced with a notepad and a biro. He handed them to Tommy. 'Write down the name and address, please.'

'Why?'

'Cause I want you to remember them.'

'I've got this.' He showed Smith the telephone directory.

'Nope.' Smith took it from him. 'I've got it.' He held it so Tommy could see the address. 'Now write it down.'

'What's the point of all this?' Smith didn't answer, so Tommy scribbled down McCracken's details. Handed the notepad back to Smith.

'That's yours,' Smith said, bagging the phone book. 'You've done well, Tommy. Don't lose that name and address. I'll be in touch.'

Tommy could hardly wait.

Smith got up and left without another word. Tommy looked at the notepad, at the name and address that meant sweet fuck all to him.

He called over the waiter, the one whose ear Smith had whispered into. 'The guy with the ski mask,' Tommy said. 'What did he say to you?'

'You don't know?' The waiter bent over. 'He wasn't your friend?'

'Just some guy I was meeting for lunch.'

The waiter looked at the table, repositioned the vase in the middle. He said, 'You want to eat?'

'I'm not that hungry, thanks.'

'More coffee?'

'Just tell me what he said.'

The waiter clasped his hands together. 'His face,' he said. 'He said it was horribly disfigured. He was the victim of an acid attack. The sight of it, he said, would put the other diners off their food.'

A likely story.

Tommy nodded and when the waiter went away, ripped off the page from the notepad and stuck it in his pocket.

THE FOLLOWING DAY Tommy got another call. Smith said, 'Hope you still have that name and address.' He didn't wait for an answer. 'Buy a *Scotsman*,' he said. 'Turn to page four.'

For a while afterwards, Tommy pottered about on his home office computer, deliberately ignoring Smith's instructions. He wasn't going to buy a newspaper just because some skinny fuck with a whiny voice and a cheap ski mask told him to. But after an hour or so, Tommy was fidgeting so much, and so unable to concentrate, that he rescued the crumpled piece of paper from his desk drawer. Not sure why, cause he hadn't forgotten the name. McCracken.

Tommy went down to the corner shop and bought a paper, resisting the urge to look at it until he was back in his office.

Page four had three stories, but the one his eye was drawn to first was the one Smith wanted him to see. It read:

KILLER ON THE LOOSE

Police said today that they had no clues as to the killer of Eric McCracken. The unmarried thirty-six-year-old was brutally murdered last night in Lochend Park as he jogged in the shadow of Easter Road football stadium. Mr McCracken, manager of the St Bernard's wing of the Meredith House Nursing Home on Parker Road West, was strangled to death with a length of clothesline left behind at the scene by the killer.

A police spokesman revealed that at present they had no suspects, and there was apparently no motive for the murder. Mr McCracken seemed to be well-liked and had no known enemies. The police have asked that anybody who might have seen or heard anything suspicious in the neighbourhood last night should contact them as a matter of the utmost urgency.

Tommy swallowed and his throat was so dry it hurt.

Eric McCracken was alive yesterday lunchtime. And Smith had known he was going to die. Which could only mean that Smith had killed him.

Fuck, no. There had to be some other explanation. But Tommy couldn't think of one.

On cue, the phone rang.

'Well?' Smith said.

His voice no longer sounded whiny. Maybe Tommy was getting used to it. 'Why did you have to do that?' Tommy asked.

'Demonstration.'

'Of what?'

'What I'm capable of.'

Tommy didn't want to think too hard about that. 'What exactly do you want?' he said.

'I told you that already. You're going to have to start paying attention.'

Tommy said, 'For Christ's sake, tell me what the fuck you want.'

'You need to control your temper. It could get you into trouble.' Silence. Then: 'Let's start with fifty grand.'

'I don't have that kind of money.'

'Don't bother with your shite, pal.'

'It's true. It's fucking *true*.' Damn, it was such a fucking lie.

'Jordan's at his brother's, right?' Smith said. 'Hope he's safe there. Wouldn't want Fraser dosing him up with cocaine.'

How did Smith know about that? The muscles round Tommy's mouth tensed, started to quiver. But, fuck it, Fraser's coke problem was hardly the best kept secret in the world.

'Nice lads,' Smith said. 'Fraser takes after you. And Jordan's got your mother's eyes.'

Tommy shouted down the phone: 'You go anywhere near my family and I swear to God –'

'What did I tell you about that temper?'

Tommy gulped air, saying nothing, a buzzing in his temples.

'Better,' Smith said. 'Speaking of your mother, very nice arse on her. For her age.'

'You sick fuck.' It took a lot to provoke Tommy, but Smith was doing a fucking great job. Tommy felt a familiar burning sensation in his stomach. He squeezed the receiver. His mother was seventy-fucking-one, for Christ's sake.

'You're in control here,' Smith said. 'Your choice. Fifty grand.'

Tommy forced himself to breathe slowly. 'If I refuse?'

Smith made a strangled sound which Tommy guessed was a laugh and then said, 'Just think about your children, Tommy.'

Afterwards Tommy had considered going to the police, but Smith had proved with McCracken that he wasn't fucking about. Before long, he decided to tell Phil about it. Nothing else for it. Anybody else in the family would have freaked and you couldn't blame them. But Phil just said, 'No problem. We'll sort this Smith cunt out in no time.'

Which is why Phil was lurking back at the bus station, hoping he'd get an ID on Smith – no reason for him to be wearing his ski mask again. If they could ID the fucker, steps could be taken to ensure he didn't cause any more trouble.

IT WAS WARM inside the taxi and it smelled of cheap air freshener and something sweet that might have been cannabis.

Tommy had been told to leave the money in a locker at the bus station, flag down a taxi and deliver the key to a pub.

And that's exactly what he was doing.

The driver eyeballed him in the rearview. Big bastard, dark shadows under his eyes. 'Youuptherevisiting?'

He had a strange accent. Transatlantic Scots. And he spoke ridiculously fast.

Then, when Tommy realised what he'd been asked, he couldn't be bothered explaining that he wasn't 'up' from anywhere, and neither was he visiting. Let the driver assume what he wanted.

'I'm from Philadelphia originally,' the driver said. Waited for a reply, but didn't get one and carried on anyway: 'Name's Duane Shweerski. Came over here couple years ago. Made some porn movies. The work dried up.' Pause. 'Drive cabs now.'

You don't fucking say.

Tommy smiled, nodded.

Shweerski didn't need any encouragement, though. Rattled on at length, glancing in the mirror every now and again, tapping a fingernail against his chin as he talked. Only stopped when he had to change gear.

He came to the end of his monologue, paused for a second or two to catch his breath, and said, 'Going out at the weekend?'

'What's it to you?' Tommy said.

Shweerski frowned. He was tapping his chin with a couple of fingertips now. 'Set up?'

Tommy was tempted to ask him to pull over, cause he wasn't in the mood for this shit. What the fuck did he mean by 'set up'? Was he warning Tommy? How could he know it was a set-up? Did he know about the money Tommy had just deposited in the locker? Did he know Smith? Was he a plant, idling outside the bus station in his taxi waiting for Tommy to appear? Was he telling Tommy it was a set-up because he was part of Smith's operation and wanted to rub it in?

'The fuck're you on about?' Tommy's stomach rumbled. He adjusted his coat to smother the sound.

Shweerski said, 'Got your bits and bobs?' And winked.

Tommy stared at him in the mirror.

'All your gear?'

Ah, *gear*. That was why he was being so pushy. Tommy leaned back, let his shoulders drop. 'I don't do drugs,' he said.

'Yeah?' Shweerski was quiet while he changed lanes. Didn't take long. He was back again, saying, 'Why not, buddy?'

Jesus Christ. This guy had a lot in common with Smith. Maybe he *was* Smith. Nah, Shweerski was twice the width of Smith and his accent was too weird to be put on. 'What's it to you?' Tommy said.

'Hey, chill the fuck out. Making conversation here, aye, yo? Fuck's sake. No need to be a motherfucker. Offering to help you out, 's all. You don't want my help, no need to get all nasty and like shit.'

The arse-faced bastard had called Tommy a motherfucker. In days gone by Tommy would have walloped him for that. In fact, he wouldn't have, much as he might have liked to. He didn't do violence. Phil would have, though, if he'd overheard. Bided his time, paid Shweerski a visit at home, armed with a length of pipe. But even in the old days, Tommy tried to behave like a civilised human being. Just cause he was involved in the occasional illegal activity didn't mean he had no morals.

'Can't tempt you with a wee rock?' Shweerski said. 'Got it right under the seat here.' He bent down to fetch it, one hand on the wheel.

The car swerved.

'Watch the road,' Tommy said.

'*No problemo.* I can drive round Edinburgh like totally blindfolded, ken.' He sat upright, bag in hand, held it out to the side for Tommy to see.

Maybe the accent *was* phoney. If he wasn't such a prick, Tommy might have suspected he was an undercover cop. Come to think of it, the one didn't necessarily preclude the other. Tommy said, 'Please just fucking drive.'

'Going,' Shweerski said, 'going,' he said again. 'Last chance.' He shook the bag.

'What makes you think I won't report you to the police?' Tommy said.

'You're a decent guy.'

Had he just forgotten he'd called Tommy a motherfucker?

'And I'm not doing any harm,' Shweerski continued. 'Why would you report me?'

'Cause you're annoying the tits off me.'

'Sorry about that. Just providing a community service.'

'And what if I'm not 'a decent guy'? What if you've got me all wrong? Could be I think you're a scumbag for selling drugs.'

Shweerski looked at him in the rearview. 'Like you're some law-abiding do-gooder? Salvation Army in disguise? Hiding a tambourine under your jacket?'

'Maybe I'm an undercover cop.'

'You ain't that, dude.' He laughed.

'How can you be sure?'

'If you were a cop you'd be one of my best customers.'

Tommy guessed the guy was blagging. Maybe the odd cop scored some coke occasionally. Maybe. Anyway, perhaps now Shweerski would shut up.

He did. For a couple of minutes. Then: 'Hey, I've got some BetaBlockers. You ever tried them? Help you chill, dude. Get rid of some of that anger.'

'PULL OVER,' TOMMY said. For the last five minutes his driver had been quiet, thank Christ. Tommy had finally got through to him that he wasn't going to buy any of his vast array of drugs, no matter how much quality gear he was missing or what kind of give-away prices were being offered.

Shweerski eased to a stop, kept the engine running. 'That's eight pounds –'

'I'm not getting out.'

'You're not?'

'Nope.'

Maybe Tommy had spoken too soon and the fucker'd be back with the hard sell again.

But, no. Shweerski said, 'So, we're just going to sit here and let the meter run?'

'Yep.'

'Your dollar.'

Tommy almost corrected him. Instead, he said, 'That's right.'

A pause. 'How long we going to sit here?'

'I don't know.'

Another pause. 'Mind if I put on a CD, then?'

'Be my guest.'

Flecks of rain streaked the passenger window, showering the sticky guts of a dead insect. Tommy looked up into the greying sky and watched a submarine-shaped raincloud drift along.

Smith had given him a residential address in the west of the city, not far from Murrayfield, and all Tommy could do for now was wait for his phone to ring.

He felt relaxed for the first time all evening. Then Shweerski started to sing along with Michael Bolton.

Seven long minutes later, the call finally came.

Smith said, 'Pay the driver and get out. I'll ring back in a while,' and hung up.

Tommy did as he was told.

The taxi drove away, Shweerski muttering to himself, no doubt pissed off he hadn't got a tip.

Tommy stared at his mobile. How long was 'a while'? He wiped a couple of raindrops off the display with the fleshy part of his palm, his fist still curled around the locker key. His palm was hot and sticky, the back of his hand cold.

He thought about calling Phil, see how things were going back at the bus station, but it'd be just his luck if Smith phoned whilst he was on the other call. Anyway, Phil wouldn't have anything to report yet cause Smith didn't have the key.

Tommy pulled up his collar. The clouds didn't look too fierce. Just a light shower, hopefully. He'd survive.

By the time Smith called, the rain had stopped and pale sunlight was squeezing through gaps in a much gentler sky. Smith went straight into his spiel: 'Follow the road up the hill. At the top, take a left. Halfway along, you'll find a hotel. Go into the bar. The lounge bar. Buy a pint, then go to the toilet. It's a single cubicle. Lift the top off the cistern, and drop the key into it. Then go back out into the bar. Stay there until I tell you to leave. If you leave early, or go back to the bus station, I'll know. Be smart and do what you're told.'

TOMMY WAS THE third customer in the pub.

The other two were a morose-looking pair seated at opposite ends of the bar. One wore glasses, or rather, he didn't, cause he'd taken them off and was playing with the leg, trying to tighten the screw with his thumbnail. The other guy wore a suit, breathed through his nose, made a whistling sound while he did so.

Tommy took up a position between them, and they all stared into their drinks, ignoring one another.

After a few sips, Tommy slid off his stool and went to the gents. It was exactly as Smith had described. Tommy lifted the cistern lid. It was heavy and very cold. He dropped the key into the water inside.

He replaced the lid and sat down for a bit. He'd just put fifty grand in a locker and was giving away the key. To some fucking fool called Smith.

Then he remembered Eric McCracken.

And wondered if he was doing the right thing in trying to outsmart Smith. Maybe he should call Phil, tell him to get out of there. But, shit, what harm could come of Phil watching the locker? And Phil could handle himself.

Unless he'd drunk himself into a stupor.

Tommy dug out his mobile. Couple of rings, then Phil picked up. 'Anything happening?' Tommy said.

Phil burped. 'Sitting here freezing my balls off. Wouldn't think it was almost April.'

'Maybe you shouldn't be drinking.'

'It's cold, Tommy. Whether I'm knocking back a few or not.'

'Move away from the door, then.'

'Can't. Everywhere you go, there are doors.'

'Only on one side, though.'

'Yeah. Where the seats are.'

'So stand up.'

'Thought I was supposed to be inconspicuous.'

'Well, you would be.'

'Nope. I need to sit down. Even if it's colder than Granny's tit.'

'Granny's dead.'

'Exactly.'

'I'll call you later.'

Tommy went back to the bar to wait for the next phone call from Smith. The two customers from earlier were still there. The barman busied himself washing glasses, running a cloth over the counter, dusting the telephone. Quiet night. Probably always a quiet night here. Tommy took long swallows of cheap lager, tasting the bitterness of the hops on the back of his tongue, thinking how much he'd have loved to be where Phil was right now.

After ten minutes or so Tommy's phone rang.

'Done?' Smith asked.

'Done.'

'Order a taxi and clear off.'

Tommy said, 'I'll walk.'

'You'll get a fucking taxi.'

'What's the harm in walking?' Tommy felt his fellow drinkers' eyes on him and lowered his voice. 'The rain's off. I could use some fresh air.'

'Do what you're told. Get a taxi. And get the fuck out of there. Go home. Put your feet up. Watch some TV with your mum and Jordan.'

Tommy clenched his teeth.

'You've a fine pair of sons,' Smith said. 'Don't do anything to endanger them. Okay?'

Tommy grunted.

'I asked you a question.'

'Okay. O-fucking-kay.'

'And don't even think about going back to the bus station.'

'Why would I do that?'

'Exactly. Just behave and everything'll be fine.'

The taxi arrived within minutes. Older driver than last time, bald guy, slightly camp, not American, didn't appear to be an ex-porn star or to have a stash under his seat and he wasn't listening to Michael Bolton.

Tommy gave him directions. Then called Phil again. 'Smith's on his way to pick up the key.'

'Cool.' Phil belched. 'Looking forward to it.'

FORTY MINUTES LATER, Tommy was in his own car again, trying to talk into his phone whilst changing gears. An earpiece would have been helpful, but he couldn't bring himself to use one. When he was nine, a build-up of fluid led to him going deaf in his left ear. Had to have an operation where they inserted a plastic tube into his ear drum. Cured the problem, but since then he'd always hated the idea of sticking anything in his ears.

He said to his brother, 'Where the hell did you find an empty flat at such short notice?'

'You don't need to know.'

'Is it one of mine?' Tommy owned quite a few suitable properties, but the last thing he'd have wanted was to use one of his own for something like this.

'Don't be dense.'

'Okay. Good.'

Phil was right. Tommy didn't need to know, and he *was* dense, and he was annoyed with himself for asking. Phil had his own life now, they both did, and it was bad enough that Tommy had dragged him into this without making it worse by behaving like an arsehole.

Phil had done okay. He could be a twat a lot of the time, but he came through in a crisis.

Tommy wasn't sure why he was so surprised. Maybe he'd forgotten how much he used to rely on his big brother.

Until five years ago, Tommy operated much of the UK distribution channels for a ring of rogue tobacco company employees. Only they weren't that rogue, from what Tommy could gather.

He was never in direct contact, handling only the return side of things, but he knew enough to suspect that the tobacco companies were aware of what was going on. They wanted to keep the prices down, keep taxes to a minimum, keep people smoking. Smuggling helped.

Container fraud accounted for around a third of the cigarettes smoked in Britain.

What happens: you export the cigarettes to business partners in Andorra or Montenegro, for, say £100K for a container of 10 million cigarettes. Because they're exported, no duty is paid on them. Perfectly legal, so the tobacco companies aren't losing out.

Then you smuggle them back into the country and sell them for a million. Everybody gets a cut of the money the government otherwise would have had, and it's still cheaper for the customer.

Tommy was good at the job, made a lot of money and didn't get caught. Phil used to help. He was customer-facing. Straight-talking, no frills. Particularly good at getting debts settled.

Anyway, Tommy had invested most of his money in the property market and some success there had enabled him to steer away from the tobacco business. No point being a criminal if you could make more money being straight. Apart from which, customs were cracking down harder all the time, making the job tougher, the risk greater and the reward less certain.

Phil should have made money too. Tommy paid him well enough. But he'd pissed it all away. Didn't do much these days – the odd bit of strongarm work, but even then he was too out of shape to be much good at it – but he did mix with the kind of people who might know where there was an empty flat in a dodgy area where you could hold some poor bastard hostage while you extracted information out of him with a cheese grater and a bottle of bleach.

Tommy didn't want to think about that. He spoke into the phone: 'You haven't hurt the lad, have you?'

'Just get here,' Phil said and gave him directions.

Apparently at the bus station things hadn't gone according to plan.

Smith hadn't shown up. Some short, spotty teenager had appeared in his place instead. Tommy and Phil hadn't anticipated this. Smith was seemingly pretty cautious for a madman. But whether Smith turned up or not, the plan had to be the same. Follow whoever, wherever. This lad was their only link to Smith. Apart from which, he now had the money. And if he got away with it, Tommy would never see it again.

So Phil had followed the kid. Then seen an opportunity and seized it.

If you believed Phil, he didn't have any choice. The lad was about to get into a car, drive off, leave Phil stranded with no Smith and no courier and no money. He'd had to make a move. A move that ended up with the lad forced to hand over his car keys and then trussed up in the boot.

No witnesses. The car was parked on a quiet sidestreet. And Phil said he'd only had to hit him once to get his attention.

Tommy hoped he hadn't hit him hard. The longer Phil had this kid in his custody, the more likely something was to go wrong. But Tommy did feel a buzz in his temples. For the first time, he had the edge over Smith. He put his foot to the floor.

Residential parking was round the back of the towerblock. Tommy pulled into a free space, killed the engine. His was the only German car alongside a bunch of Nissans and Ford Fiestas. He wasn't so much concerned about not having a permit as he was that the car would be gone when he returned. Or if not the whole car, then at least the wheels.

There was no sign of life. Not even a couple of neds hanging around who could watch his car for cash. It wasn't as if it was that late. Must be a big football match tonight, or something. Only about a third of the lights in the towerblock were on, though. Maybe all watching the game at the pub. Missed opportunity, in any case. Kids these days had no entrepreneurial skills. Too fixed on trying to get Asbos.

Tommy walked over to the entrance. No security system. He swung the door open, stepped inside. A couple of guys sitting on the stairs turned their backs to hide something. Not difficult to guess what. One of them had a needle sticking out of the crook of his arm.

If you didn't know better, you'd think Edinburgh had a bit of a drugs problem.

Tommy took the lift up to the seventh floor. Got to the door. Knocked.

PHIL LET HIM in. Led him down the corridor by torchlight. Just like Phil. Always prepared. The real last boy scout. Even wearing a pair of gloves to avoid leaving fingerprints. And for once he didn't have a can of beer in his hand.

There was a slight smell of damp and something unusual. Sweet but hard to place. A bit like popcorn but, more likely, dead mice.

At the end of the corridor, Phil opened the door. Handed Tommy the torch.

The door creaked open and Tommy shone the light around the room. Bare floorboards. Wallpaper hanging off the walls. Not good for soundproofing. Minimal furniture. A two-seater settee. And a dining chair. A plate-glass door led into another room, probably the kitchen.

Smith's teenage courier was sitting in the chair, straining against the packing tape that was holding him there. He looked far closer to Jordan's age than to Fraser's. Too young to be involved with someone like Smith.

His shoulders rocked and a faint buzzing sound came from him as his moans vibrated against the tape over his mouth. There was a lot of tape. Between attaching him to the chair, and stopping him making a noise, Phil must have used most of a roll.

Tommy shone the light into the courier's eyes, making him blink, screw up his face. 'Find out where Smith is yet?' Tommy asked Phil.

'Being polite. Waiting on you before we start.'

'Okay,' Tommy said. 'You want to remove the tape from his mouth?'

'You think that's wise?'

'How else is he going to answer?'

Phil shrugged, walked over to the courier who stopped rocking as the heels of Phil's boots clicked on the floorboards. 'You going to be quiet?' Phil said.

The lad nodded, wide-eyed.

'Speak when you're spoken to,' Phil said. 'And not any other time. Okay?'

Another nod. He seemed keen to get on with it, which was promising.

'We just want you to answer a few questions,' Tommy said. 'Then you can go.' He was struggling playing the tough guy. Must be pretty scary to be hit, stuffed in a boot, taken to an empty dark flat in a highrise and interrogated by a couple of guys who didn't appear to be messing around.

Tommy jumped as a phone rang. He didn't think the boy noticed.

Phil put his hand into the boy's jacket. Slid out his phone. Moved it into the light. 'Says 'Dad',' Phil said. 'Ain't that fucking sweet? Want me to tell him what's going to happen to his little boy?'

'I don't think so,' Tommy said.

'Okay.' Phil dropped the phone onto the floor and thumped his heel down on it half a dozen times till the phone was in pieces.

'Shit,' Tommy said.

'What?'

'Never mind.' There had been the chance that Smith had called the boy, or vice versa, and there would have been a record of his number in the phone's call log. Nothing they could do about it now, though.

Phil took his glove off, teased the end of the tape away from the boy's chin. Then ripped it off in a sudden jerk.

The boy yelped. The tape probably took some facial hair with it. Then again, maybe not. He didn't look old enough to have any.

'Told you to be quiet,' Phil said, balling his fist.

'I will,' the boy said, teeth chattering. 'Just don't . . . don't hurt me.'

'Ready to talk, then?' Tommy said.

The boy nodded.

'That's good. Answer a few questions and you can go home to Mummy and Daddy. Okay?'

He nodded again.

Tommy said, 'Who hired you?'

'Don't know her name.'

Her? Tommy looked at Phil. The little bastard was having them on. 'Try again.'

'What do you mean?'

'There's no 'her'.'

'There was. There *is*. A lady. I'm telling you the truth, man. She was short, about my height. Old. About sixty. I'm not lying. Why would I lie? Come on, man. You gotta believe me.' He breathed quickly, gasping for air between his sentences.

'This 'lady'. She have a name?'

'No. I mean, yeah, probably. But I don't know what it is.'

'She just hired you to look after a big pile of money.'

He pinched his eyes against the light, looked away. 'I don't know about any money.'

'What do you think's in the bag?'

'Dunno.'

'Have a guess.'

'I dunno.'

'You didn't look?'

'Didn't have time.'

That was probably true.

'You didn't ask?'

He shook his head.

Tommy waited. Then said, 'So, this sixty-year-old lady whose name you don't know. Why did she choose you?'

'Dunno, man. It's a mystery.'

Tommy gave him a minute to see if he'd say anything else. He didn't. 'A mystery,' Tommy said. 'I'd say so. It's a real fucking puzzle.'

'Look, I dunno. Please. You gotta believe me. She just asked me if I'd do it and I said yes.'

'Just walked up to you in the street, this stranger, and propositioned you?'

'Yeah.'

'Asked you to go fetch her bag out of a locker?'

'Yeah.'

'Why?'

'What do you mean?'

'Did she say why she needed you to do it?'

'She just asked and I said yeah.'

The boy's legs were shaking so hard the chair rattled against the floorboards.

'You didn't ask yourself why she wanted you to get the bag?'

'No.'

'Didn't worry there was a bomb in it?'

'No.'

Tommy held the light steady, watched the boy's Adam's apple bob up and down as he swallowed.

'She offered me money,' the boy said. 'Not the money in the bag. I mean different money. Out of her purse. I didn't ask why.'

'You got this money now?'

'In my pocket.'

'How much?'

'Fifty quid.'

'Not much, is it?'

'Only half. I was going to get the other half later.'

Tommy sighed, said to Phil, 'You want to check his pockets?'

Phil said, 'Not particularly. I don't doubt he's got the fifty quid. Hardly a fortune.'

'Fair point.' Tommy breathed in through his nose. 'What's your name?' he asked the boy.

The boy paused.

'Don't bother making one up.'

The boy said, 'Grant.'

'Well, Grant. I'm going to go out to the car and get my toolbox. Got all sorts of things in there. Screwdrivers with the ends filed to a point. Hacksaws. Powerdrills.' He remembered there probably wouldn't be any electricity here. 'Cordless, of course. All charged up and ready to go. I'll just be five minutes. When I come back, I want to know the truth, or I'll start doing some carpentry on you. Okay?'

'It *is* the truth. I'm telling you, man. I'm fucking telling you the fucking truth.'

'No need to swear.' Tommy turned.

Grant started to scream. It was short-lived, though, cause before Grant had time to take a second breath, Phil was right on top of the lad, arm locked round his mouth, stifling his cries.

Tommy carried on walking. 'You want the torch?' he said to Phil.

'Nah,' Phil said, puffing as he held onto Grant. 'We'll have a fucking great time in the dark, won't we, Grant?'

Tommy went out into the corridor. Opened the flat's front door, but stayed where he was and let it swing shut with a bang. Then he crept back along the corridor, popped into the nearest room. A bedroom. The bed was still there. No other furniture, though.

He was about to sit down on the bed but smelled that sickly sweet popcorn/dead-mouse odour again and decided to stay standing. Looked at his watch. He'd give it five minutes.

It'd be so different if Smith was in the sitting room with Phil instead of Grant. If Smith was in the chair, Tommy might have actually gone out to the car to fetch his toolbox. Assuming he had a toolbox. Nah, course he wouldn't. Not his style. But Phil would. Only question would have been whether Tommy would have let him.

Stupid kid just had to tell them the truth instead of making up shit. If Phil had half a brain he'd be describing to Grant what he could expect once Tommy came back. And Grant would be crapping himself.

That's if he'd got Grant to shut up by now.

Tommy listened, but couldn't hear anything other than the distant thump of a downstairs neighbour's music. He turned off the torch. The music immediately seemed louder. He couldn't hear so much as a whisper from the sitting room, though.

Phil probably still had the poor fuck in that chokehold.

Tommy had always steered clear of this kind of crap. Knew that Phil had to get rough now and then but he'd never wanted to know about it. But until now, nobody had ever threatened Tommy's mother and children.

They had to convince Grant to reveal the identity of Mr fucking Smith. And once they had that information, Phil would have a quiet word with Smith and that would be an end to the violence.

Simple.

Okay, Smith was a killer and maybe it wouldn't be so simple but Tommy didn't see a whole lot of alternatives. He'd like nothing better than to bring all this to an end without anyone getting hurt. Once Grant told them where his boss was, they'd sort something out. Just knowing who Smith was would give them enough leverage for him to back off.

Yeah, it was going to work out fine.

Tommy wondered if maybe enough time had passed now for Grant to believe he'd been out to the car and back. But it was only a couple of minutes since Tommy'd last looked at his watch. Mind you, Grant was probably too scared to tell. Still, it wasn't worth the risk.

Tommy slipped off his shoes. Didn't much fancy walking on this floor in his socks but he didn't want to risk making a noise. He shuffled along the corridor. Crouched down by the sitting room door and placed his ear to the keyhole.

'. . . a machete,' Phil was saying. 'Sliced off the guy's arse cheeks.' He laughed. 'I know. You're thinking that's pretty funny. No? Anyway, you can't ever walk again. No arse cheeks, no walking muscles. You know that? Hard to find a pair of trousers that fit, too.'

Pause. Tommy heard himself breathing.

Then: 'Not laughing?' Phil said. 'Right. Cause I'm not joking. You know that. Just tell me who hired you.'

'I told you.'

'The old lady? Sticking with that still? Well, it's your arse.'

'She hired me to take the bag, deliver it –'

'Deliver it?'

'Yeah. That was the plan.'

'When?'

'When? When she told me the plan.'

'No, you prick. When were you supposed to deliver it?'

'Eleven.'

'Tonight?'

'Aye.'

'Where?'

He paused. Swallowed. 'Car park.'

'Which one?'

Another pause. 'Greenside.'

'It's closed by eleven.'

Tommy wondered how the fuck Phil knew that. He had to be bluffing.

'Oh.'

The bluff worked.

'Don't lie to me again,' Phil said.

'Okay, sorry.'

Pause. 'Where?'

'I can't tell you.'

Phil said, 'You'll tell me when I start drilling holes in your kneecaps.'

'Warriston Cemetery,' the kid blurted out.

Strange venue, Tommy thought, but Grant sounded like he was telling the truth. Warriston Cemetery was a notorious cruising spot for Edinburgh's gays. Plenty privacy behind the tombstones, but the last place you'd expect a bagman to deliver fifty grand. In cash. Maybe that was the idea.

Smith was a clever bastard.

It was about time Tommy got his shoes back on, got in there and found out exactly who Grant's employer was.

'GOT MY TOOLS.' Tommy shone the torch into Grant's eyes. Made him squint.

'Don't need them,' Grant said. 'Tell him,' he said to Phil.

Phil told Tommy what he'd already overheard and Tommy pretended it was news to him.

Tommy kept the beam directed in Grant's eyes. Otherwise Grant might spot that Tommy's other hand was empty and realise there was no toolbox, that it was all a bluff.

Tommy said, 'I don't know that our young friend's telling the whole story.'

'I am,' Grant said. 'Honest.'

'Hmmm,' Tommy said.

Grant's eyes shone in the light. Tears leaked down his cheeks. He said, voice thick as though he had a cold, 'What can I do to make you believe me?'

'What do you think?' Tommy asked Phil.

'Get the drill out,' Phil said. 'Do an elbow. See if he sticks to his story.'

Tommy's stomach rose a couple of inches at the image. He forced it back down, then said, 'Sounds like a plan.'

'No,' Grant said. 'Please don't. Please. Please. *Aaah.*' His torso went rigid. He grinned. No, he was grimacing. Like he was in pain. '*Aaaah,*' he said again, and his head slumped forward and he didn't move.

Tommy swept the light over him, up and down, and then up and down again, finally resting on the crown of his head.

'Fuck was that?' Phil said, eventually.

Tommy said, 'Really bad acting. I think that was supposed to be a heart attack. That right, Grant?'

No response from Grant. He kept his head down.

'Grant? Wakey-wakey.'

Grant still didn't move.

Tommy said, 'Stop fucking about.'

Phil said, 'Hey,' grabbed him by the hair, lifted his head up. Grant's eyes were closed. He didn't appear to be breathing. Phil smacked his cheek.

No reaction.

Phil was just about to strike a second blow when Grant charged forward. He tried to butt Phil but Phil stepped out of the way and Grant, still bound to the chair, plunged into the darkness.

There was a crash, like somebody'd just smashed a window, and then a clatter and Grant said, 'Oof,' and then, 'Ahhhhh.'

Tommy swung the torch in the direction of the sound.

Holy shit.

Grant had just run headfirst into the plate-glass door, and burst out most of the glass. He was either wedged in the doorframe or something was holding him up a couple of feet off the ground.

He wasn't making any noise at all now. The only sound was something dribbling onto the floor.

PRELUDE TO A SAVAGE NIGHT: THE PARKS

'WHERE'S GRANT?' ANDY Park asked, looking at the door of Effie and Martin's tiny council flat, expecting his younger son to walk in any second. Little bastard was late again.

'He called when you were in the toilet, Dad,' Effie said.

'How long's he going to be?'

'He's not,' she said, looking at Martin.

'Not what?' Park said.

'Effie means he's not late,' Martin said.

'He fucking is.' Park looked at his watch. 'Time do you make it?'

'Dad,' Effie said. 'Grant's not coming.'

Park couldn't believe he was hearing this. Ever since he'd got out of prison, he'd visited his wife three or four times a week. Effie usually joined him in the evenings. And he made sure Grant tagged along on Saturdays. Fair enough, the wee bastard was a teenager and had his own life to lead, got bored sitting around with Liz, but she was his mother and the least he could do was put in an appearance once a week.

'He says it's too upsetting,' Effie said. 'Meredith House is a shithole. And, anyway, Mum doesn't know who anybody is. Grant says she won't notice he's not there. He says she's . . . gone, Dad.'

'She's not *gone*, Effie.' Park was inside when Liz had tried to kill herself. Saw her once afterwards while he was locked up. Everybody agreed that prison visits wouldn't have done either of them any good. But he'd seen her regularly these last six months. It was hard, knowing the medical experts had given up on her. Called her chronic. But what did they know.

'Dad, Grant's right. Her body's here but her mind's elsewhere. She doesn't recognise any of us.'

'She does,' he said. 'She just has no way of showing it.' She was locked up inside herself. Park knew all about being locked up. Liz was experiencing a 24-hour bang-up, not even getting out for meals and a quick canter round the exercise yard.

'And Grant says he can't stand that new guy.'

McCracken. The prick who had taken over Liz's wing. The type who had no hesitation about cutting corners if it meant making profits to impress his employers.

First thing the fucker had done was move another resident into Liz's room. Park told him his wife needed her privacy. McCracken said there was nothing he could do. And smirked.

'Let's go,' Park said. 'We'll pick Grant up on the way. You coming, Martin?'

MRS H SAID, 'Hello, I'm Mrs H.'

Mrs H was Liz's new roommate and she introduced herself to them every visit. She got up off her bed, held out a hand.

'Already met,' Park said and eased past her. The beds were only a couple of feet apart. The room wasn't that much bigger than his old cell and looked far less lived in. Smelled just as bad, though. That useless bastard McCracken needed to get the drains fixed.

Mrs H sat down again. Ran her fingers over her quilt cover, tracing invisible patterns.

'We're all here,' Park said to Liz. She was lying on her bed wearing a pair of dark-brown trousers and a lilac cardigan that was far too big for her. She looked like something had sucked all the flesh out of her body. He bent down, took her hands in his. They were cold, the bones sharp. 'Grant was really busy but he put off what he was doing to come along. Isn't that nice?'

Grant waved from the doorway. 'Hi, Mum.'

'Come over here,' Park told him.

Grant shuffled over, nearly tripping on Mrs H's fluffy slippered feet.

'Waste of time,' Mrs H said, looking up. 'She doesn't know who any of you are.'

'Get out,' Park said.

'This is my room.'

'Get out.'

'I will not. The soldiers are on my side.'

Sad old fuck was a total loophead.

'Let's take Mum for a walk,' Effie said.

'Good idea,' Park said. 'You like that, Liz?'

She didn't look at him. He squeezed her hand, which was a little warmer now. She didn't squeeze back.

Mrs H said, 'She's whiffy. They don't change her.'

Park sighed. So that's what the smell was.

OUTSIDE LIZ'S ROOM, Park bumped into Moira, one of the carers. Asked her how come his wife was allowed to lie in her own filth. Moira said they were busy, she'd sort her out just as soon as she could. Park said, 'Don't bother. Just tell me where McCracken is.'

Fifteen seconds later: 'You run this shithole,' Park said to McCracken, barging into his office. More of a broom cupboard than an office. Just enough space for a desk and a pint-sized filing cabinet, a visitor's chair.

Park didn't sit down.

McCracken leaned back, locking his fingers behind his head to show Park his beefy arms. He didn't lean back very far before his head touched the wall.

Park had seen muscles before. Lot of muscles in jail. Muscles didn't mean shit. Park said, 'My wife's not an animal.'

'Who's your wife?'

He knew who Park was. They'd spoken before. He was deliberately being an arse. 'Liz,' Park said. 'Elizabeth Park.'

'Oh,' McCracken said, unlocking his fingers, levelling his chair. 'I remember you.' He leaned forward, steepled his index fingers under his chin. 'You're the jailbird.'

Jailbird? Jail-fucking-bird? 'I've done my time, you poncey twat. Fuck off.'

'No need for that kind of language, Mr Park.'

'Don't change the fucking subject. Liz needs looking after.'

'I'm aware of what Mrs Park needs.'

'So do something. Get your staff to take her to the toilet.'

'We don't always have the time or the staff.'

'Make the time. Hire more staff.'

'It would be better for everybody if we could catheterise her.'

'It isn't better for Liz. It's been tried before. She doesn't like it. She pulls it out.'

'And yet I'm told she doesn't move of her own volition.'

'That's how much she doesn't like it. You're not sticking one of those up her again. That's fucking final.'

'Fine. So what do you suggest?' McCracken smiled, showing his teeth. Perfectly straight and white, the kind of teeth you wanted to splinter with a hammer.

'I don't run this place. You do. Why the fuck should I be suggesting anything? Do your fucking job.'

'I'm sorry,' McCracken said. 'These things happen.'

'Not to my wife, they don't. And while I'm at it, she used to be a big lass. Can't weigh more than six fucking stone now. Her face looks like a skull.'

'You're not happy with the care she's being given, why don't you look after her yourself?'

Park couldn't believe the fucker had said that. 'If I could, I'd take her out of here right now.'

'Be my guest. I can always use a spare bed.'

Course, there wasn't any room for Liz at Effie and Martin's. As it was, Park was sleeping on the settee. And Liz had to be clothed, fed, bathed, taken to the bathroom, and God alone knew what else.

Park didn't think he'd be much of a nurse. Effie had the part-time hairdressing job, which meant she wasn't around all the time. And Martin wasn't flesh and blood, so they couldn't expect him to help out.

They stared at each other, Park and McCracken, the cunt.

'You're a fucking disgrace,' Park said. 'You're supposed to be looking after her. You're going to start doing that.'

McCracken picked at his teeth with his thumbnail.

It was as if the guy *wanted* a kicking. Park asked, 'You know why I was in prison?'

McCracken shook his head. 'Let me guess.' He pretended to think. 'Paedophilia?'

Patience. 'Fireraising,' Park said. 'I like burning things. Buildings mainly. Wouldn't mind if there was a person got stuck in one of them, though. You do night shifts?'

McCracken ran his tongue over his teeth. 'You threatening me?'

'You fucking better believe it.'

'I don't scare easily.'

'How about your family? You got a wife? Kids? Mother? I can find out. Maybe they scare easily. I'll roast the fuckers if I have to. Every single one of them. You want to play with me? I like games, Mr McCracken. And I'm very fucking good at them.'

McCracken looked at his fingernails. Cleared his throat. 'You're unbalanced.'

'Fucking right, I am.'

'I don't respond to threats.' He held up his hand to stop Park interrupting. 'But I do believe in doing my job. I'll make sure your wife's well cared for.'

Park waited.

'What?' McCracken said.

'I want to see you do it.'

'Now?'

'Now.'

McCracken sighed, picked up the phone. He spoke to someone, told them to look in on Mrs Park, make sure her incontinence pad was changed, see if she was hungry. He looked at Park, eyebrows raised.

Park nodded. That was a start.

When McCracken put the phone down, Park said, 'And I expect you to apologise to her in person.'

'But she doesn't –'

'What was your wife's name?'

McCracken stood up. 'Get the fuck out of my office.'

Park leaned across. 'No need for language like that,' he said. 'You going to apologise to Liz?'

'I'm not apologising,' McCracken said, 'to a fucking cabbage.'

Park gripped the edge of the desk, squeezed.

'What?' McCracken said. 'You look like you want to say something.'

BACK HOME, EFFIE put what Park was thinking into words: 'We need to get Mum out of there.'

Park said, 'Maybe McCracken'll be okay now. He acted tough but I think I scared him.'

'Didn't sound like it.'

She was right, of course. Park was just trying to stay positive. Cause once he started going down that negative path, there was no going back.

Martin said, 'Liz could stay with us. Be a bit cramped.' He looked around the pokey sitting room. 'But we could manage. For a while.'

'Appreciate the thought, Martin,' Park said. The lad kept surprising him, and in a good way. 'But we couldn't manage. You're already overcrowded with just me staying.'

'She could sleep on the settee with you,' Martin said.

'You and Eff are getting married. Be having kids of your own before you know it.' Park noticed Effie glance at Martin. 'You won't want us around.'

'But if there's no alternative,' Martin said.

'There's always an alternative,' Effie told him.

'Exactly,' Park said. 'I'll find her somewhere nice.'

'Costs money, though, Dad.'

'I know,' he said.

'The kind of money that doesn't come legally.'

'You've looked into it?' he said, quietly.

'Had to,' she said. 'When Mum first . . . became ill.'

He didn't know that. The things he'd missed by being inside. 'So how much are we talking about?' he said.

'Won't get a lot of change out of thirty grand a year.'

'Holy shit,' he said. 'I need a drink.'

COUPLE OF WEEKS later and Park had knocked back more than a few. He shook the last drips from his penis and zipped up. Long time since he'd had a piss outside.

'Come on, Dad,' Grant said.

Park hoped the lads didn't mind him taking a leak. No doubt they'd have done it too if they'd needed as badly. Although Effie'd said Martin was a bit shy. Maybe those two only did it with the lights out. He should ask sometime just to see Martin's face.

He'd thought at first that Martin was gay, the way he wore cravats all the time. That Effie was like his, whatever they called it . . . beard.

'Oops,' Grant said, indicating something behind Park, with a nod.

Park turned. Ah. Bloke in a cap and vest, with handcuffs and CS spray accessories, no doubt been standing there getting a good eyeful of Park's own accessory. A gazer. And no shame about it either. If this was a public toilet, here was one cop who'd get done for cottaging, no question.

Park wondered whether he should call the cop on his homosexuality, but decided not to. No point winding him up. He looked pretty wound up already, mind you. Probably hadn't found anybody to arrest for a good five minutes.

Grant was looking at Park. At the cop. Back at him. Trying not to laugh.

The cop said, eyes still on Park, 'You need to go home.'

Like fuck he did. The night was young and he was conscious. Liz was free. He was looking forward to snuggling up with her later. But not now. It was far too fucking early. 'Fuck off,' he said.

''Scuse me?'

'You heard.'

The cop eyed him up. Likely wondering if he could take him. Ah, hell, not like *that*. Wondering if he needed to call for backup or if he could handle Park all on his own.

Probably could, too. Park's stomach felt full with all the drink. Maybe he could knock the cop's hat off and puke in it. Maybe he should ask first. Be polite, wouldn't it?

The fucker was still standing there looking at him.

'What?' Park said.

'You just urinated in a doorway, pal.'

Pal. Park hated being called somebody's pal when he clearly wasn't. Really fucking got him steamed. Anyway, he did what he always did when he was accused of something: denied it. He said, 'Not me, *pal.*'

The fucker sighed, like Park was the one being a prick, and said, 'I saw you.'

'No, you didn't.'

The cop placed his hands on his hips, shook his head. He said to Grant and Martin, 'You pair with him?'

Park said, 'Leave them alone, you fucking bully.'

Grant said, 'Dad. Shhh.'

The fucker ignored Park. Spoke to Grant, 'You need to get him home.'

'Not going home,' Park said. 'Got more drinking to do.'

'You don't.'

'Do. Just said so. You should listen.'

'You're drunk.'

'Nope.'

'You want me to take you down to the station?'

'Like to see you try.'

See how brave the fucker was now. Showing off, the cop was. Probably fancied Martin. Waving his authority about like it meant something when everybody knew it meant cock all. Policemen liked a bit of GBH but only on their own turf. Get them outside, quiet street like this, they didn't fancy their chances one on one. Or one on three if you counted Grant and Martin.

The black-capped cuntbastard took a step closer. And another. Such fucking balls. William fucking Wallace, he was. The original Old Bill.

Pretty close now. Trying to look hard. And him just a wee guy, too, no bigger than Grant. Had his work cut out. Glass jaw, no doubt, no matter how tight it was clenched. Hands at his side now like he was some cowboy about to reach for his gun. Only he didn't have a gun. Just a truncheon and a can of doctored deodorant.

Sorry, not a truncheon. A fucking baton, they called it. Extendable. If the cop didn't back off, Park would take it off him, extend it fully, and shove it up his arse for him.

That'd teach him to accuse an innocent person.

The cop came to a halt, said, 'You can't urinate in door-ways.'

'Didn't,' Park told him.

'You were clearly doing so. I saw you.'

'Not me.' Park paused. 'You must have imagined it. You see anything?' he asked Grant and Martin.

'Wasn't looking,' Martin said. Grant shook his head.

'Been taking drugs or anything?' Park asked the cop.

The cheeky bastard ignored him, pointed to the puddle on the ground. 'So what's that?'

'Puddle.'

'Exactly. A puddle. A puddle of urine.' He pronounced urine to rhyme with wine.

'Could be anything,' Park said. 'Puddle of water. Clear soup. Perfume.'

'It's urine.'

They stood in a group looking at the puddle.

'If you say so,' Park said. 'Hard to tell without sniffing it. Want to get on your knees, have a go?'

'I don't need to,' the cop said. 'It's fucking urine.'

'Maybe,' Park said. 'Not mine, though. Not mine –' he paused, winked at Grant – 'urine.' Rhyming it with wine.

'Fucking is.'

'Nah.'

'It's fresh.'

'If you say so.'

'It's still trickling down the pavement.'

'So it is.'

'You're still denying that was you?'

'Right.'

The cop sucked his lips in and said, 'You were facing the door.'

'That a crime?'

'Why were you facing the door if it wasn't in order to urinate?'

'Interesting door,' Park said. 'Just having a good look at it.'

'Jesus,' the cop said, his fingers clenching and unclenching by his side. 'Go home.'

'Nope. I'm going drinking.'

'You're not.'

'Going to stop me, are you?'

'Mr Park,' Martin said. 'Andy. Give it up.'

'Right. Give him my fucking name, why don't you, Martin?' Park shook his head, said to the cop, 'Come on, then. Let's see what you've got.'

The cop's facial muscles were all tight. 'Take him home, please,' he said, this time to Martin. Then to Park: 'If I see you again tonight, Mr Park, *Andy*, you're in the cells.' And he walked away.

Fucking minced off.

Park said, 'Don't turn your back on me, you fucking coward. Hey, I'm talking to you. Come back here and clean up your piss.'

The cop stopped. Turned. Spoke slowly and quietly: 'Go home before I lose my temper.'

'Oh, I'm scared now. Maybe so scared I'll piss myself. Or I would if I needed.'

The fucker gave him the finger.

Park held himself back. Couldn't go around causing any serious damage. Although being arseholed took the edge off his reaction. And he was most definitely arseholed.

Cause he was so fucking happy that Liz was out of that shithole. Had to celebrate. Effie had said, 'Go out, enjoy yourselves.'

Which they'd done. Even Grant, who was on orange juices and cokes on account of looking too young to get served. He claimed he looked his age, but that didn't help, cause looking seventeen was no fucking good.

'He's gone,' Martin said.

And he had. The cop had rounded the corner.

'You know it's not his fault,' Grant said.

'What you talking about?'

'You're taking it out on the policeman because of McCracken.'

McCracken. Pissbastardfuckwankercunt. Grant was right. He might only look his age and be extremely short but he was a smart lad.

Park had visited Liz that afternoon.

SHE WAS LYING on her bed, pillow over her face.

Mrs H said, 'I'm Mrs H, how do you do? Shhh. She's sleeping.'

He grabbed the pillow off Liz's face, chucked it at Mrs H.

Liz had a Tesco bag on her head. He pulled it off, nestling the back of her head in his palm. Her hair was warm and damp.

She was breathing, thank God. Eyes open. Unblinking. Looking right through him.

He said to Mrs H, 'You do this, you old fuckhead?'

'Language,' she said. 'Any more of that and I'll arrest you.' Then she spoke some gibberish that sounded like German.

Park raised Liz into a sitting position, lifted her off the bed. She weighed scarily little and it was remarkably easy to move her into her seat.

She stared at him. Or through him. He kissed her forehead. Leaned towards Mrs H, who was still spouting some crazy lingo. 'What did you think you were doing?'

'Can't I help her sleep? Sometimes I sing to her. She likes that. But she likes the dark and the quiet better.'

'You're a dangerous fucking fuckwit,' Park said.

He didn't want to leave Liz in the room with her. He took his wife's hand, encouraged her out of the chair, walked her into the corridor. She was happy to go where you led. As long as you moved slowly.

McCracken wasn't in his office. Park bumped into one of the nurses, a new one, didn't know her name, got her to track him down.

He went back to Liz's room, waited patiently. When the fucker arrived, Mrs H introduced herself to everybody again, then Park calmly told him what had happened.

McCracken said, 'You don't need to worry about it.'

'I don't?'

'Mrs H has a predilection for such antics.' He folded his arms. 'Don't you, dear?'

Mrs H said, '*Achtung.*'

'What's a fucking 'predilection'?'

'A tendency. But it's never caused any harm, Mr Park.'

Park balled his fingers, squeezed. 'Is that right?'

'Sure. Mrs H doesn't want to hurt your wife. Correct?'

Mrs H nodded. '*Schweinwaffen.*'

'Was the bag tied at the bottom?' he asked Park.

'No, but Liz could still have died.'

'Don't get melodramatic.' McCracken unfolded his arms, scratched his upper lip.

'Don't tell me what to do. I demand you move that fuckhead out of here.'

'I already explained. That's not possible.'

'My wife can't stay here.'

'Fine,' McCracken said. 'Take her away.'

'That's it?' Park asked him.

'Seems to be.'

'You really don't give a shit about her, do you? Wouldn't have mattered to you if she'd suffocated. She's just a fucking vegetable as far as you're concerned. She'd be better off dead, right? That'd free up a bed for you, after all.'

McCracken looked at Liz and said, 'I can't comment on that.'

'I fucking bet.' Park swallowed, shook his head. He said, quietly, 'Get out of my fucking sight.'

McCracken stepped towards the door, paused as if he was about to say something, then walked out of the room.

Park bundled some of Liz's things together. However tight the space at Effie's, Liz wasn't staying here a minute longer.

Park called Effie. Told her what had happened.

'McCracken said she'd be better off dead?' Effie said. 'I'll swing for that bastard.'

'Don't worry,' Park said. 'He won't get away with it.'

PARK LOOKED DOWN at the puddle in the doorway. A long thin strand of piss wove along the pavement.

'Come on, Dad.' Grant grabbed his arm. Tugged.

'Where we going?' Park asked.

'Home to our beds.'

'Ah, away and rub it.' He grinned at him. 'You getting some, son?'

'Fuck's wrong with you, Dad?'

Martin took his other arm.

'So,' Park said, 'this is gay. Where're we really going?'

'The copper was right,' Grant said. 'You've had enough.'

He stopped. His son and future son-in-law, who was all right if a bit poofy, carried on a step, jolted, stopped too. Park said, 'Don't want to go home yet.' He sounded like a little boy, even to himself.

'So, what do you want to do?'

He thought for a minute.

'Come on,' Grant said, tugging his arm again.

'Don't suppose we can go clubbing?' Park said.

'No.' That was Grant. Martin shook his head.

Park said, 'Not even a baby seal?'

HOME. YEP. FUCKING brilliant. Course, some people wouldn't call it home, cause he didn't have a bed at Effie's, just a settee. But he'd experienced worse.

Not too long ago his bed was a pile of cardboard and a bunch of newspapers in one of the lanes at the back of Rose Street. Fine when it was dry. But there was nothing more depressing than soggy cardboard. Beat sleeping in cemeteries, though. He'd done that plenty.

Thanks to Yardie. Should never have chucked him out. Park had heard last week that he was back inside, six-monther for possession. Blow. Only enough for a couple of joints. Served the bastard right, though.

Park had finally agreed to stay with Martin and Effie. Just till he got himself sorted out. Not much room for them all. One bedroom. One small sitting room. One galley kitchen. One corridor bathroom. They managed, somehow. It'd be tough now with Liz staying. But they'd work something out. Christ, Park had lived three to a cell for one memorable four-month stretch. A cell originally designed for one occupant. Now *that* was tough.

You know, he probably should be getting home, like the lads said. See Liz.

'Don't know why we put up with you,' Grant said. 'Pissing in the street, man. Threatening cops. You're no kind of example, Dad.'

'Don't know why I put up with *you*,' Park said. 'Slagging me off. Not letting me go drinking.'

'You love him,' Martin said. And he wasn't taking the piss.

Funny how he came out with stuff like that, matter-of-fact and all.

'Martin,' Park said, 'I love all my kids.' Anything happened to any of them, he'd fucking . . . well, he'd fucking rip in half any bastard who messed with them. In a manner of speaking. Cause he couldn't actually do it. Even assuming he could rip through a human torso, as soon as he saw any trace of *nnnnngah* that was him gone.

Like at Yardie's party, for instance.

Park had moved into Yardie's straight from jail. This was before he was homeless, long before he moved in with Effie and Martin. He was supposed to be staying with Yardie till he got his own place, which wasn't likely to happen cause he couldn't be arsed looking for somewhere.

He needed a job. He had a couple of computer qualifications he'd picked up inside, plus his previous experience in retail and all that bollocks. But nobody wanted a thief and a fireraiser working in their shop, especially when the thief had been sent down for nicking computer equipment from his place of work and then setting fire to the premises. Prejudiced fucks. It had been good stuff. State of the art. Hard to resist. And he'd had to cover his tracks somehow.

Anyway, a job was a long-shot, so he'd been planning on dossing at his mate Yardie's until he overstayed his welcome. One of the hardest things about sleeping rough was smelling damp and sour, like you'd left your clothes in the washing machine too long with the door shut. At Yardie's, he had access to running water and soap. No excuse not to smell nice. Technically, he was staying at his mate's mum's, Yardie not being the houseowner. He'd met Yardie inside. Yardie was black and twenty-five years old. Yardie's mum was white and over seventy.

Park had got a surprise when he first met her. But neither she nor Yardie ever explained and Park never asked. None of his business. If there was ever a Mr Yardie, he seemed to be long since gone.

Old Mrs Yardie couldn't have been kinder to Park. Truth was, he liked her a lot more than he liked her son.

They lived in a nice house. Money was tight but she coped. Only drawback, it was about ten miles west of Edinburgh. In the country.

Yardie threw a party one night when Old Mrs Yardie was off staying with her sister in Kent. He went to a lot of trouble, preparing fancy nibbles. Sausages on cocktail sticks and squares of cheese and Pringles with dips. That kind of crap. Park didn't think anybody would turn up cause the place was so fucking hard to find.

Martin and Effie had come along. Just engaged. All night, she fiddled with his hair, long and blonde. Hers was too short for him to play with. Martin was beefy, Effie looked like a boy with tits. He wore a big collar. A cravat. Other kinds of 70s gaywear. There was lots of touching, holding hands, wistful smiles. Enough to turn your stomach if you were at all sensitive.

Park ignored it, butted in, started talking to Martin. Bloke might be dressed like a Frenchman, but he was a good listener.

Could have had a good conversation going if Effie didn't keep sticking her tongue down Martin's throat every couple of minutes.

A while later, the lovebirds stopped pecking at each other long enough to join Park in taking the piss out of Yardie's mates, a bunch of mutton-headed blissed-up neds. Yardie was showing them his prize possession: a shitty little closet chain.

Closet chains were just like handcuffs but with a long chain between the cuffs. Several feet long usually. Designed to allow the wearer – usually a con attending a family funeral or wedding – to use the bathroom in privacy without the risk of him escaping through the window. He'd wear one cuff and his escort would be on the other side of the door wearing the other. Had to keep the door ajar to let the chain through, but that still gave the con a little dignity while he did his business. But Yardie's closet chain looked to be on the short side. Three, maybe four feet long. He'd nicked it from a prison officer's home. The screw shouldn't have had it there, so it never got reported stolen.

Yardie's mates had paired up, tried it on, and now two of them had the chain stretched tight about three feet off the ground and a third was about to jump over it. Park hoped he'd trip.

Effie pointed out the girlfriend of one of the mutton heads. Effie knew her vaguely. Rumour had it she swung both ways, Effie said.

Park got on well with lezzers. And this one was a looker, too. Not that he was going to hit on her, him being a married man and all, but there was no harm in saying hello. He left the happy-couple-to-be in the corner to snog for a while, grabbed a bottle of white wine and went off to talk to the dyke.

She wasn't very talkative, though. Any topic of conversation he brought up, she replied with a one-word answer. He thought long and hard and came up with a topic he was sure she'd be interested in. Muff diving. Told her it'd been a while, but that was something he'd always been good at. Did a mean butterfly kiss.

She dropped her drink and ran off.

Seconds later he was on the floor with her boyfriend looking down at him, clenching his fist and snarling. No, really: snarling. Park had never heard anything quite like it.

The boyfriend hadn't actually hit him. Just shoved him sideways onto the ground whilst Park was off-balance picking up the lezzer's glass. Pretty embarrassing. And totally uncalled for. Wasn't as if Park had been chatting her up.

But even if he was, it wasn't as if this guy was married to her. And she swung both ways, so he probably wouldn't ever be married to her, cause if he was, she'd only be able to swing one way. If that was technically possible. And if she swung both ways, then she'd need to be able to swing the other way, cause that was in her nature. Which is why she couldn't ever marry him. Stood to reason.

Not that he managed to explain it to himself as rationally as this, cause he was fuming at the time and incapable of thinking clearly enough to put on his own trousers.

As Park got to his feet, an audience gathered round, all the fun of jumping over a closet chain forgotten for now. Rage was thermalling through Park, heating him up from the inside till his face was all toasty on the outside. He felt a muscle tug in his cheek.

Park tried to hit the cocksucker on the point of the chin rather than on the nose or mouth, which is where he'd have preferred. But that was easier said than done. He caught the lip full-on, and it burst and spurted *nnnngah* blood almost straight away. Came out all thick and red and spelling disaster.

All the energy drained out of him, saliva built under his tongue, that weird nausea not like he was going to be sick but something much more specific. Happened every time he saw blood. Had done for as long as he could remember. Since he was three, to be precise. Vision blackened at the edges, bells rang, chest tightened, knees gave way. If he managed to get his head between his knees, it passed after a few minutes. If not, he fainted.

Haemophobia. Or the term he preferred: blood-phobia. It was his biggest embarrassment.

Apparently, after he'd fallen to the floor, the ned boyfriend had seized his opportunity, brave as a bull with an extra-thick lip now Park was on the deck, and given him a few smacks round the head and a couple of kicks in the ribs. That's what it felt like, anyway, and Effie corroborated as much afterwards. The kicks, she said, were pretty half-hearted. And the kicker was wearing trainers. But, still.

Effie had stepped in. None of the other lads had been bothered about their mate kicking a bloke. Thought it was a bit of a laugh, in fact, egging him on, cheering and that. But they weren't at all happy about their mate kicking a woman. Which didn't seem fair to Park, even if the woman in question was his daughter. But despite the injustice of it all, Martin and Effie hauled him away, and thanks to their intervention Park was spared a more serious doing.

Later, in the bedroom, on top of a thick duvet, something cold pressed to his cheek.

Effie moved the cloth, dabbed his forehead.

He turned his head.

Effie knelt on the bed, leaned over him. 'You okay?' she said.

'Long time since I was in bed with a lovely woman,' he said.

Martin cleared his throat.

'You're not *in* bed,' Effie said. 'You're on it. Anyway, how does your face feel?'

'Hurts when I stretch it,' Park said, opening his jaw wide, stretching his lips. It hurt, exactly like he'd said it did. 'Ow.' Maybe overdoing the sympathy card, was he?

Effie said, 'Don't fucking stretch it then, you bumshite.'

That was nice. Being called a bumshite. No, really. Hardly anybody felt comfortable enough with Park to call him anything other than sir or cunt. He tended to provoke extreme reactions. Bumshite was good. There was an intimacy in the word that made him smile.

Anyway, that's why Park had to be careful when he got violent.

Yardie threw him out of his house the next day, claiming that he'd been there too long already. Truth was, he'd thrown him out for belting one of his friends. But, anyway, whatever. Yardie was an arsehole and it didn't matter what had pissed him off. Park missed Yardie's mum, though. She made great pancakes.

Park was homeless for a couple of months until Effie and Martin had finally persuaded him to stay with them till he got himself sorted. Sweet as a honey-dunked nut, that was. He owed them.

So right now, much as he'd have liked to go clubbing just to annoy the copper who'd ordered Martin and Grant to take him home, he was happy enough to head off to bed. Well, head off to settee. Point was, he wasn't heading off to collapsed cardboard and newspapers. And tonight he'd have Liz to curl up next to.

'HOW WAS GRANT?' Effie asked, pressing a button on the TV remote.

'Wee bastard,' Park said. 'Wouldn't drink. And then he wouldn't let *me* drink. I'm still thirsty.'

'Should have seen your dad with the policeman,' Martin said.
She asked, 'What policeman?'

'I never got parole,' Park said. 'So I don't have to be nice to the fuckers.'

'You didn't hit a policeman, Dad?'

'Wish I had. Now, never mind that. How's my girls? What've you been up to?'

They were on the settee, next to each other. Liz already looked better.

'I'm good,' Effie said. 'We watched a movie about this guy who stores the souls of dead people in a hotel in his brain.'

'And I thought it was just me,' Park said. 'Any good?'

'I liked it. Thinking about going to bed now, though. Mum's tired.'

'She had her medicine?'

'Yep.'

'She say anything?'

'Dad, she never says anything.'

'Don't give up hope, Eff.'

'She's been farting a lot. In fact, it's time she had her pad changed.' She turned to face Liz. 'Eh, Mum? You a bit smelly?'

'I'll do it,' Park said. 'You and Martin get off to bed.'

'You sure?'

'What, you think I can't change a nappy?' Park said. 'Changed yours often enough. I'm a fucking dab hand. Off you go.'

'I don't mind.'

'Go on,' Park said. 'Fuck off.'

Once they'd gone he spent a couple of minutes trying to guess where Effie'd put the nappies. He knew they were somewhere, cause he remembered taking them from the Home.

No joy, so he went to ask her. He stood outside the bedroom door and listened. Martin was telling her about the cop and the puddle. Park knocked on the door.

Effie answered in a black dressing gown. She apologised. She'd stuck the nappies out of the way, on top of her wardrobe. She shouted to Martin to fetch them.

He brought them over, wearing a matching dressing gown, towel wrapped round his neck. He handed the nappies to Park.

'We'll need to get more tomorrow,' Effie said.

'Don't we have enough?'

'Even if we take her to the toilet every couple of hours, there's no guarantee she won't have an accident between times. She can go through three or four a day.'

'She can? That's a lot of nappies.'

'Incontinence pads,' Effie said.

'That's too many sylla-whatever-they're-calleds.'

'Syllables? Try 'pads', then.'

'Fuck's wrong with nappies?'

'Babies wear nappies. Mum's not a baby.'

That was Park told. 'Oh, I'll need a nightie for her too.'

Effie told him where to find it and suggested some wipes might come in handy to clean her with.

He said goodnight again, and eventually got all the gear gathered round him in the sitting room, and then tried to get Liz to lie down. She wasn't great at following new instructions. You could get her to walk easily enough by taking her hand and leading the way. She'd sit if you gave her a chair. She'd lie down if you pulled back the bed covers. But getting her to lie down on the floor proved to be a challenge.

Park lay down first, hoping a practical demonstration would help.

But she wouldn't look at him. The TV was still on, some chat show, volume low, but she wasn't looking at that either. She was staring straight ahead at nothing in particular.

Park got to his feet, wedged his hands under her arms and lifted her towards him. He balanced her easily with one hand, scooped her legs up with the other. Held her in his arms for a minute, then got down on one knee, then the other. Laid her down gently, like she was asleep and he didn't want to wake her.

She was wearing a skirt, zip at the side. Got that off okay, just tearing the fabric a bit before he realised he'd have to lift her bottom up for her. Course, that meant having to press against the nappy and risk squashing its contents. Not a good idea. So he figured out how to roll her onto her side, tug the skirt down, then roll her onto her other side, tug that down. Did that a few times and the skirt came off.

'Easy, sweetheart,' he said.

The smell was much stronger now. Big difference between changing a baby's nappy and changing an adult's. Much meatier.

The nappy was baby blue. Had a thin green line running up the centre of it. He pulled the tabs apart and it opened.

'Ah, Jesus,' he said, the stink getting up his nose. 'Sorry, Liz, but that's rank.'

He raised her legs, held them out of the way while he folded up the nappy.

Grabbed a wet wipe. Cleaned round her arsehole where some shit had smeared. Used another to clean her anus. A third wipe, he cleaned her vagina.

A rash dotted outwards towards her thighs.

Wiped that, too.

This was how they used to fuck. Liz lying on her back, her legs over his shoulders.

Within seconds, he was as hard as a clenched fist.

Shit, piss, a nappy rash. That's all it took. He was a sick bastard.

He lowered her legs. Her thatch of near-black hair reached to her belly button. And the hair was thick. He remembered that. It was always thick and wiry. He liked it that way. Wild and out of control.

Fuck it, he wanted her.

Was there something wrong with him that he felt like this? She was his wife and she was half-naked and he hadn't had a shag in over five years. Couple of sneaky blow-jobs from a bloke with a shaved head who stank like a horse, but that was all.

Not as if he'd be doing something wrong if he fucked her now. If she could make a choice one way or the other, she'd want to do it too. Right?

But she couldn't make a choice.

There were other options, of course. He could go elsewhere, pay for it. Liz wouldn't mind. She wouldn't know anything about it. But he didn't want sex with just any woman. He wanted Liz.

He bent over, kissed her. Her lips were dry, unresponsive.

He should get rid of the nappy, the used wipes, get her ready for bed.

But first he lay down beside her, placed his cheek on her belly. The chatter on the TV dulled.

She was warm and soft and her belly rumbled. He wondered what she was trying to say.

BEEF STEW FOR dinner the next night. Martin had made it, and like everything he cooked, it was de-fucking-licious. Afterwards, they all sat in the sitting room, sinking a few pints, Effie and Martin snuggled up on the settee, Liz beside them. Park sat on the arm until the pressure on the base of his spine got too much, then switched to the floor by Liz's feet.

'Want my seat?' Grant said. He was sitting in the only armchair.

'I'm fine here.'

They were all here. Well, apart from Richie, Park's eldest. Right at this moment, he was probably in the prison gym 'getting big', or slobbing it in front of the TV. If he was out of his cell. And gagging for some beer. That's what you missed inside. More than sex.

Still, Richie could do the time. You don't become a hit man unless you're prepared for the consequences. Although he'd never imagined what it would do to his mother when she found out. Nobody'd imagined that.

Christ, Liz.

Maybe she'd like some beer. He asked her.

'No,' Effie said. 'Are you fucking mental?'

'Just a glass.'

'She's not used to alcohol. And, anyway, she's had enough liquid for one night.'

'Dad's an expert nappy changer now,' Grant said. He laughed.

'It's not funny,' Park said. 'And it's true. I am.'

'That's debatable.' Effie didn't think he'd done that great a job last night. She'd given him some advice earlier: 'If Mum does a number two, get her to stand in the bath. Much easier to clean her under the shower.'

He'd try it next time and see.

Anyway, didn't look like Liz was getting any beer.

They watched some reality show, then an oldie DVD Grant had got from a friend at work. Park rarely watched modern movies. Too much blood. So Grant was always on the look-out for old classics for his blood-shy dad. *God's Little Acre*, this one was called. A comedy about a poor crazy hick family. Turned out to be every bit as sad as it was funny.

When that was over, Grant left, giving his mum and Effie a hug and a kiss, shaking hands with Martin, and not sure what to do with his dad. Park helped him out, giving him a hug but foregoing the kiss.

Martin put some music on. Lesbo-pop, he said. Russian.

It sounded all right. Park was even humming to himself when he went to get more beer from the kitchen.

He wondered when he'd get a chance to speak to Effie. All day they'd been talking about what they were going to do with Liz. Long-term. Then Effie'd whispered to him that she had an idea, but she wanted to talk to him about it when they were alone. By which she meant, not in front of Martin.

It was getting late now, and Park was hoping Martin would head off to bed soon so he could hear what Effie had to say. But when Park returned from the kitchen, Martin was talking about his mother and bed still looked a long way off.

'We have our ups and downs,' Martin said. 'Mainly ups, though.'

'Don't remember my mum,' Park said.

Effie said to Martin, 'She died when Dad was three.'

'And as for my dad,' Park said, 'he scarpered as soon as he found out my mum was pregnant.'

Effie said, 'Well, my dad's pretty cool.' And smiled at him. 'And my mum's pretty cool, too.' She put her hand out, stroked her mother's greying hair.

'My mum gave us her old settee,' Martin said.

'Very kind.' Park felt bad he hadn't been able to help them smarten the place up too. Been nice to have got them a chair or something. 'How come I've never met her?'

'She's . . . ,' Martin said. 'It's complicated. She's . . . don't know the right word. Fragile, I suppose.' He looked at Effie, his hand playing with the neck of his pale-yellow polo-neck jumper.

'Since your dad . . . ?' Effie said.

'Yeah,' he said. 'No, before that. Didn't help, though.'

'Since your dad . . . ?' Park repeated.

'Let Martin tell you in his own time,' Effie said. 'If he wants to.'

Martin said, 'It's okay.'

'You don't have to say anything,' Effie said to Martin.

'It's about time your dad knew,' Martin said.

Effie gave his shoulder a squeeze.

Martin's face seemed to thin and grow older as the muscles tightened. 'My dad,' he said, glancing at Effie, then back to Park, 'was murdered.'

'Jesus fuck.' Park took a swig of beer. 'When was this?'

'Ten years ago,' Martin said, struggling to light a fag even though there was already one smouldering in the ashtray.

Park wasn't going to pretend he wasn't interested, however hard this was for Martin. 'What happened?' he asked. 'Wrong place at the wrong time, kind of thing?'

Martin lit his cigarette at last, sucked hard. Then said in a strangled voice as he breathed out, 'He was involved with the wrong people.' He bit his lower lip, tapped his fag in the ashtray. 'Drug smugglers. Dealers.' He closed his eyes. Opened them again. His eyelashes were moist. 'This is boring,' he said.

'Far from it,' Park said. 'Carry on. Please.'

Martin stubbed out his cigarette, then picked up the other one and crushed it smokeless too. 'Dad was an alchy.' He picked at the label on his beer bottle. Loosened an edge. 'Got worse as he got older. Had a gambling habit, too. And it was worse when he was drunk.' He tore a strip off the label. 'Eventually he got in some serious debt. And then, as if he hadn't already fucked up enough, he did something really stupid.' He crumpled the label in his fingers, pinged it into the ashtray. Missed. He picked it up and dropped it in. 'He ripped off his employers, the dealers.'

'Got found out, of course,' Effie said. 'He was made an example of. They took him to Almondell Country Park. You know it?'

Park nodded. He knew where it was. Never had occasion to go there, though.

'The place didn't matter,' Martin said. 'Not for Dad. Middle of the night. His hands tied behind his back. Could have been anywhere quiet.' He lowered his head. Effie stroked the back of his neck till he looked up again. 'He was blindfolded. Never saw the blade.'

Oh, shit. Park felt the blood rush from his head like someone had scooped out a big hole in the back of his skull. 'They stabbed him?'

Martin looked pained, exactly as if somebody had just stabbed *him*. 'Cut,' he said. 'They cut . . .'

Park put his hand to his throat. It felt tight. He coughed.

Martin thought he was making a suggestion. Shook his head. 'Decapitated.'

'Man,' Park said, glad he was sitting down. He leaned forward, head between his knees.

'Cut his hands off, too.'

'Oh, Jesus.' Park's fingers curled towards his palm as he imagined steel slicing through the barbed-wire tattoo on his wrist. His vision went black at the edges but he fought it, stayed conscious.

'You okay, Dad?'

He blinked hard. Sweat trickled from the corners of his eyes. 'Dad?'

'Sorry about this,' he said. 'Yeah, I'll be fine.' He kept his head down and said, 'So why the fuck did they do that, Martin?'

'Suppose the plan was to get rid of the pieces. Lose the head. Lose the hands. Make the body hard to identify. But they were disturbed and ran. Left Dad behind.'

'Jesus,' Park said. 'That's . . .' He couldn't think of what to say. He concentrated on breathing.

'Dad?'

'I'm fucking fine, Eff.' He batted her hand away.

Martin said, 'I think Dad was going to use the money to do a runner. Otherwise he'd have paid off his debts.'

'Would have been too obvious,' Effie said. 'Money goes missing. Your dad's debts are cleared. Wouldn't take a genius to figure out what had happened.'

'That's what we figured,' Martin said. 'And things weren't great between him and Mum.'

'Because he was fucked up?' Park said.

'That. And he was abusive sometimes. A lot, actually. She wouldn't have minded if he'd left.'

'Still.' Park's head felt almost solid again. 'He was your dad.' He dared to sit up. Took a moment to confirm, but it seemed like he'd beaten it. Good. Didn't want to pass out again in front of Martin. 'Nobody deserves to come to an end like that.'

Martin looked at him. 'He wasn't a great dad, but, yeah, the truth is I miss him.'

They were quiet for a while. Then Park said, 'Hope the bastards paid.'

'What bastards?'

'The ones who killed him.'

Martin let a burst of air out through his nose. 'Still walking around.'

'They let them out already?'

Martin held his breath. Then: 'They've never been in.'

Park absorbed the information. 'The murderer's never been caught?' he said.

'Sorry,' Martin said. 'I can't talk . . .' He got up, put his hand to his brow and walked out of the room with Park calling after him. Effie followed him.

Park got off the floor, slowly. Still not a hundred per cent.

He took Martin's seat on the settee, said to Liz, 'Did you know anything about all that?'

Impossible that Liz had put on weight already, but that's what it looked like. Couple of pounds at least. Maybe she was just happy.

He took her hand and held it. 'You're looking very sexy,' he told her.

He'd almost polished off his beer by the time Effie returned, alone. 'Martin okay?' Park asked.

Effie closed the door. 'As okay as he can be. Have to keep an eye on him. He gets depressed sometimes.'

'I've never seen him depressed.'

'There's a lot you haven't seen. A lot you don't know. Squeeze up.'

Park let go of Liz's hand and edged along. Effie sat next to him, tucked her legs under her bottom.

'Fuck it.' She reached for Park's beer. He gave it to her. She took a sip. 'You've heard one story. You might as well hear the other.' Another sip, emptied it. 'When he was a kid, ' she said, 'Martin tried to hang himself.'

Park had new information coming at him from all angles tonight.

'That's why he keeps his neck covered,' she said. 'Big scar from the rope burn. It still embarrasses him.'

'Makes sense,' he said. 'I suppose. What happened?'

'All I know is he was only ten at the time. Didn't get it right. Not enough of a drop. His mum found him choking to death and cut him down. He says he was playing. It was an accident.'

'You don't believe him?'

'I know when he's lying. It was deliberate. A cry for help.'

'I need more beer,' Park said. 'You want one?'

She nodded.

Park grabbed two beers out of the fridge, removed the caps. Felt fine now. The nausea gone. Back in the sitting room, he handed a bottle to Effie.

She pressed it to her cheek, closed her eyes.

Park didn't want to talk about her boyfriend trying to hang himself twenty-odd years ago. Especially if Martin claimed it was an accident. Hell, that was his business. But Park did want to hear more about the murder. He asked her, 'Anybody have any idea who killed Martin's dad?'

'Yeah. In fact, that's what I wanted to talk to you about.' She opened her eyes, yawned. 'I'm sorry. Looking after Mum's hard work. I'm out tomorrow, by the way. You'll have to watch her.'

'Fine,' Park said. 'Carry on.'

'The fucking bumshite who arranged the hit on Martin's dad,' she said. 'Back then this guy was a dealer. Or a smuggler. Did a roaring trade in illegal cigarettes, apparently. Eventually made enough money to turn legit. Invested in property and made a fortune.'

'Martin's dad's death was a hit?'

'Yep.'

'And you're sure it was this dealer guy who put out the contract?'

'The bastard said he was going to have him killed. Told Martin's mum.'

'Jesus. She tell that to the police?'

'Yeah, but he had an airtight alibi. Course he did. Wouldn't have wanted to get his hands dirty. Didn't do it himself. Like I said. It was a hit.'

Park had an idea what was coming. Postponed it by asking, 'And this was just because Martin's dad ripped him off?'

'Pure and simple. He wouldn't give them their money back. Claimed he knew nothing about it. But they were convinced it was him. He had access. Motive.'

'It was just money, though? What a bunch of cunts. What's this dealer guy's name?'

She smiled at him. 'Savage. Tommy Savage. And this isn't just a case of taking Martin's mum's word, Dad. You know how Richie used to tell me everything?'

He knew what was coming. Fuck, he knew.

Park swallowed more beer. His elder son had a lot to answer for. Park was glad Richie was in prison, no access to beer. Best place for him. Park said, 'You're saying your brother . . . ?'

'I am.'

'Does Martin know?'

'Course he doesn't.' She smiled again. It didn't last. 'I can't tell him my big brother took out his dad. I have to keep that a secret from him all the time. It's killing me.'

Park shook his head. No, that wasn't something you could say to your betrothed. 'Eff, how come Richie knew who'd hired him for the job? I'd have thought the names of the people taking out the . . .'

'Expurgations,' she said.

'. . . aye, them, would only be known to the Spanish guy.'

'Carlos?'

Park nodded. Not someone he'd ever met. But Carlos was the guy who set up the contracts for Richie. Took the orders, if you like. Arranged payments. Richie called him his agent, thought very highly of him. Never breathed a word about the Spaniard when he was arrested.

When Richie got sent down, it hadn't come as a surprise to Park. Everybody's luck runs out sooner or later. Park knew what his son did. Effie had told him early on (those two were close, almost like twins), knew Park wouldn't snitch on his son.

Problem was Liz. She hadn't known that her big boy killed people for a living and after she found out, she changed.

'I asked Richie to find out who'd placed the hit on Martin's dad,' Effie said. 'He asked Carlos. Carlos said it was Tommy Savage. And Carlos has no reason to lie.'

'So this Tommy Savage hired Richie to kill your boyfriend's dad,' Park said. 'That's fucked up.'

'I can't let Savage get away with it.'

'Course not.'

She shifted in her seat, inched closer to him. 'I have an idea how to sort it out. Make everything work out for the best.'

'I'm listening.'

'We need to make Tommy Savage pay,' she said. 'You agree?'

'Certainly seems that way. What're you thinking?'

'He deserves to die,' she said. 'But he's stinking rich. Could be worth a lot to us alive.'

Park couldn't quite see how. It wasn't as if they could blackmail Savage. They didn't have any proof he'd ordered the hit on Martin's dad. Just had Carlos the Spaniard's word, and he wasn't exactly likely to spill to the authorities if Savage refused to pay up.

Park must have looked puzzled cause she said, 'We can use Savage's money to get Mum into a decent home.'

'I like that idea,' Park said, nodding slowly. 'I like it a lot.' He looked at Liz. 'But how do we get it?'

'Well, here's the clever bit. We threaten him.'

'Okay. Think that'll work?'

'As long as we prove we're serious.'

'Go on.'

'We tell him we're going to kill somebody. That's the threat.'

'And we prove we're serious by . . . ?'

'Doing it.'

'Right,' Park said. He thought about what she'd just said. 'You think we should actually kill somebody to show Savage we mean business?'

'Yes.'

Park didn't like to appear stupid in front of his daughter but he couldn't follow her line of thought. He asked, 'How does that work?'

'If Savage sees we're prepared to kill someone,' she said. 'And he knows he's next, then he'll pay up. We have something on him. He's guilty. He can't go to the police. Course he'll pay up.'

'And if he doesn't?'

'The only reason for not killing him is to get some money out of him. If he won't pay up, he might as well die.'

'But just suppose he doesn't pay up, then we'll have killed somebody for nothing.'

'Not if we kill someone who deserves it.'

Park paused. That was interesting. 'You have somebody in mind?'

'Think about it.'

He thought about it. Shook his head.

'Isn't there one person you'd really like to see dead?'

He wasn't there yet.

'Someone Mum would like to see dead? Someone who treated her like shit, never changed her pads, called her a fucking cabbage, let some poor old madwoman nearly suffocate her?'

'Fuck, aye.' That cunt McCracken. He could see now how all this might work. Kill McCracken to show Savage they meant business. Then blackmail Savage. Bleed him dry. Use his money to get Liz in a new home. Maybe tap him up for a bundle to give Effie and Martin a nice wedding. And Martin would be avenged for his father's murder, even if he could never know the ins and outs of it.

Only one problem. Park had never killed anyone. 'If only Richie was around,' he said.

'I can manage,' Effie said. 'And Grant offered to help.'

'You told Grant?'

She said nothing.

'Before you told me?'

'Actually,' she said. 'It was Grant who came up with the blackmail idea. I would have been more than happy to kill the fucker.'

Park believed her. She really took things personally sometimes. 'So Grant knows about Martin's dad?'

'He knows everything. He's cool, Dad.'

'Yeah,' Park said. 'It's not that I don't trust him. I'm just not too sure about involving him. He's got his own place. Well, his own room. And a job. Making a life for himself. And I don't imagine killing someone's going to be that straightforward.'

'He wants to do something for Mum,' Effie said. 'Don't shut him out.'

Park ran the palm of his hand down his face. 'If we do this, we need to do it right. I'm not going back to jail.'

'We'll be very careful.'

'Effie,' he said. 'You're a fucking lunatic.'

'Look who's talking,' she said and smiled. 'You think we can do it?'

Park weighed McCracken's life against Liz's comfort, and there was no contest. Having a good reason to kill McCracken was a godsend. Fuck, even a bad reason was fine. He could do this, no problem. A few tips from Richie and he'd be solid.

'Well?'

He nodded. 'But you stay out of it,' he said. '*I'll* handle it.'

Effie looked disappointed but she didn't argue. 'I'll look into homes for Mum in the morning, then,' she said.

NEXT MORNING HE'D gone out for a walk in the brisk March air, left Effie to make her calls in peace.

'All the homes are full,' she said when he returned. She'd heard him at the door and came to meet him.

'All of them?' He closed the door.

'The nice ones, yeah. There are a couple with vacancies but I got the impression they'd be every bit as bad as McCracken's.'

'Fuck that.' He shrugged out of his coat. 'No point taking her out of that shithole to put her into another.'

'Got one that'll take her two months from now.'

Jesus. 'That long?'

'Best I could do. And they'll need a month's deposit and a month in advance.'

He looked for somewhere to hang his coat. The pegs on the back of the door were all used. 'Got any good news?'

'I'm just telling you what I found out.'

'I know, ' Park said. 'Sorry. I'm pissed off, though.'

'Look,' she said. 'The deposit and all won't be a problem once Savage pays up. So if we look on the bright side, at least this gives us plenty of time to plan how we're going to do this.'

'I suppose.' He tried to hook his coat on one of the pegs. Couldn't get it to stay there. Tried another. 'One thing, though, Effie.' He tried the last peg. His coat hung there for a second, then slipped off and slumped onto the floor.

'Yeah?'

He picked up his coat, held it to his chest. 'Me and Mum can't stay with you till then. It's just not practical.'

She shuffled her feet, head bowed. 'You think Martin doesn't want you?'

He put his coat back on, fighting to get his right arm in the sleeve. 'We're already on top of each other. It was crammed when I was staying on my own. But with Mum here too, it's just not going to be workable. Two months of that and we'll be at each other's throats. It's nothing to do with Martin.'

She still wouldn't look at him. 'You'll take Mum somewhere, get out of our hair. That it?'

The coat was on. He zipped it up. 'You think I won't cope?'

Now she looked up at him, eyes big and fiery.

'Effie, don't be mad at me.'

'I'm not, Dad. It's just a bit of a shock. You sure you'll cope with Mum?'

He thought about what he'd have to deal with. He'd dealt with the worst of it already. He'd have to cook for her, medicate her, make sure she got some exercise. No problem. Only thing that bothered him was that Liz might fall over, cut herself. He'd be no use to her then.

And then he had a thought that instantly dried out his mouth. He said, 'What if she has a period?'

Effie laughed. 'She stopped having those while you were inside.'

'Then I'll be fine.' He put his hands in his pockets. 'I've made up my mind.'

She nodded, knew him well enough not to try to persuade him otherwise. 'Dad, we'll expect to see you and Mum a lot. You have to promise. If you need a break, bring her round here.'

'Yeah,' he said. 'Course.'

'Any idea where you're going to go?'

He was thinking, he'd always got along just fine with Yardie's mum and with her son back inside, there was a chance she might like some company again. 'If it's okay to borrow the car,' he said, 'I'll take Liz for a spin, go check something out right now.'

OLD MRS YARDIE was delighted to see him. She ushered him into the house, all smiles and slow-walking for Liz. Not that Old Mrs Yardie galloped along at a great speed herself, but Liz did like to take her time.

Mrs Yardie led them through the big hallway into her sitting room. 'You should have said you were coming,' she said. 'I'd have made pancakes. And I've no coffee. Will tea do?'

'No need to bother,' Park said.

'It's no bother.' She stood there staring at him.

'Lovely,' he said.

She went off to make the tea.

'Nice, eh?' Park said to Liz, leading her to a chair.

Flecks of spit gathered between her lips. She sat down.

'You'll like it here,' he said.

When Mrs Yardie returned with the tea – pot, milk jug, sugar bowl, fancy cups, all on a brass tray – Park got to his feet to take it from her.

'I can manage,' she said.

Park took it anyway and placed it on the coffee table.

Old Mrs Yardie took a seat on the settee, leaned forward. 'How does she like it?' she asked, nodding towards Liz.

Park wasn't sure. He never made tea. Liz never drank it. 'White, no sugar,' he said.

'And yourself?'

'Same,' he said. Then, 'No, I'll have some sugar, too.'

They chatted for a while, Park commiserating with her on Yardie's return to jail. She said he deserved it, didn't know where he'd got the drug habit from. And that he was in her bad books from the day he'd asked Park to leave.

She said, 'If I hadn't been away at Maud's at the time –'

'What would you think about me moving back in?'

She looked at him, cup frozen mid-route to her lips.

'Just temporary,' he said. 'Couple of months. No more than that.'

'Well,' she said. 'Well, I have your old room upstairs still. I don't see why not.'

'And Liz,' he said.

Old Mrs Yardie turned to look at her. 'Goodness,' she said. 'She's no trouble. Such an angel.'

'Isn't she?' Park said. 'Is that a yes, then?' he asked. 'We'll pay twice what I was paying before.'

'Oh, no need,' Old Mrs Yardie said. 'Just pay the same. You keep your money. You young folks need it.'

Park stood up, bent over and took her hand. 'I wish I could do something for you,' he said. 'To say thanks.'

'Maybe you can,' she said. 'I was just thinking . . . If you didn't mind looking after the house for two or three weeks, I could go see Maud down in Kent. She's not well at the moment. But I hate to leave the house empty.'

'Just let us know when,' Park said. 'We'd be delighted.'

'As long as you promise you won't throw any wild parties.'

FOUR DAYS LATER and they'd settled into their new home. Old Mrs Yardie was off visiting her sick sister. Took the train, left her car keys with Park. Which made it easy for Park to take Liz with him when he went to Florida Al's.

Park had never been to the tanning studio. In fact, he'd never been to any tanning studio. He was happy with his skin the way it was.

The guy behind the desk, blonde hair streaked blue, said, 'Can I help you?'

He didn't look Spanish and he didn't sound Spanish. Park said, 'Where's Carlos?'

'Out back, smoking.' He motioned Park to the rear of the salon. 'Door's open,' he said.

'My wife needs somewhere to sit,' Park said.

'Only got the seat I'm sitting on,' the guy said.

'That'll do,' Park told him.

In the alleyway at the back, a small bronzed guy, looked about twenty, was taking a long drag on a cigarette. 'Who are you?' the guy said.

'You Carlos?'

'I ask first.'

'You're too young to be Carlos.'

He smiled. 'I have the face of the youth.'

'My son's a bit like that,' Park said. 'Not the one you worked with. The other one, his little brother.'

'And you are?'

'The Expurgator's dad.'

Carlos didn't react. 'What do you want?'

'I want your gun,' Park said.

The Spaniard stared at him. 'I do not know no Expurgator.'

Park said, 'Park.'

Carlos shrugged. 'I know no Park either.' He paused. 'Maybe where I walk my dog?' He grinned.

Park smacked the cigarette out of his hand. Grabbed his throat, pinned him against the wall. 'I'll pay you,' he said. 'Cash.' He squeezed. 'Lots of it.' He squeezed harder. 'Just give me your gun.'

Blame Effie. She'd pointed him in the right direction.

She'd said, 'You should get yourself a weapon, Dad.'

And he'd said, 'Where would I get one of them?'

'*Carlos has a gun.*'

'*But I can't use a gun,*' he'd told her.

'*You know that. But the guy you're pointing it at won't.*'

'*And why would Carlos give me his gun?*'

'*Cause you're Richie's dad. And cause you'll pay him.*'

'*Don't have any money, Eff.*'

'*But you will. Lots of it. You can pay him then.*'

'*You know,*' he said. '*You've got a real head for business.*'

The Spaniard whimpered. Made gagging noises. His voice-box vibrated beneath Park's fingers.

Carlos didn't look as if he was going to be a threat. Too busy choking.

Park let go and Carlos doubled over, coughing like a sick dog.

Park waited patiently, although he was tempted to knee him in the chin to help straighten him up again.

Eventually Carlos unbent of his own accord. His eyes were bloodshot.

Park said, 'Two grand.'

'You can't offer *el dinero*,' the Spaniard wheezed. 'I am not who you think I am. This Expurgator, he is not someone I know. *Dinero* or no *dinero*.'

'Three.'

Carlos paused. 'Why you think I have a gun?'

'I spoke to my son.' A lie. 'Richie said you'd let me borrow it.'

'Four.' His voice sounded just fine.

'Three five.'

'*Si.*' The little man put his hand behind his back, reappeared with a gun. 'I could have shot you when you were strangling me.'

Park wrapped his fingers round the gun, eased it out of the Spaniard's grip. 'You need balls to shoot someone.'

Carlos smiled. His lips trembled under the strain of holding it. 'Money?'

Park aimed the gun at the Spaniard's forehead. Kept his arm steady. 'And now I can shoot *you*.'

'But you won't.' Carlos was sweating.

'You saying I don't have balls?'

Carlos said, 'Three thousand five hundred. Cash. Now.'

'Like fuck.'

'Is my gun. We had a deal.'

'Your gun, eh?' Park said. He lowered it. 'Where's your receipt?'

'I have no receipt. I don't buy no Glock in a supermarket.'

'I think I'll keep it, then.'

'But is mine. You don't understand. Is a Glock. Is very difficult to find a Glock in this city.'

'Yeah?' Park walked away. Stopped. Said, 'Tell you what, I'll give it back to you when I'm done.'

'If you don't,' Carlos reached into his pocket and took out his cigarettes, 'I will send someone to fetch it.'

SAVAGE NIGHT
8.30 P.M.
VEHICLES

PHIL PAUSED AT the traffic lights. Polished off his beer, tossed the bottle. *Clink.* A big pile rattled around on the passenger seat, dripping onto the upholstery. He didn't give a shit, though. Grabbed the last one and cracked it open.

The car lurched forward. *Shit.* He wrenched the handbrake on. Fine. No problem. He shouldn't be driving, so he was told. Well, fuck 'em, he'd drive if he wanted. His head wasn't throbbing, not at the moment.

He'd taken a real whack that night, though. Hell of a lump.

'As big as an ostrich egg,' the doctor had said. Young guy, neat beard, liked to grin.

Phil had tried to sit up, but the doc eased him back down.

'Not yet,' the doc said. 'Just going to take an x-ray.' He showed his teeth.

'Of the egg?'

The doc didn't reply.

Phil couldn't understand why the doc had lied. Ostrich eggs were massive and the lump on his head was never that big. Didn't seem to be any rhyme or reason to it.

Anyway, the swelling had gone down now.

Phil slugged some more beer. His skull still felt tender but at least it was back to its normal shape. No longer felt like somebody else's.

'No lasting damage,' the doc had said.

Well, maybe, but Phil was finding it hard to think straight. Mind you, he always did, if you asked Tommy. Thought Phil was stupid. Told him so, as often as possible. Oh, not straight out: 'You're thick as mince.' Not since they were kids, anyway. He was more subtle these days. Little digs. But enough of them and they scoop out a hole big enough for a body to fall into.

Phil felt himself topple forwards, heard the blast of a car horn, jerked himself upright.

Tommy was the brains, you see. Phil was the muscle. Phil did what he was told. Which was fine. If that's what people thought. There wasn't much Phil could do about it. Everybody had their own opinions. Didn't really matter. An opinion wasn't right or wrong, by its very nature. Just an opinion, eh?

Phil's opinion was that Tommy was nothing. Not without Phil. Which was why Phil was behind the wheel when he shouldn't be. For Tommy's sake. Shit, he didn't mind. Although it'd be nice to get thanked occasionally. Never happened, though, not once. Tommy took him for granted, the bastard. Any time he was in trouble, Phil sorted it out. And the fucker never even remembered Phil's birthday.

Phil burped, a real belter from the back of the throat.

Well, Tommy was in real trouble now. And Phil was sorting it out once again. Yeah, fuck the missed birthdays. Birthdays were for kids. And Phil was the forgiving sort anyway. Phil never missed one of *his*, though. Not once in the best part of fifty years. Well, maybe when they were kids. No money to buy presents, then. But, you know, he'd never missed an adult birthday. In however many years that was. That was it. Not that he cared. They were just birthdays.

Dad said, 'Blow out your candles, Phil.'

Phil took a breath and blew so hard he thought his eyes might pop out. Seven of the candles went out. One flickered but the flame didn't die.

'You didn't do it,' Tommy said.

Phil punched him in the ribs and Tommy started to cry.

Dad sent Phil to his room. On his fucking birthday.

The traffic lights finally changed. Must be some malfunction. They'd been on red far too long.

Phil couldn't get going though, cause there was a guy halfway across the road. An old geezer, stooped like a beaten kid, wearing a long pale coat that dragged along the ground. Needed a walking stick and didn't have one.

Phil revved the engine, hooted the horn, pointed his bottle at him. None of that helped so Phil made a face.

That hurried him up a bit.

The geezer turned near the kerb and waved. Taunting him, the old fuck.

Phil should get out and smack him one, teach the bastard a lesson. Might have done just that, but Phil had a meeting with Martin Milne. Probably didn't want to get into a fight, anyway, even with an old git. Just in case he landed a lucky shot. Phil wasn't at his peak. But he'd had the x-ray and his head was fine. They'd kept him in the hospital overnight as a precaution. But he was home by lunchtime.

He couldn't remember being hit. Remembered bits afterwards. It was all like he was drunk, though.

Lying there on the ground for ages, stiff and cold, feeling like somebody'd dropped the back end of a truck on his head. Finally he'd got it together and scrabbled to his feet. Knew he ought to phone an ambulance but also knew he shouldn't. He wasn't sure why.

What should he do, then? Phone somebody. Get out of here. Go home. Go to bed. What had happened? That's how he was thinking. In fucked-up snatches.

He took out his phone. Looked through the names in his contacts. Only one made sense: Tommy. He remembered Tommy. Where was he? Phil looked for his brother and thought he saw him, but it was just a tombstone lying on the ground like a flat person. There was no sign of Tommy.

Phil called him. No answer. Phil wanted to leave a message but couldn't think of the words. He hung up and called again. Same result.

So he took another quick look around, couldn't see anyone, just more flattened tombstones, and staggered down the path.

He'd lost something. No idea what. Flashes of something bright, shiny, sharp. The information was in his head, but the harder he tried to locate it, the sicker he felt. Just out of the graveyard, he fell to his knees and spewed. Didn't help him remember, but he felt better. A little.

Dizzy, legs about to give out, he walked down the path. He had to sit down before long. Thought about staying there. But he had somewhere to go. Not home, no. Another place. Where sick people went.

Hospital! That was the fella.

He got there, but it was a mystery how. He couldn't remember a thing.

Taxi? Wasn't possible. It wouldn't have stopped. He looked drunk and taxi drivers didn't like alkies.

But somehow he'd made it.

Yeah, everything was stop-start. For a while. With chunks of time missing.

The doc said, 'Turn your head to the side.'

'I'll be sick.'

The doc grinned. 'You have to turn your head to the side.'

He did. And was sick.

Sometime later the doctor said, 'You're feeling better.'

'I am?'

'Are you?'

'I think so.'

'Your head still hurts?'

He nodded. Bad idea. It hurt.

'Can you tell me your name?'

He could.

'And your address?'

He could.

'That's great,' the doctor said. 'There are some gentlemen here to see you.'

They weren't gentlemen. They were cops.

They asked him what he'd been up to. How he'd hurt his head.

'Fell,' he said.

'The doctor tells us you were hit.'

'Don't remember.'

'So you didn't fall?'

'Don't remember.'

They handed him a card and told him to phone if his memory returned.

When Phil left the hospital, first thing he did was call his mum. He'd already called Tommy several times that morning. In the toilets. Private. In case. But no joy. He remembered more of what had happened in the cemetery. Couldn't remember being hit and hadn't seen who'd hit him. But no prizes for guessing.

Smith had taken Tommy. Cunt.

'Where is he?' Mum said when Phil called.

'Where's who?' He knew it was stupid as soon as he'd said it. He was the stupid one all right.

'Tommy. Who do you think?'

'Hoping you'd be able to tell me.'

A long shot. But, no. Tommy hadn't gone home. Mum thought he was with Phil. Thought he'd stayed over. She was pissed off with him for leaving her with Jordan. Not that she minded but he could have given her some warning. She was pissed off with him for not answering his mobile too.

Phil made some shit up but it didn't calm her down. Since when had Tommy started sleeping around like a teenager? Phil wasn't sure.

'New girlfriend. You know how it is.'

But she didn't. She hung up.

Phil knew why Smith was doing this. He had no idea who Smith was. Or how he fitted in. But Phil knew what it was about.

Smith was playing some kind of blackmail card. Holding something over Tommy. But Tommy was clean, always had been. Phil did the dirty work. Tommy didn't have the stomach for it. Had the brains, yeah, but those weren't much good sometimes.

That Milne cunt. That's what this was about.

You try to do something for the best and somebody fucks it up. The fucker was a professional, too.

This hired killer was chopping Milne up, everything all fine and dandy. Then some lovey-dovey couple spots him. It's two in the fucking morning, in the woods. Nowhere's fucking safe. So the killer leaves the body. He runs. It's touch and go. But he gets away with it. Milne's dead, which is a start. But not what Phil wanted. Phil wanted him disappeared, all neat and clean.

Next day Tommy finds out. Says, 'Somebody cut Greg Milne's head off. Why would anybody do that?'

Phil shrugged.

Tommy pushed. 'You think of a reason?'

Phil said, 'Cause he was a thieving bastard?'

'You saying *I* had a reason?'

Phil said, 'Thought you'd already said that.'

'What do you mean?'

'You told Jean you were going to kill him.'

'Jean?' Tommy said. 'Jean. The wife. Right. You still shagging her?'

Phil said nothing. He twisted the ring she'd bought him, round and round his finger. Quarter turns. A Viking longship. Silver. He'd had to take it back and get a bigger one. The new one fitted like a charm. Nobody'd ever bought him jewellery before.

'Cause if you are,' Tommy said, 'the police will want to speak to you.'

'It's over. Long time ago.'

Tommy said, 'Where *were* you last night?'

Phil said, 'Party at Harris's house. Drank beer. Watched some porn. Fell asleep.'

'Cosy.'

'What're you saying, Tommy?'

'Sure you weren't with her?'

'You don't believe me?'

Tommy eyeballed him. 'You have anything to do with what happened to Milne?'

'Jesus,' Phil said. 'You not listening? What do you take me for?'

Tommy continued to stare at him. Phil held his gaze. Easy.

'Okay,' Tommy said, looking away. 'Just wondering.' He scratched an eyebrow. 'Who do you think it was?'

'Killed Milne? Guy was an alchy,' Phil said. 'And a thief. And in debt up to his eyeballs. Fuck knows who he pissed off.'

Tommy didn't want to know. Not really. Which was fine with Phil. Let Tommy think everything was above board. He was a funny guy. Smuggling fags was okay. No violence, though. Of that, Tommy certainly didn't approve. Definitely no killing.

About a week later Phil met with the Spanish kid, Carlos. He looked about twelve, immediately demanded the rest of his money. As arranged. Phil wouldn't give it to him, though.

'Half-arsed job,' Phil told him. 'No way.'

'I tell the police,' Carlos said.

'Tell them what?'

'Thomas Savage hires a man to kill Greg Milne.'

Phil smiled. 'What makes you think I'm Thomas Savage?'

'Your car,' Carlos said. 'When we meet first, I have it checked. Registered to Thomas Savage.'

Phil said, 'Okay.' He paid the man. Let him believe his lie. It was Tommy's money, anyway. Phil had nicked it to set up Milne. Easy. The fucker shouldn't have hit Jean. Nearly broke her fucking jaw.

PHIL NEVER SLEPT with Jean again. She was convinced Tommy'd had her husband killed. Phil was a reminder, so she said. He looked nothing like Tommy and pointed that out. They did try. A couple of times. But it didn't work for either of them. She had some kind of breakdown, not for the first time. He wanted to help. He made her worse, she said.

OUTSIDE THE PUB, Phil pulled into a parking space.

He looked around, checked his watch. He was early.

Even so, there were lights flashing at him from a Ford Escort van.

He tossed his last bottle of beer onto the pile and climbed out of the car. A bit unsteady on his feet. Drink'll do that. He walked over to the van pretty much in a straight line. Could always sober up when he had to.

Martin Milne reached across, opened the door. He didn't look like his dad.

Phil got in. Said: 'You know where Tommy is?'

'Patience,' Martin said. Drank beer from a bottle. 'We're going to Fraser's. Need to speak to your nephew, too.'

Fair enough. Speak to Fraser about his dad. Phil hadn't said a word. Not cause he was scared of Smith, just didn't want Fraser phoning the cops. Couldn't trust the spoiled prick. Hadn't spoken to Mum either. She didn't want to. She was still pissed off with Tommy for buggering off. Two weeks was a long time, right enough. But it was fine with Phil. Meant he had less explaining to do.

Phil slotted home his seatbelt and stretched his legs. 'Not scared I'll hurt you?' he asked Martin.

'You won't.'

'You're sure of that?'

'Mum said you were cool,' Martin said. 'Not like your brother. I'm no threat to you. You're none to me. That right?'

Phil nodded. Martin had asked as much on the phone. Had Jean told him?

'Keep it a secret,' she'd said.

'Why?' Phil had wanted to know.

'My husband's just been murdered. How do you think it'll look?'

She'd had a point. Phil never told anyone other than Tommy.

'How is your mum?' Phil asked.

'Good.' Martin reached over the half-height steel partition behind the seats and produced a carrier bag that clanked in a promising kind of way. 'Help yourself,' he said.

In the bag were half a dozen bottles of beer. Way to go. 'Don't mind if I do,' Phil said. 'You want another?'

'I'm fine.'

Phil opened the bottle and took a sip. Tasted like shit. Foreign crap. Couple of sips later, though, it wasn't so bad. He raised the bottle to Martin.

Big guy, Milne's son. Could easily go to fat. He needed to take care of himself. Wore that cravat thing round his neck. Drove very carefully. Came across like a bit of a nonce.

But Phil wasn't looking forward to having to kill him.

He couldn't think of anything to say. He downed more beer. Needed it. He watched the scenery, the pretty lights out of focus. Felt good, though. He had a nice buzz going. Couple more long pulls. Yeah. Nice.

Tired, though. So fucking tired. Hadn't slept properly for ages. Not like him at all. Tommy was missing. His fucking little brother was missing. Phil shouldn't have let that happen. 'We going to be long?' he asked.

'Twenty minutes?'

Time passed.

Phil felt the beer bottle slide out of his fingers. It rolled over his leg. Dropped to the floor with a thud.

'Whoa!' Martin said.

Phil mumbled, 'Just beer.'

'You want to pick it up?'

He couldn't. No way. He was far too tired. 'Just leave it, eh? Nearly empty, anyway.'

Martin shrugged.

'I'll grab fifty winks.' Phil smiled at him. 'Wake me up when we get there, eh?'

'YOU ASLEEP?' MARTIN asked Phil Savage a couple of minutes later.

No sooner had he said he was going to catch some sleep than Savage had slumped towards Martin, landing with his head in his lap. Martin almost pranged the van, but managed to shove Savage's head out of the way so that the guy's plump cheek rested on his thigh and Martin was still able to reach the gearstick, even if he couldn't get at the handbrake. Since it was quite a drive out to Fraser Savage's house, it was probably a good thing that his uncle was out of sight.

'Wake up, you fat ginger bastard,' Martin said.

No reply.

Sleepy Head had convinced Martin's mum that he'd had no involvement in his dad's death. But Martin wasn't so sure. Phil Savage was exactly the kind of man who would have killed Martin's dad. And even if he hadn't, the dirty fucker had slept with his mum.

He deserved everything that was coming to him.

Martin had had two weeks to tell himself this over and over. Which was just as well. He'd needed it. But he was ready now. This was not something he was going to fuck up. Whatever

Effie and her dad thought. Oh, they never said as much, but he knew they didn't think he had it in him.

'Well, I fucking do,' he told the unconscious man. 'You wait and see.'

He'd make Effie proud of him.

Fifteen minutes later, and the warm, wet patch on Martin's jeans was spreading towards his crotch. He'd been warned that GHB could induce some powerful reactions: spasms and vomiting weren't uncommon.

But he'd managed to sneak a look and he was pretty sure Savage was drooling on him rather than spewing.

Still, he was glad when he pulled into Fraser's driveway. He drove round the back of the house. Out of sight, not cause of the neighbours – there weren't any – but to ensure Fraser didn't spot the van when he came back with Effie.

When Martin lifted Phil's face off his leg, the damp patch instantly cooled. Definitely drool, but he'd have to get rid of all his clothes afterwards, anyway, so whether it was sick or drool really wasn't a big deal. He had to stop flustering. It didn't matter.

He shook Savage. No response. Shook him harder. Nothing. He was hardly breathing. Had to look closely to detect the rise and fall of his chest. Could have been fooled into thinking he was already dead.

Martin lit a cigarette. The smoke hit the back of his throat, fired a dart of adrenalin into his brain.

Getting into the house would be no hassle. Park had given Martin a key. And Effie had got the number for the burglar alarm the night she'd gone back with Fraser. Martin hadn't liked that, but there was nothing he could do about it. He trusted her enough to know that nothing had happened, but still.

He'd take in the bag first – a few tools, dropcloth, plastic footwear, shit like that. Then he'd take in the tub. Could do it all in the bathroom, yeah, but the bathroom was upstairs and that would mean hefting Phil Savage all the way up there and then back down afterwards. Much more straightforward to do it in the sitting room. They'd worked it all out.

He had to stick to the plan. That was the only way he'd get through this.

Mr Park, *Andy* (couldn't get used to calling him that), wanted Fraser to see what they'd done to Phil. He wanted Fraser distracted so that Effie could do her thing. Which seemed pretty sadistic to Martin. He'd said so to Effie and she just said, 'Yep, and?' And he wasn't sure, so he shrugged, and she said, 'That's the whole point, Martin,' and he nodded.

As for Martin's role in this, yeah, he'd considered waiting till they were in the house before spiking Savage's drink. He'd weighed up the pros and cons with Effie and decided there was less risk doing it this way. Doctor the beer before handing it over, then the only risk was that Savage was going to say no, but according to Effie he was a pisshead so that was unlikely. Or that he'd notice the beer was a bit flat. If he had, the plan had been to kill him in the car park. Wait till he was buckled in, then reach into the back, get the knife out of the bag, and chib him where he sat.

This way was better. Meant Martin hadn't had to drive around with a corpse for a passenger, which wouldn't have been any fun if he'd been pulled over. At least with Sleeping Beauty next to him, Martin could have claimed Savage was blutered and if the cops hadn't believed him, he could have invited them to check Savage's pulse and see for themselves.

Martin took a last drag of his cigarette. He couldn't put this off forever.

'I'll be back in a minute,' he said to Phil.

Still no reply. Good.

Martin left Phil asleep in the van and walked round to the front of the house. He sucked in a lungful of air. Then he opened the door, found the alarm panel and keyed in the code.

PRELUDE TO A SAVAGE NIGHT: THE SAVAGES AND THE PARKS

PHIL TOOK THE torch from Tommy and shone it on Grant's motionless body, highlighting the gleaming patches where blood dripped through the lad's shirt and trousers.

Tommy looked away, said, 'Fuck,' for what had to be the twentieth time. His stomach was only just holding out. Felt like a terrified rabbit was trapped inside him, trying to kick its way to freedom.

As far as Tommy could gather, Grant had rammed the door with his head, punching a hole in the glass large enough for his shoulders to fit through. Whatever his velocity he was never going to make it through the doorway strapped to a dining chair. So he'd slumped down onto what appeared to be a horrifically sharp wedge of broken glass and was stuck there.

Tommy took a step back. 'What're we going to do?'

Phil said, 'I think we should fuck off.'

'You what?' Tommy said. 'We have to do something for him.'

'Like?'

'Call an ambulance?'

'What about Smith?'

'Fuck Smith.'

'He'll still be wanting his money.'

'Fuck the money.'

'We could go to the cemetery.'

'How does that help Grant?'

'Forget Grant for a minute,' Phil said. 'Right now we have to think about us.'

'Fuck's sake, Phil. There's no time. Look at him.'

'We'll make time.'

Tommy breathed in through his nose, out through his mouth. No good. Wasn't just his stomach, his heart was hammering away too. He took a few rapid breaths. 'We have to take him to the hospital.'

'You're not listening.'

'Fuck, Phil, he's going to –'

Phil smacked Tommy hard on the cheek. 'Calm the fuck down.'

Tommy stared at his brother, cheek stinging. Said nothing for a while. Then: 'Phil? What the fuck have we done?'

'It's okay.'

Phil raised his hand and Tommy flinched, thinking he was going to get hit again.

But Phil lowered his hand onto Tommy's shoulder and squeezed. 'It's a mess,' he said. 'But it'll be okay.'

Tommy wasn't so sure.

'You all right, Tommy?'

'I don't know.' His teeth were chattering. That fucking rabbit was still pounding away inside him. His skull felt like it was shrinking.

'You going to pass out?'

Tommy shook his head.

'Then you're okay. I need you to listen. Can you do that?'

'Yeah,' Tommy said.

'Good. Now here's what I was thinking. Grant was going to go to the cemetery with the money, right? We can go instead.'

'Okay,' Tommy said.

'But how do we explain that to Smith?'

'You asking me? It's your suggestion.'

'Maybe we don't need to. If Smith's waiting there, he might wonder why we're showing up instead of Grant. But we can just tell him Grant never turned up.'

'Turned up where?'

'At the bus station.'

'Grant was never supposed to turn up. Not as far as we were concerned. ' Tommy felt as if somebody'd rubbed every inch of his skin with a cold cloth. He ignored it, forced himself to concentrate. 'I was supposed to leave the money in the locker, drop off the key and go home.' He shivered. 'And that was the end of the story. You weren't supposed to be there. And we weren't supposed to know about Grant. And he's fucking dying while we're standing here talking, Phil, for Christ's sake.'

'I'm not thick,' Phil said. 'I know all that.'

'So why're you suggesting such a dumb idea?'

Phil aimed the light at Tommy, made Tommy put his hand in front of his face.

''Cause I *was* there,' Phil said, lowering the torch. 'And we can just admit to it. What's Smith going to do?'

'So if Grant didn't show at the bus station, how come we know to go to the cemetery?'

'Now that,' Phil said, 'is a much better question. I'll have to think about it.'

Phil shone the light over Grant again. Dark lines dribbled down what remained of the glass in the door. A finger twitched. And again.

'We have to fucking do something, Phil.'

'How about this, then?' Phil said, ignoring him. 'Grant did show. But we gave him a doing and he told us where to meet Smith.'

'If that's what you want.'

'We have the money. And we wanted Smith's identity. But maybe we can go one better.'

Tommy didn't know what he was talking about. 'Let's get Grant some help.'

'Fine,' Phil said again, shining the light up and down the glass, tracing what looked like paint drips. 'Just tell me what you want to do.'

'I told you,' Tommy said. 'Call an ambulance.'

'They'll contact the police.'

'It was an accident.'

'Yeah,' Phil said, 'but I fucking hit him. Kidnapped him. Taped him to a fucking chair. And then we scared him. So much, he tried to do a runner. Through a plate-glass door. The police might not agree it's an accident.'

Tommy couldn't think. He felt as if somebody'd taken the top off his head and drizzled honey all over his brain. He said, 'So what do you think we should do?'

'Well,' Phil said. 'First, *we* don't tell the cops anything. I'll phone in. Won't give my name. Tell them I heard a disturbance. Shouts and screams. I'll exaggerate. Make it seem urgent. That way, Grant's got a chance. If he has enough blood in him.'

'And then?'

'We have a choice, Tommy. One option is to do nothing. You take the money. Go home. Wait for Smith to get in touch. Wait for him to do whatever it was you were so scared of before tonight. Cause nothing's changed. Apart from how mad he'll be when he finds out about Grant. The boy's got to be somebody he knows. Might be his little cousin. Or his nephew.'

'You have to be so fucking negative?'

'Or we can do what I suggested,' Phil said. 'Go to the cemetery and nail the bastard. Get him out of your life once and for all.'

'Nail him?'

Phil nodded. 'Yeah.'

'You mean what I think you mean?'

'Nobody'll know.'

'I'm a businessman. I can't go around . . . nailing people.'

'Look at Grant here.'

'He's an accident.'

'So I heard. You're making a mistake, Tommy.'

'I can't take the chance.'

'You never could,' Phil said.

'Fuck you,' Tommy said. 'Let me think about it.'

'There's no time to waste thinking.'

Phil was right. Besides, Tommy couldn't think. 'Maybe we could just scare him a bit.'

'Now you're talking,' Phil said. 'We'll need weapons.'

'Oh, Jesus, Phil. That's too much.'

Phil said, 'We're not going to scare him by pulling faces. And he might not be alone.' He paused. 'Just for show.'

'You know where to get guns?'

'You any idea how hard it is to get guns in this city?' Phil said. 'And with this kind of notice? Tell you what I *can* get, though.'

PHIL DROVE. HE'D always been the better driver and speed was essential.

Tommy clutched the bag on his lap, listened to the revs of the engine. He felt better now, more together, although there was an odd pressure in his head like he hadn't slept in days, and his hand was shaking and he didn't seem to be able to stop it. At least he was able to think straight. Enough to know that he had to take charge. Couldn't have Phil in control or they'd both be fucked. 'What're we going to do with the money?' Tommy said. He couldn't take it home, stash it somewhere safe. No time for that.

Phil glanced at him, at the bag. 'Maybe we should have left it with Grant.'

'The police would find it.'

'Not if we don't call them.'

'Jesus, Phil,' Tommy said. 'Keep your eyes peeled for a phone box.'

It was safe to make the call now. They'd put enough distance between themselves and Grant that there was no fear of getting flagged down in the vicinity, asked awkward questions like why they were in possession of fifty grand in cash.

'You sure you want to?' Phil said.

Tommy just looked at him.

Took a couple of minutes, but they found one. It was empty. Probably meant the fucker was broken, though.

'You mind doing it?' Tommy said.

Phil didn't say anything, just opened the door and scuttled out of the car. While he made the call to the police, Tommy watched some drunk lads walk past, scooping chips into their mouths. He had to look away or risk throwing up.

He closed his eyes, banged the back of his head off the seat, said, 'Fuck', under his breath. Did it again, harder and louder. And again.

Kept it up cause it stopped him thinking about what had happened. After a while his hands stopped shaking.

'You shouting about?' Phil said when he came back.

'How'd it go?' Tommy asked him. 'They believe you?'

Phil put the car in gear, headed off. 'I said I was a neighbour. Heard a noise. Went to see what was going on. Found the door open. Wandered inside. Saw somebody lying in a pool of blood. Yeah, they believed me.'

'Good.'

'Yeah,' Phil said. 'Fucking terrific.'

They didn't speak for a while, long enough for the tremble to creep back into Tommy's hands. He checked his watch. 'You want to put your foot down?' he said. Time was tight if they were going to make the rendezvous with Smith in the graveyard.

'And get stopped for speeding?'

Tommy looked at the speedo. 'Sorry,' he said. 'I'm sorry, Phil. I'm fucking sorry.'

'Yeah, no big deal,' Phil said. 'Anyway, we'll be at Worm's soon. Maybe he'll look after the money for you.'

Tommy knew Phil's mate by reputation only. Something of an eccentric. Worm claimed he hadn't slept in twenty years. 'I'm sure he's a great bloke,' Tommy said. 'But if he looked in the bag and saw all this cash, he might be tempted to keep it.'

'You'll just have to keep the money on you, then.'

'I'm not leaving it in the car. Some joyriding bastard'll be off with it in no time.'

'Keep it on you, I said.'

'Can't take it to the cemetery.'

'Why not?'

'Smith'll love that.'

'Doesn't matter what Smith loves. He's going to be dead meat in an hour or so.'

Tommy got a flash of Grant, wedged in the doorway, blood running down the glass, blood dripping onto the floor. Tommy couldn't handle any more bloodshed. 'Dead meat?' he said.

'In a manner of speaking. You're not chickening out, are you?'

Tommy looked at his brother. 'No,' he said.

''Cause I can go to the cemetery alone.'

'Don't wind me up.'

'I'm serious. I'll go to the cemetery. You take the money somewhere safe.'

'I can't let you do that,' Tommy said.

'Think I can't handle Smith?'

'I think you might handle him too well.'

Phil banged the steering wheel with the heel of his hand. 'You want to keep an eye on me?' He puffed his cheeks out, nodded slowly. 'Okay, look, you keep the money on you. We find Smith. We . . . sort him out. Nothing too heavy. Just enough for him to get the message. Threat's over. And you get to keep the money. Okay?'

Tommy swallowed. 'That easy, eh?'

Phil speeded up a little. 'Don't see why not.'

Tommy wished he had a tenth of his brother's confidence. He wanted to reach over and give his arm a squeeze. Then he remembered the slap in the face. He could still feel the warmth in his cheek. He kept his arm by his side.

'One thing I'd like to know,' Phil said. 'What did you do that pissed this guy off so much?'

Tommy paused. Good question. 'I've no idea,' he said.

'Come on,' Phil said. 'You can tell me.'

'Honestly,' Tommy said. 'I haven't a clue.' The closest he'd come to an answer was the nursing home guy's death. That was supposed to be significant. 'The name McCracken mean anything to you? Eric McCracken?'

Phil slowed down, pulled into a parking space near a bizarre concrete building that looked like it'd been built in the sixties. He switched off the engine, took his gloves off. 'Nope,' he said. 'Not a bloody thing.'

WORM WAS EXPECTING them. Or so he said. So why he opened the door dressed in what looked like a hospital gown was a puzzle.

Phil made the introductions without commenting on the gown. Worm glanced at the bag in Tommy's hand, then led them inside. The gown was open at the back and Tommy got an eyeful of Worm's hairy arse as he waddled along the corridor in front of them.

Tommy looked at Phil, who shrugged.

The walls were decorated with lots of paintings of military scenes. Battles, regimental marching, cannons, swords. Lots of swords.

The sitting room was spacious, looked comfortable and reeked of dope. A long-haired blonde slouched on the sofa, struggling to keep her eyes open. She was wearing a hospital gown, too. She said hello to Phil, got to her feet, shook Tommy's hand. 'Make yourselves at home, gentlemen. You'll have to excuse me.' She padded across the room. 'I'm dog tired. Gotta catch some shut-eye. Have to do the sleeping for both of us.'

Her gown was open at the back, too, her buttocks smooth and nicely chubby.

'Night, Simone,' Worm said. And to them: 'Want a drink of something?'

'Beer,' Phil said.

Tommy said, 'We're in a bit of a rush.'

'Cool,' Worm said. 'Wait there. I'll get my girls.'

He vanished, returned shortly afterwards with a bottle of beer and a couple of swords. A big bastard, and a smaller one. He gave the beer and the big bastard to Phil.

'Two-handed claymore,' Worm said. 'Has its restrictions. But it's a nice weapon. Here.' He took it from Phil. 'Heavy beast. Five and a half pounds. You're probably best not to try cutting or thrusting. Takes a bit of getting used to. Just dunt the fucker over the head with it. Slap like that, he won't get up again in a hurry.'

To demonstrate, Worm thumped the blade on the arm of the sofa. 'Have a go,' he said.

Phil took the sword and tried a few practice dunts.

Tommy's sword was a handmade *katana*, a Japanese samurai sword that Worm boasted he'd paid only forty quid for on eBay. The seller was some idiot who thought it was one of those crappy imitations, apparently. He had several *katanas*, but this was a real bargain. Even came in a sharkskin sheath and Tommy was more than happy to let it stay there.

'Try it,' Worm said. 'It's nice and light.'

'Got to get moving,' Tommy said.

'Try it,' Worm said. 'It's nice.' He paused. 'And light.'

The guy was wearing a fucking open-arsed smock and yet Tommy felt threatened by him. He'd better do it. After all, Worm was letting them borrow the weapons. True, they were paying a hundred quid for the privilege of doing so, and that was more than Worm had paid for them in the first place. But, still. If the guy owned the weapons, he probably knew how to use them.

'Okay,' Tommy said. 'Just a couple of swings.' He slid the sword – the *katana* – out of the sheath. It was long, curved, with a single sharp edge.

'Stand clear,' Worm said, dragging Phil back towards the wall.

Tommy squeezed the handle, looked at his reflection in the blade.

'Ready,' Worm said.

Tommy didn't move.

Phil said, 'What're you waiting for?'

Tommy raised the sword, held it for a second, then took a swing. Just a little one, as if he was chopping the end off a carrot.

'Another,' Worm said. 'Get the hang of it.'

He tried again.

'Bigger swipe,' Worm said.

He took a bigger swipe. Didn't feel at all like he was in control of the bloody thing. Slight misjudgement and he was in danger of slicing a chunk out of his thigh with the follow through.

'And a thrust.'

Tommy sighed. Took a breath. And thrust his arm forward.

'You have to say 'heeyuh' when you thrust,' Worm said.

'Fuck that.'

'Go on,' Worm said. 'It's rude not to.'

Phil was smiling, trying to hide his expression behind his upended beer bottle.

Tommy said, 'I don't really care.'

'I'll take my sword back then.'

'You can't. We've paid you for it.'

'Not yet, you haven't.'

Tommy dipped his hand into the bag of money at his feet, took out a hundred quid and chucked it on the sofa. 'Have now.'

'Money's no good.'

Tommy stared at him for a minute. 'You think it's counterfeit?'

'I didn't say that,' Worm said. 'Phil wouldn't do that to me.'

'Then what?'

Worm said, 'The money's no good cause you haven't said 'heeyuh'.'

'I'm not going to fucking say 'heeyuh'.'

'Then give me my sword back.'

'I don't want your fucking sword,' Tommy said.

He sheathed it, threw it on the sofa. Picked up his bag and let himself out. He ran to the car and got inside, trembling all over.

After a bit, he lowered the window, clutched the bag hard to his chest. The breeze cooled his face.

He thought about driving away, leaving Phil. But Smith would be there tomorrow. And the next day. And Grant –

Tommy moaned. They'd fucking killed him. Jesus fucking Christ.

Tommy wanted to bite something. Anything. As long as it was hard enough to break his teeth on. There was a burning pain in his stomach and he wanted more of it. He deserved more of it.

He was scaring himself.

A couple of minutes later, Phil appeared. He crouched down outside the car, face in Tommy's face, beer breath in Tommy's nose, and pushed the handle of the *katana* through the window. 'Take it.'

'I don't want it.'

'Worm was just having a laugh,' Phil said. He paused. 'He likes you, you know.'

Tommy took hold of the handle and said, 'Hee-fucking-yuh.'

THE GROUND SMELLED damp, the grass fresh from the earlier rainfall. Splashes of moonlight trickled through the clouds onto the path ahead.

Tommy needed to pee. Felt like someone was scraping the inside of his bladder with a razorblade. Told himself it was just a side-effect of the adrenaline. Likewise the dizziness and the swishing of the sea in his ears and the ball of fire in his gut.

He had to ignore his body and saunter along towards Warriston Cemetery, nonchalant, like Phil. Never mind that he was carrying a bag containing fifty grand. Or that Smith was hiding out there in the dark. Tommy had a Japanese *katana*. He was a hard bastard. Nothing to worry about. Maybe he should unsheath the sword. If the moonlight caught it just right, it would look mighty impressive and Smith would surely think twice about trying anything.

Or they'd bump into Smith on the path as he was leaving, and Tommy'd get a fright and drop the sword. Thanks to Worm, they were late, and Smith wasn't going to hang around forever.

'You know where we're going?' Tommy whispered.

Phil whispered back: 'Straight ahead. Can't miss it.'

Tommy fought against the instinct to turn and run.

Eventually they came out into a clearing but Tommy only finally knew they were there when he banged into something solid and his heart trampolined off his stomach. He jumped back a foot expecting to see a moonlit ski mask in front of him. Turned out he'd collided with what was one of the few gravestones still upright. As he looked around, he saw that somebody'd been having a lot of fun knocking them over. He could make out half a dozen dotting the ground close by.

Apart from the toppled gravestones, it was too dark to make out much else.

'Sword,' Phil whispered.

Tommy looked at him.

'Get it out.' He moved off.

'I was just going to,' Tommy said to his back. He unsheathed the *katana*. Tried to be quiet, but couldn't avoid the faint sound of scraping steel. Phil turned. Tommy pulled an apologetic face that Phil probably couldn't see.

Phil shook his head, the prick. It wasn't that loud.

Tommy couldn't carry everything, so he laid the sheath on the ground and trailed his brother along another path which arced round the lefthand side of the cemetery, sword in one hand, money in the other. Phil advanced slowly but steadily, both hands wrapped round the handle of his claymore, looking straight ahead. Tommy wished they hadn't had to leave the torch in the car. Phil reckoned a torch would have made them too conspicuous and he was right, but Tommy felt conspicuous anyway.

Something crunched underfoot. If drawing the sword had been a whisper, this was a full-blooded yell. Tommy stopped in his tracks, held his breath. Phil turned again, glared at him. Tommy didn't need that look to tell him what he'd just done. If Smith was around, he now knew they were here, torch or not. That stupid fucking noise meant they'd lost any advantage they might once have had.

He'd stalk them now. Maybe he was already lying prone on the grass over there, masquerading as a collapsed headstone, wearing night vision goggles, sniper rifle ready to fire.

Tommy readjusted his grip on the sword.

Phil started to move again. They edged along the path, Tommy on his tiptoes. He didn't stand on anything else noisy and they didn't encounter a soul. At the end of the path, Phil crouched down. Laid his sword on the ground, flicked on his lighter. The path swung into a hidey-hole. Couldn't tell whether it was man-made or just a naturally cave-shaped thicket.

Phil said, 'Give me your sword. Mine's too big.'

Tommy handed it over and Phil headed inside.

Tommy peered in after him. 'Anybody there?'

'It's safe,' Phil said. 'Come on in.'

Inside, Tommy stumbled. Hard to steady himself with his bag of money clutched to his chest. He kicked something solid and it skittered away. Felt like there was ice underfoot.

Phil took a bottle out of his pocket, screwed the top off. 'From Worm,' he said. 'One for the road. Want a sip?'

Tommy shook his head.

Phil took a long swallow, sword tucked under his arm, then bent down, lowered the flame of his lighter so they could see what they were stepping on. Cigarette butts, beer bottles, condoms. Lots of condoms. A rubber carpet of them. No wonder walking was so tricky.

'Minging,' Phil whispered. He straightened up and ambled round in a circle, poking things with the *katana*.

'What you doing?' Tommy asked him.

'Looking.'

'Yeah, obviously. For what?'

'Wondering if there might have been an arrangement to leave the money tucked away somewhere in here.'

They'd not managed to pinpoint the exact spot for the handover before Grant had tried to escape, but Tommy could only assume that Phil was shitfaced if he believed this was it. 'Looks like it gets pretty busy in here,' Tommy said.

'Not busy now.' Phil carried on looking around as he swigged his beer. Crouched down again, scanned the debris on the ground.

Smith wasn't here. He'd gone home, fed up of waiting for Grant. Maybe he thought Grant had stolen the money. Yeah, he'd be after Grant now. Definitely no point hanging around any longer. Tommy took a step to the side, barging into Phil.

Phil lost his balance, put his hand out to stop himself, dropped his beer. 'Fuck,' he said. 'My hand's stuck in this fucking muck.'

'Shouldn't have left your gloves in the car,' Tommy said.

'You can be a real fucking twat sometimes.' Phil straightened up. 'Could have hurt myself on your fucking sword, too.' He elbowed Tommy out of the way and walked back outside, trying to shake the crap off his hand.

Making a noise now. Tommy could hear him. *Thump, thump.* Stamping his feet, the bloody child. Don't suppose it mattered now that they'd raised their voices. This whole thing was a waste of time. They weren't going to find out who Smith was, weren't going to get an opportunity to scare him into leaving

Tommy alone. It was a stupid idea. If Tommy hadn't been in a daze from what had happened earlier, he'd never have agreed to come here in the first place.

He followed Phil outside, intent on dragging him home.

'Phil, we should go −' The blow blindsided him. First he knew, his head exploded with pain. Centre of the blast was just forward of the crown, and it radiated out to every millimetre of his cranium. Somehow, even in the darkness, his vision deteriorated. His eyes watered and he felt sick. There was something very wrong with him.

The bag of money dropped to the ground and he sank to his knees. It felt like his skull had shattered. He moved his head to the side and could feel the pieces of bone breaking loose inside. He hoped he was wrong about that.

Fireworks went off in his stomach. Vomit spurted out of his mouth in a couple of neat sprays.

He heard a movement behind him, and turned, head pounding with the effort, just in time to see Phil's claymore rushing towards him.

PARK WAS TWITCHING mad. Got like that sometimes so that his cheek muscles would start doing a kind of merry dance. Just happened, and then went away once he'd calmed down.

He'd waited for Grant at the cemetery, hoping no one thought he was hanging around for a quick bumming. Prime spot for a bit of buggery-pokery. But the place had been deserted. Too cold, no doubt, for that kind of thing. Although he'd had a very pleasant experience once with Liz in the snow. Anyway, he'd waited, hands in his pockets to keep warm, and Grant didn't show. After a while, Park began to get bad feelings about the whole thing. Something had happened, or Grant would have arrived with the money by now.

Grant had called him just after leaving the bus station. Said he was on his way to the car. He had the money. Said he'd drive around for a bit, make sure he wasn't being tailed, then head for the cemetery. Park thought he was being over-cautious but told him it was an excellent idea. And that was the last he'd heard from his son.

Park had called him half an hour later. No reply. Park left a brief message. Then tried again, fifteen minutes after that. Left another message. Called once after that and still Grant wasn't picking up.

He wasn't going to call again. If Grant wasn't answering his phone, no amount of repeat calls would change that. The boy'd get in touch when he could. And Park would wait as long as necessary. He had a lot of patience. Prison had taught him that.

Yeah, either Grant would call or he'd turn up with the money.

But that wasn't what had happened.

Park laid the fuck-off sword on the ground, checked to see if the Savage brothers were breathing. He wouldn't have cared if it wasn't for the fact that he needed them alive so he could find out what had happened to Grant. Well, to be precise, he needed *one* of them alive.

He opened the bag that Tommy Savage had dropped. The sight of the cash inside was enough to make the twitch in his cheek go away. So the Savages had come here to deliver the money. But then Park realised that if they had the money, they must have Grant too. And his cheek started twitching all over again.

Problem now was he didn't want to hang around. Might need to perform a spot of interrogation, and it was better to do that where the sound wasn't going to carry.

He had a choice to make. Phil Savage was a fat bastard, who probably wouldn't even fit in the boot. Tommy was much lighter and far more likely to talk. There was the money and the swords to carry too. He didn't want to leave any evidence. And he wasn't prepared to make two trips.

So, the only question was what to do with Phil. Phil Savage had a rep as a bit of a hard man. Provided muscle for his brother's little tobacco empire for a while. Yeah, Park had done his homework.

He couldn't risk drawing *mnnngah* blood, not even by moonlight, but he could strangle Phil if he wanted. Or maybe he could just snap his neck.

But did he want to risk drawing attention to himself before he'd found Grant?

Tricky one.

Fuck, Phil Savage would keep. Hard man reputation or not, he looked as soft as shite in a wet bag. He could bring it on any time he wanted. Park would be ready.

Park slotted the swords through the handles of the bag. Hoisted Tommy Savage over his shoulder, bent his knees to pick up the money.

Just as well he'd spent so long in prison gyms. He might be a skinny bastard, but he'd got big enough to bench press 350 pounds, which came in handy at times like these.

Out of the cemetery. Along the path. Had to ditch one of the swords, the longer one he'd used to lamp Fat Phil, cause it kept tripping him up. Heaved it over a wall into somebody's garden.

And on he went. One small step after another.

Finally he arrived at the car, out of breath, thigh muscles on fire. Put Savage in the boot. Removed his shoelaces. They were nice and long and did the trick. Park bundled him up good and tight.

TOMMY AWOKE IN the dark, foul taste in his mouth, a vibration jarring his bones, his skull throbbing, stomach burned raw and desperate for a piss. Barely had time to register that the steady purring sound he was hearing was a car engine when a sudden movement bounced him an inch or two in the air. He landed on his hip. No time to groan, cause he was immediately jolted backwards. Something hard pressed into his back. When he tried to move away he realised his hands and feet were tied.

He could feel the ligatures cutting into his wrists and ankles.

His armpits prickled, sweat broke out on his forehead, his shins, the base of his spine. His chest felt tight and when he realised he wasn't breathing, he gulped in a lungful of air that tasted of car exhaust.

The boot was a tight fit. He was lying on his side, legs bent. He rolled forwards, away from the object digging into his back. The car went over another bump and jounced him again.

He yelled. Not so much in pain but because he couldn't bear the thought of what might happen to him. He wasn't going to think about that. Had to concentrate on the here and now. He yelled again. The sound didn't have anywhere to go. It filled his skull, deafened him, made his head ache even more.

What could he do? Could he do anything? He was having a hard enough time remembering to breathe.

Oh, Jesus fucking fuck. This wasn't happening.

His heart was beating too hard and too fast.

Even if he managed to undo these fucking bindings, he wouldn't be able to get out of the boot. Could hardly just lie back and kick it open. Or could he? And then what?

But if he got his hands free he could get to his phone and call for help.

'I'm in a car boot.'

'Where's the car?'

'I don't know.'

In any case, he realised, when he moved, that his pocket was empty. Smith had taken his phone.

Tommy lay in the dark, ignoring the stabbing pain in his bladder, trying to steady his heartbeat, breathing as evenly as he could, trying to guess when the car would hit another bump so he could roll with it. Focus on the present. Be philosophical. Laid back. Phil would be proud of him.

Christ, he hoped Phil was okay.

As a kid, Phil was the one who'd dive off the highest diving board, the one who'd stand up to the school bully, the one who tried smack. Phil was the great adventurer. He'd be fine.

But, fuck, Tommy shouldn't have listened to him. They shouldn't have gone to the cemetery. Phil had got him into a right fucking brilliant adventure now, hadn't he? Shit, though, he couldn't blame Phil. It was his own fault. Should have just paid up and gone home. Well, he was paying for it now.

Fuck, his heart was hammering. And his bladder was bursting. Wasn't as if he could ask Smith to pull over while he got out and took a leak. Smith could be planning on taking him all the way to Dundee, for all Tommy knew. No way he could hold on for that long. Maybe he should just let go. He'd feel so much better. But the thought of the stink and the discomfort were just too much.

Maybe Smith wasn't ever going to let him out. Maybe his plan was to push the car into the Forth and watch Tommy drown.

Why the fuck did he have to go and think of that?

Despite what it meant if he wasn't allowed out of the car, it was worse to mull over what might happen once Smith stopped and got out. He'd open the boot, and then what? Lop Tommy's head off with the samurai sword?

Jesus, Tommy almost wet himself.

He was shaking so much he hardly noticed that he hadn't been jolted around in the last couple of minutes. But he noticed now, and realised that the car was slowing.

His heart kicked into a new gear. Rattled in his ribcage. He could hear the echo in his ears.

The car came to a halt. The engine died. The door clicked open, slammed shut.

A few seconds later, the boot opened. Light shone in his eyes.

Then Smith's voice: 'Where's Grant?'

Oh, fucking fuck fuck fuck.

'It was an accident,' Tommy said.

PARK GRABBED THE fucker by the ear. Hadn't even touched him and the cunt was screaming like a teething baby. Park got hold of the other ear and yanked him out of the boot. Well, not quite. He got stuck and squealed, and wouldn't budge no matter how hard Park was pulling, and Park didn't want to end up with a torn ear and *nnnnngah* bleeding wound and all that would entail, so he had to let go and lift him out, like he really was a fucking baby.

Once Savage's shoulders were over the lip, Park grabbed an ear again and yanked hard. Savage dropped to the ground. Yelled for help.

Park let him lie there for a bit. He could shout all he liked. Nice quiet spot. Not much chance of anybody being around this late. Park thought about what he'd said. *It was an accident.* Jesus, that could mean any number of things. None good.

Savage's yells turned to whimpers before long. Then he just lay there, quiet, making occasional spastic eel-like wriggling movements.

Park said, 'Tell me about the accident.'

Savage squirmed a bit more.

'Well?'

'No.'

That was honest. 'No choice, Tommy. If you tell me, I'll make it quick.'

'Oh, God,' Savage said. 'It was an accident.'

'You need help to focus?' Park said. 'I can help. Could be that a little pain will do the trick.'

And then Savage started talking, words spilling out in a garble.

Eventually, Park got the gist of it: Fat Phil had collared Grant, they'd both interrogated him, and Grant had run straight into a plate-glass door when he tried to escape.

Park tried to block out the images that flashed in front of him. It was tough, but he managed. 'Is he badly hurt?'

No reply.

'Huh?'

Still no reply.

Park lost control. Kicked Savage. Several times. Kicked him till the stinking bastard pissed himself. 'Is he cut up bad?' Park asked.

And then Savage explained, between gasps, about the broken pane, the shard of glass. About Grant landing on it.

Park sat down before he fell over, breathed deeply. 'You took him to the hospital, right?'

Savage said, voice trembling, 'We did what we could.'

'And what was that?'

'We called for help.'

Park thought he might spew. 'Jesus Christ. You left him?'

'It was a fucking accident.'

Park said, 'Is he alive?'

'I don't know.'

'You don't fucking know?'

'Last time I saw him, yes, he was alive.'

'Well, Tommy,' Park said. 'You better start praying that's still the case.'

'WHAT ARE YOU going to do?' Tommy asked. He was sore and damp and his eyelashes were wet.

Smith was sitting next to him. Been there for about five minutes now. Not saying anything, not moving, not doing a fucking thing. His reaction wasn't what Tommy would have expected. No rage, no violence.

Tommy didn't want to interrupt him. He wasn't forgetting that Smith most likely had their swords in the back of his car. Not that Smith needed a weapon, with Tommy trussed up like this. If Tommy had the freedom to move his limbs he might be able to fight back. Okay, he wouldn't. But maybe he wouldn't feel so utterly helpless.

Fuck, Smith had killed already, just to prove a point. Wasn't as if there was a line he wasn't prepared to cross. He'd already fucking crossed it.

This silence was terrifying. If Tommy was going to be killed, he wanted to know about it now.

He raised his head. It hurt like the kind of hangovers he used to get in his late twenties. The ones just before he accepted that he wasn't so young any more and couldn't drink like he used to. The ones that Phil got too but ignored. 'I've been honest,' Tommy said. 'That's got to be worth something. Could've told you a pack of lies.'

Smith looked at him. Looked away again.

Tommy breathed in, then out, slowly. 'Who is he?' Tommy said. 'Who's Grant?'

Smith stared.

'You have the money,' Tommy said. 'Why does Grant matter?'

'Why,' Smith said, his expression not changing, 'does Grant,' he said, 'matter?' He got to his feet.

This was it. Tommy should have kept his mouth shut. He was all set to beg. He'd do anything. Didn't care. Anyfucking-thing. All he wanted was to stay alive.

Smith ran his hand over the chin of his ski mask. Then he put his hand in his pocket. Tommy expected to see it reappear with brass knuckles, a Stanley knife, a lock-back knife. Maybe something worse. A grenade, maybe.

But, no, it reappeared with a phone.

Must have been on vibrate, cause Smith answered it: 'Effie,' and walked around the side of the car towards the bonnet.

Tommy was lying a few feet beyond the rear bumper and couldn't see a thing. Might have been able to position himself so's he could look under the car, get a glimpse of Smith's feet, maybe, some indication of where he was. But Smith had turned off the headlights and it was dark out here.

And Tommy couldn't hear him now either. Which meant he had to be far enough away to give Tommy the chance to escape.

Could he get to his feet, though? Probably. But then what? He'd be in a similar situation to Grant. Only, unlike Grant, he wasn't tied to a chair. And there wasn't a plate-glass door around.

He could just about make out trees, left and right. Behind him, it looked clear for a few feet at least. A track. Maybe it led to a main road. If he could reach it, he'd be able to flag down a passing car by standing in front of it. Dangerous, but worth a try, surely.

But fuck standing up. If he did manage to get to his feet, he'd have to hop all the way there. Which was going to take more energy than he possessed. Plus it would take ages. Far longer than the likely duration of Smith's phone call. There was a better option. He could roll himself there.

No sooner had the idea occurred to him than he twisted round and shoved. His hip hurt from all the banging it had taken in the boot. And his side was bruised from the kicking Smith had given him. But he rolled over. And again. And again. Wasn't sure, but he thought he might be rolling at an angle towards the side of the track, into the woods or whatever was there. Might be a ditch, though.

He adjusted his course as best he could. Gave himself another push. And another. Felt like he was building up some momentum now. If only he'd been on a slope.

He wondered if Smith had finished his call and was coming back yet. What would he think when he found Tommy had gone?

And that spurred Tommy on to roll more quickly.

Something sharp dug into his arm. He tried hard not to cry out. Succeeded. But the bastard stung. Whatever it was, it had stuck there.

He completed another rotation. Started another. And when he put pressure on his arm, the foreign object pressed in even harder. His eyes were wet again. And he was biting his teeth together so hard his jaw hurt. His head was spinning now with all the rolling around.

One more. Just one rotation at a time. He could do it.

A half turn. And his chest struck something solid. Something in his way. Something that moved.

'Fuck are you trying to do?' Smith said.

Smith's hand was on Tommy's throat, knuckles pressing into his chest. Then he lifted Tommy to his feet. The skinny bastard was strong.

Tommy waited for the blow, sure that Smith's rage had won out. Tommy winced. Closed his eyes. Peeked through narrowed slits.

But Smith was just standing there. Tongue flicking in and out of the mouthhole of his ski mask.

Tommy swayed, ankles tied together so tightly it was hard to stay upright. He took a half hop backwards.

Smith grabbed him. And said, quietly, 'What did I ever do to you?'

Tommy said the only thing he could think of: 'Nothing.'

But Smith wasn't listening. He said, 'That was my daughter. Told me she had bad news.' Smith laughed. Then he shouted so loudly Tommy thought he saw the trees cringe: 'You believe that? Huh? Bad fucking news?'

'I'm sorry,' Tommy said. 'How bad?'

PARK WALKED INTO the waiting room, knew he'd come to the right place. He'd followed the coloured lines on the squeaky clean floor as he'd been told at reception, but he wasn't always sure whether they were going forwards or backwards. Anyway, he'd got here to find a couple of cops talking to Effie, her hair all mussed up.

'How bad is he?' Park had asked her on the phone.

'They won't say. Just get to the hospital, Dad. He needs you. We all need you.'

'I'm a bit out of town right now,' Park said. 'I'll be along as soon as I can.'

'What happened, Dad?'

'I'll explain everything when I see you.'

'Explain now.'

'Effie –'

'Dad, I have to know who did this to my little brother. Fucking tell me.'

So he did.

'The Savages were torturing him?'

'Looks that way.'

'We have to find them.'

'I've already got Tommy.'

'Wish you could make a mess of him. Leave him for me. I'll do it. Can you get his brother too?'

'We'll work something out. I'll see you soon.'

And there she was, blowing her nose. Martin, pristine and cravatted as ever, with his arm round her. Liz sitting on her own, nobody paying her any attention.

Effie caught Park's eye, shrugged Martin's arm off her shoulder, ran over to her dad. She flung her arms round his neck, said, 'It's not looking good.' Leaned into him. Her tears dripped onto his skin, hot, then cold.

Park didn't trust himself to speak. He held her.

Martin looked over at him, a wistful expression on his face. The cops were doing the same.

After a while, Effie pulled her head back, dabbed at her eyes.

Park said, 'Can I see him?'

She shook her head. 'He's in theatre.'

In theatre. Being operated on. Under the *nnnnngah* knife. On account of the Savages.

'When will we know?' Park asked.

'As soon as they've finished,' Effie said.

Which could be any time. Nothing like sitting around a hospital waiting room wondering whether your son was going to die.

One of the cops was strolling over. Talking to the cops was one way to pass the time. But there were others. Maybe Park should sneak back to the car. He'd parked a reasonable distance from the hospital, walked the rest of the way. Even though he'd knocked Savage out again, and gagged the fucker, he might wake up and be able to move enough to make a noise. Kick the boot lid or something. If he was going to do that, it was better he did it on a quiet stretch of road rather than where people were going to and fro at all hours.

But Park couldn't leave right now. He needed an alibi before the police spoke to him. He knew how they worked. Knew that in their twisted minds he was a suspect. Do a five-spot and, in their eyes, you were automatically the sort of sick bastard who'd kill his own son.

He whispered to Effie, 'Did you tell them I was at home with you this evening?'

'Of course.'

She was a good girl. Didn't even have to be primed. 'What was on TV?'

'We watched a movie.'

'Which one?'

'The one Grant brought round. *God's Little Acre.*'

That was one he could remember. 'And afterwards?'

'You went home.'

'To Old Mrs Yardie's?'

'That's where you live.'

'But the police don't know that.'

'Which is why they couldn't get in touch with you.'

Park nodded. 'And why was Mum at yours?'

'I'm her daughter. Why not?'

'Good point,' he said. He eased Effie to the side. 'Go talk to her. See how she's taking it.'

'She's no idea what's going on, Dad,' Effie said. 'You know that.'

'Do it for me,' Park said. 'Your mother needs someone to comfort her.'

The cop smiled as Effie passed him. He moved towards Park, close enough for his breath mints to mask the antiseptic hospital smell for a second. 'Mr Park? A few moments of your time?'

And a few moments was all it took. Even a cop could tell Park was hurting.

When the doctor arrived to speak to them, Park knew what he was going to say.

A CONSULTING ROOM. Desk, chairs, a bench for the patient to lie down on, a plastic curtain.

Bright light.

Everything shimmering.

Trippy.

Death was like this.

Park wondered if Grant had died like McCracken. Did death look the same?

McCracken.

'Sit down, please,' the doctor said, poker-faced.

It was probably a cop who'd told McCracken's old man.

There were only three available chairs. Liz, Effie and Martin sat. Park stayed on his feet, behind Liz, hands on her shoulders. The doctor offered Park his seat. Park shook his head. He needed to hold onto something.

Imagined himself walking out of the building. Going to the car. Getting Carlos's gun out of the glove compartment. Opening the boot. Shooting Thomas Savage.

But that was letting him off too lightly.

Park had needed to get McCracken alone. And that required patience. No point trying to do it at the Home. Too obvious. So Park found out where he lived easily enough. It was in the phone book. Park kept an eye on McCracken's house for a couple of days when he was on day shifts, and on both occasions noted he took an evening jog round Lochend Park. Third day Park went for a jog too. Piece of cake. Didn't matter that McCracken spotted him.

Park's kneecaps were jigging up and down. Couldn't stop them.

He didn't want to hear this.

McCracken had slowed down as Park headed towards him.

Park too. Came to a stop right in front of each other.

'The fuck you doing here?' McCracken asked, sweat dripping off his nose.

Park felt Carlos's gun digging into his thigh through his jogging bottoms. Gun in one pocket. Clothesline in the other. 'Can't a man go for a jog?'

'Haven't seen you here before,' McCracken said.

'Don't normally hang around slummy areas like this.'

McCracken said, 'So why today?'

'Business,' Park said. 'Locally.'

'Oh,' he said. 'Right.'

Park knew McCracken wanted to say something cheeky but was holding back. Almost a shame to kill him, him being so well behaved and all.

'I'm very sorry to have to say this,' the doctor said.

'You cold?' McCracken said, looking at Park's gloved hands.

'Bit chilly, aye,' Park said. Clapped his hands together. Managed to stop himself from shivering. Didn't want to overdo it.

'Better get going, then,' McCracken said.

Didn't ask about Liz. Not a fucking word.

'You're not going anywhere,' Park said. 'Get on your knees.'

Effie said, 'Oh, Jesus, no.'

Martin started to cry.

Liz farted, high-pitched and slow as a sigh.

Fucker didn't do as he was told.

'On your fucking knees,' Park said.

McCracken stared at him, shook his head.

And fucking turned away.

Park pulled the gun out of his pocket, changed his grip, ran after McCracken and thumped him hard in the back of the neck with the butt of the weapon. That *dropped him to his knees. Park hit him again. Twice.*

He swayed.

Park took the carrier bag out of his pocket. Stuck it over McCracken's head.

No, they hadn't mentioned that in the papers. That was the kind of detail they liked to keep to themselves.

Whipped out the clothesline. Coiled it round McCracken's neck.

Wrapped it tight.

Sole of the foot between his shoulder blades.

Steady.

Pulled the fucker's head towards him, pushed his torso away.

'Cabbage, eh?' Park said. 'You want to know who the fucking vegetable is?'

The doctor said,

Yeah, maybe he shouldn't have left the clothesline behind, but it didn't matter.

'Grant's . . .'

He'd nicked the clothesline from a supermarket. Same supermarket he'd got the

carrier bag.

'. . . heart'

He'd worn gloves. No way they could connect him to McCracken.

'. . . stopped.'

'STOPPED ON THE operating table,' Smith said, voice level, low, not whiny at all. Tommy didn't know how he'd ever thought Smith's voice sounded whiny.

Tommy's balls squeezed so tight he felt the ache in his belly. He shook his head, hair wet from where one of these lunatics had poured some fizzy juice over him to wake him up. Christ, he really hadn't needed another whack on the skull.

Smith continued, 'My son is dead.'

Grant was Smith's fucking son.

Of course Tommy had suspected that all along. He just hadn't allowed himself to believe it. Because therein lay madness, or heart failure. And yet, despite being petrified, he felt a tiny surge of excitement that he'd at least be able to identify Smith now.

Once Tommy discovered who Grant was, and that'd be pretty much public knowledge, he'd be able to track down his father. But he also realised that the information was going to be futile cause he wasn't going to get a chance to use it. Smith wasn't going to let him go now.

'My brother,' the girl said, sounding older than her tiny stature suggested. If Grant was her brother then she had to be the Effie who Smith had spoken to on the phone. Unlike Smith, she wasn't wearing any kind of mask. Neither was the other bloke, who didn't say anything. But it was dark and Tommy couldn't make out their faces very well.

'It was an accident,' Tommy said. Or tried to say. Impossible to speak with the gag on. He wanted to make himself heard. Maybe Effie would believe him. She'd understand.

Smith lurched forward suddenly and Tommy balled up tight inside the boot. Smith leaned over him, slipped the gag off. 'You wanted to say something?'

'Yeah,' Tommy said, licking his lips, wetting them. 'It was an accident.'

Smith said, 'You kill my son. Then you insult my intelligence.'

'No, no, no.'

'And you're no doubt thinking to yourself that you don't deserve this.'

'I don't know what I'm supposed to have done. I mean, about Grant, yes. It was —'

'An accident, I know,' Smith said. 'But if you're not responsible, who is?'

'You.' Tommy went cold. What the fuck had he just said? The last thing he wanted to do was antagonise this bastard. But it was true.

'Bollocks,' Smith said.

'You fucking are.' Tommy couldn't restrain himself. 'You're the one who started all this shit. If it wasn't for you, your son would still be alive.'

'You believe that?' Effie said.

'Fucking right I believe it.'

'You don't accept any responsibility for your own actions?' The girl again.

What could Tommy say to that? He said nothing.

'I didn't start anything,' Smith said. 'You did.'

'What the fuck did I do?'

'Staggering,' Smith said. 'The level of denial. I almost believe you.'

'Tell me what I did, for Christ's sake.'

'Now that,' Smith said, 'would be fucking pointless. I suggest you have a good hard think about it.' He closed the lid and everything turned dark.

Tommy could still hear them, though.

'You pair go home now,' Smith said. 'I'll take it from here.'

'Like fuck you will,' the other bloke said. 'I mean, I want to help.'

'Me, too,' Effie said.

Smith said, 'I don't think so. I can handle this.'

'I don't care,' Effie said. 'I have every right to carve that piece of shit into a dozen pieces.'

'And so do I,' the other bloke said. 'I've lost a brother-in-law. Just about. Are you going to tell us what's been going on? I'd really like to know how Grant got involved with Tommy Savage.'

'You know him?' Smith said.

'Yeah,' the bloke said. 'His brother slept with my mother.'

'Did he?' Smith said. 'Edinburgh's such a small place.'

'No offence, but I don't buy that it's a coincidence.'

'Look,' Smith said, 'an opportunity to make some money came along, Martin. It looked easy. Went tits up.'

'Why didn't you tell us?'

'No need.'

'Why Grant?'

'Okay,' Smith said. 'I knew about your connection to Savage. Did some asking around. Found out he was a suspect in your father's murder. I couldn't involve you in this cause I thought you'd be upset.'

'*Now* I'm upset.'

'I'm sorry.'

'Yeah,' Martin said. 'Well.'

It was quiet for a while. Then: 'So what are you going to do with him, Dad?' Effie said.

'Let me think about it.'

The voices grew muffled. After a bit, the car door clicked open. The engine started and they were moving again.

Tommy was left to his own imagination.

This Martin bloke had to be Greg Milne's son. Tommy hadn't recognised him. Hadn't seen him in years, and he was thinner then. But Phil had slept with Martin's mother. And Tommy was a suspect in his dad's murder. It was him, all right. Had to be.

Tommy doubted that protesting his innocence would make any difference.

He just wished he knew what the fuckers were going to do to him.

WHAT MCCRACKEN HAD done was nothing in comparison with what the piece of shit in the boot was guilty of.

Tommy Savage was a dead man.

Only questions were when and how.

Effie and Martin had taken Liz back home with them from the hospital, leaving Park free to do what he must. Only, he didn't know what that was yet.

He didn't know where he was headed. Just knew he had to keep driving. Didn't want to stop because if he stopped he'd have to decide what to do with Savage. Kept driving. Watched the lines in the centre of the road, knew they were leading somewhere, like the lines on the floor at the hospital. Kept driving. Didn't want to stop. Cause if he stopped . . . Kept driving. Piece of shit in the boot. Didn't know where he was going. Just kept driving. Watched the lines. And kept driving.

Till he realised he was in a trance. Not a proper trance, but a trance-like type of thing. A near trance.

Keep on driving.

And work it out. Work out what to do with the fucker in the boot. Work it out.

Wasn't easy.

Savage had fucked up by having Martin's dad killed. And

now he'd killed Grant. And he'd probably get away with that murder too if it was left to the police to deal with.

Taillights up ahead. Getting closer. He eased off the accelerator.

The punishment had to fit the crime. Or, rather, the crimes. And that was the difficulty. Park thought about the money. Fifty grand, which he'd handed over to Effie for safe-keeping. He'd have been reasonably content with that twenty-four hours ago. Paid for top quality care for Liz for a year, plus enough left over to give Martin and Effie a decent wedding. Everybody would have benefited. And he could have gone back to Savage for more when they ran out.

But what he wanted now was for Savage to feel the way *he* felt. He wanted Savage to know how it felt to lose someone he loved. For starters.

An image of Grant sliced in half by a sheet of broken glass zapped into Park's head.

Buzzing in his brain. Ears ringing. He felt faint.

Shit.

He lost control of the car for a second, swerved into the next lane. Just the blood. The thought of it. He knew that anything he arranged for Savage had to be just as messy. Which was why he needed help. Couldn't do it himself, much as he would have liked to.

Times like these he missed his mother.

Wondered how things might have been if she hadn't had her accident. The kids would have had another grandmother.

Park couldn't remember the incident at all. But from what was put together afterwards, it appeared his mother had tripped and fallen in the kitchen. Cracked her head open on the floor tiles. He was alone with her, three years old. She'd died instantly, so he was told. Certainly, she wouldn't have regained consciousness.

When they found young Andy Park, two weeks later, he was filthy and starving. He'd ransacked the cupboards and the fridge, found enough chocolate biscuits and cheese and milk and juice to sustain him. Just. And he was covered in his mother's dried blood. It was all smeared on the floor around her head and he'd been crawling in it.

Funny thing, during that fortnight the only clue the outside world had that anything was out of the ordinary was a neighbour who noticed a couple of letters sitting outside the front door. She thought it odd, but picked them up and posted them through the letterbox. He liked to think he'd been responsible, that he'd posted those letters back into the outside world, his way of asking for help. But if he did, he was probably just playing a game. Maybe if he'd tried it later, when his hands were covered in blood, she'd have noticed the tiny bloody fingerprints on the envelopes and called the police.

Anyway, the blood phobia resulted from a gradual under-standing of what had happened to his mother. At least, that's what the doctors told him. And he didn't have a better explanation.

So, much as he wanted Savage's punishment to fit his crimes, he couldn't participate directly himself. Would have been great if Richie wasn't in prison. But Park had other family. He could rely on Effie. And Martin seemed to be up for it too.

Park saw a signpost. He was approaching Almondell Coun-try Park, the woods where Martin's dad had met his end.

He slowed down. Turned off his lights. Nudged the car past the gatehouse and into the deserted parking area.

THIS IS IT, Tommy.

Tommy hardly noticed the various aches and pains of his body now. His hands were numb. Couldn't feel his feet either. He could ask Smith to cut him loose and he'd still not be able to help himself.

He'd fall over, claw at the ground.

Let me think about it?

That's what Smith had said to his daughter. Had he decided? Did he want her help? Or was he going to carry this out himself?

If Smith was alone and they were in the middle of nowhere, it'd be pretty fucking clear what he'd decided.

When the boot opened, Tommy blinked his eyes into focus, started talking straight away. He had no means of defending himself other than with his tongue. He said, 'You don't want to do this. You really don't.'

'I don't want to touch that slavvery gag again,' Smith said, hoisting him over the lip of the boot. 'But I will if you don't shut up.'

Tommy fell onto gravel. Smashed his kneecap into the ground. He remembered feeling that exact pain when he was a kid learning to ride his bike and falling off. Welled up in his knee, then pulsed, made him gasp. Just like it was doing now. He fought it and said, 'If you kill me, they'll find you.'

'Yeah?' Smith reached down, lifted him onto his feet.

Tommy said, 'They always find murderers.'

Smith looked at him. 'You, of all people, should know that's not true,' he said. 'You winding me up?' He reached into the car and reappeared with a sword. Worm's *katana*.

'Oh, Jesus, shit, no,' Tommy said. 'Fuck, no, good God, no.'

Smith was alone and they were in the middle of nowhere. The signs weren't good.

Smith bent down, freed Tommy's legs. 'Let's walk.'

Tommy's breathing was shaky. So were his legs. He took a step. His knee throbbed. He stumbled. Stamped his feet. Some feeling was coming back into them. He could feel his shoes loose, the laces removed. Acid burned in his stomach.

Smith pushed Tommy ahead of him, and Tommy led the way down a path into the woods.

This didn't look entirely unlike the place they'd just left. For a minute, Tommy wondered if Smith had driven in a big circle.

Some kind of woods. Probably wouldn't be able to see much once they got into the thick of it. Too much leafy cover. Maybe Tommy could use that to his advantage somehow. But how? *Think. Think, you stupid bastard.* If he didn't think, he was going to die. He was smarter than this fucker. He had to believe that.

Now would be a good time to prove it.

SAVAGE NIGHT
10.45 P.M.
FRASER'S HOUSE

EFFIE UNWRAPPED THE clothesline from around Fraser's neck. It had dug into the skin, and she had to tug hard to free it. But it popped out at last and when she let go, Fraser slumped forward, his face banging off the side of the tub.

'Ow.' Martin appeared in the kitchen doorway again, naked, one transparent plastic-booted foot on top of the other. 'Is he . . . ?'

'Yeah,' she said.

'Good,' Martin said. 'We've done okay, babe.'

He didn't move from the doorway. Last thing she wanted to see right now was his sexy-messy body. Caused a tingle in her yoni just thinking about it.

She said, 'Three things. You shouldn't have let Fraser see you.'

'I thought you'd finished with him.'

'Well, I hadn't.'

'I know. I saw that. But I didn't realise at the time. Why didn't you wait till the roofies had taken effect?'

'They had.'

'Not completely.'

'I'm impatient, Martin.' She shrugged. 'Anyway, don't change the subject.' She paused. 'Two. You shouldn't be smoking. That's risky.'

'I'm tense, you know. What's three?'

'You should have cut Phil Savage's hands off by now. What's kept you?'

'Sorry, boss.'

He moved towards her, but still she didn't look up. His foot, his calf, his thigh, entered her vision. She turned away before she saw any more.

'I didn't have time.' He placed his lips on her cheek, drew back. 'The head took longer than I thought.'

She nodded. 'No trouble otherwise?'

'He never suspected a thing. Took the beer, went out like a light.'

'Not like Fraser here.'

'Affects people differently.'

'I just wanted to slow him down.'

'You did that okay.'

'How do you feel?'

'Fine. How about you?'

'Fine.' She closed her eyes momentarily because she couldn't trust herself not to look at him. 'Where did you put Phil's head?'

'In the kitchen. In a carrier bag. I got sick of it staring at me.'

She looked at him.

'The eyes wouldn't close. No matter how hard I tried. And I did. Kept at it for ages. But they kept springing open. Fucking freaky.'

'Don't be a girl, Martin.'

She walked past him into the kitchen. The bag was on the worktop next to the sink, a large Evans' carrier. Martin must have got it from his mum: she was a big lady.

Effie opened the bag, lifted out Phil Savage's head by the hair. With her other hand, she gently thumbed an eye shut. When she raised her thumb, the eye sprang open. She tried the other one. Same result.

'See?' Martin said, in the doorway.

Effie hadn't known that dead eyes could refuse to close. Who knew they were so stubborn. She lowered the head back into the bag. 'Back to work,' she said to Martin.

She took off her clothes. Once she was naked, she opened the holdall that was resting on the counter, took out a pair of gloves and snapped them on. Put on a pair of booties. She found the spare hacksaw and rejoined Martin in the sitting room.

Martin had started on Savage's wrists. About a third of the way through the left one. The blade was sticking. She could hear it. A wet crunch. Pause. Another.

She stared into the pool of blood, her reflection rippling as Martin moved his blade jerkily through the corpse's wrist.

TEN MINUTES LATER, Effie was wrapping Phil Savage in a sheet she'd found in Fraser's linen cupboard. Well, she was wrapping Phil's torso in it. His head was still in the carrier bag in the kitchen.

She said, 'He's heavy.'

'Tell me about it,' Martin said. 'It was a real pain getting him into the tub.'

'I'm impressed.'

'You should be.'

'I said I was.'

'So you should be.'

She looked at her boyfriend. His head tilted to the left. He was streaked with blood and sweat. The hair on his chest was matted, dried red. She looked down at her own chest.

A mess. As if she'd been given five minutes to paint the room red on pain of death. She gazed up at Martin. 'You okay?' she said.

'Never better.' His lips twitched.

Liar. She'd have to watch him.

After all, it wasn't as if he'd grown used to killing people. Not like Richie, Effie's big brother.

EFFIE HAD UNEARTHED Richie's secret early on, right after his third hit. Actually, he'd been smoking blow very heavily around that time, and although she'd noticed something was amiss, she'd never have guessed what the problem was. She didn't need to, though. He made a confession to her.

'Effie,' he said, and she remembered the pub they were in, a bit out of the way, but one of the few places in Edinburgh they could find draught Beamish. They were big fans, rated it much higher than Murphy's or Guinness, and regularly made the trek to the other side of town for a pint or two. He slid a cigarette out of his pack, held it out for her to light. She grabbed one for herself. Both heavy smokers in those days. 'We're close, right?'

They were. They'd never argued, not since adulthood anyway. She nodded.

He leaned in, spoke in her ear. 'I have to tell you something.'

She turned her head towards him. Said in his ear: 'Tell me.'

He did. At first she didn't believe him.

'A hit man?' she said. 'Bumshite.'

But he wasn't smiling. 'Is that so hard to believe?'

'Yeah,' she said. 'It is. What're you playing at?'

'I'm serious,' he said. And he looked it.

'Fuck, Richie,' she said. 'Fuck.' She took a drag of her fag. 'Fucking hell.' Her hand was shaking. It wasn't that she was scared of him, though. She had nothing to fear from Richie. No, her hand was shaking with excitement. 'How many?' she asked him. 'How many people have you . . . ?'

Turned out the one he wanted to tell her about, the one that had fucked him up a bit was the last one, hit #3.

'That's why I was in Manchester,' he said. 'Ugly hole of a place.' This was way back in the days before the Arndale bombing. He'd done another hit there afterwards in '99 and said the place was unrecognisable. 'The target worked in an Italian restaurant.'

'Target? That the word you use?'

Richie shrugged. 'Why not?'

'They use it on TV, in the movies.'

'I know,' Richie said. 'I think that's where Carlos gets it all from.'

'Who's Carlos?'

'Tell you later,' he said. 'Anyway, I tried to figure a way to smuggle in a handgun, hide it behind the cistern in the toilet.'

'Like in *The Godfather*.' All movie-romantic like. He was young. Effie was a year younger, and knew exactly how he felt.

He smiled, his eyes lighting up. 'Too many complications, though.'

In the end, he'd opted for something much easier. At least, superficially.

'I befriended the target,' Richie went on to explain. He looked away, stared at the wall for a bit, then said, 'He was gay. I went back to his flat with him and suffocated him with his pillow.' He looked at the wall again. 'Afterwards. While he slept.'

Effie said, 'You got too close.'

'I know.'

'You won't make that mistake again.'

'No.'

'Tell me about Carlos,' she said.

He did. Spanish guy living in Edinburgh and arranging contract killings using a tanning salon as a front. She never believed in him completely till she met him a few months later.

'Tell me about the others,' she said.

She was fascinated and had remained so. She knew that wasn't how she was supposed to feel, but Richie felt the same way and he said it was just the way their minds worked, that they were special. She wasn't sure about that. But they were different, no doubt about that. Maybe it was genetic. Their dad didn't think like anyone else she'd ever met either.

From that night on, Richie told her everything. After a while, it was almost as if she was there on every job. She'd asked him more than once if she could go with him, but he wouldn't let her.

Which was something she was glad of the time he nearly got caught in the woods at Almondell. She remembered him telling her about it, and she was so wrapped up in the story that when she moved her arm to brush his hair off his face, she realised she was sweating under her armpits, beneath her breasts, behind her knees – just as if she'd hightailed it through the woods too.

She didn't know at the time that the target was Martin's dad. But she did now. And she wished she didn't.

Living with the knowledge of who'd killed her boyfriend's dad carried a lot of responsibility. She'd had to tell Dad. There was no way round it. She just hoped he'd be able to keep his mouth shut.

If Martin knew . . . well, he couldn't be allowed to. She couldn't tell how he'd respond. Maybe he'd blame Richie. She could see how that might happen. From a certain perspective, Richie was to blame. But Richie was just someone being paid to do a job. If it wasn't him, it would be someone else.

If Martin knew . . . shit, she couldn't let it lie. Well, if Martin knew what Richie'd done, maybe he wouldn't love her any more. There, she'd said it. That's what she was scared of.

But there was no reason for Martin to think Tommy Savage had farmed out the hit to a subcontractor. No reason for him to suspect Richie.

Sometimes she wondered how much she felt about Martin was on account of guilt at what Richie had done. She'd never know.

She loved Martin, though, whatever. And he loved her too. She couldn't afford to be scared.

Tonight's job with the Savages was complicated. Richie would have probably turned it down if Carlos had offered it to him. Course, this wasn't a contract Carlos would have been negotiating. This was from the heart, not the pocket.

They'd planned it together. Her, Dad, Martin. Richie'd helped. Hard to dispense advice from behind bars – they wouldn't even let him out for his little brother's funeral, the bastards – but he'd managed to get access to a mobile a couple of times and chat for a few minutes. Phones were small enough to smuggle in these days, though it made her wince to think about how that was done. He'd taken to calling her his apprentice. And if she ever considered following in his foot-steps, the Apprentice had a certain ring to it. Richie was known as the Expurgator. Effie's idea, although she hadn't come up with the name, just the suggestion that he needed one. The name had come from the title of a book he'd found in a charity shop. But contract killing wasn't for her. She'd never be the Apprentice. She liked people too much. Most of the time.

Between them all, they'd agreed who to kill, and how and where. She was glad Martin was here. Dad couldn't be around, of course, but he was happy keeping an eye on Tommy Savage. And somebody had to look after Mum.

It was good for Effie and Martin to do something together. This was as much for him as it was for her. She just wished she could explain to him how much.

THE FIRST TWO killings were over, but carving up the bodies was a painfully slow process. Martin had finished sawing through Savage's wrists, which just left Fraser. You wouldn't think a person would have so much meat and bone and sinew to get through. Not that they were in a hurry, but still. Effie had a new respect for butchers.

She'd didn't mind the mess, though. Never had a problem with blood. Haemophobia ran in some families, but not theirs. It was just Dad.

Phil Savage was wrapped up nice and snug in the hall by the door. The sheet he was rolled up in was smeared in blood but nobody was going to see it. The sheet was just a handy way of conveying him out of the house and into the van later, without making too much of a mess.

Okay, she couldn't postpone this any longer. They'd stripped Fraser. Stuffed his clothes in a bag with his uncle's. Slung the body into the tub.

Time to get on with it.

This might be hard, no matter how right it was.

She put the hacksaw blade to his neck.

It *was* right. No fucking doubt about it.

WOULD HAVE BEEN nice if the weather had stayed dry. But, no. Started to rain when Mum and Dad arrived. They'd all sat around drinking. Took awkward sips and smiled sadly at each other. Dad kept saying, 'I can't believe he's dead,' till Effie told him to shut up.

He wouldn't. After a while, she got out a crossword book. Tried to keep herself amused. Block out Dad's whining.

Dad hadn't been the one who'd looked after Grant. Twelve years old, Dad's off to prison. Then Mum tries to end it all and fucks it up, leaving Effie to bring up her little brother. And was Effie whining?

Martin got up, offered everybody more drinks. Tea or coffee?

Dad came over, crying. Put his arms round her, set her off.

Sat like that till Martin came back from the kitchen and he started too.

Mum was the only one dry-eyed.

They managed to block out their grief for a couple of hours by planning what to do with the fucker chained up at Old Mrs Yardie's.

Decided on a few things there and then.

– They'd make him suffer as much as they were suffering.

– No women or kids were to get hurt.

– Effie would get to know his elder son, Fraser.

– Martin would handle Phil, the brother.

When the limo arrived, Effie couldn't face it. A car journey, even a slow one, was going to make her sick.

She walked. Arm in arm with Martin, who looked smart and sombre.

The rain was just a drizzle. Still, should have worn a hat. But she liked the spongy-damp way her hair felt when she touched it.

She walked slowly, hoping she'd never arrive.

But the church was local, and they got there in under ten minutes.

The service was weird. Seeing people you never see otherwise. Cousins who only appear at weddings and funerals. Aunt Joyce, who Effie thought had died long ago. Everybody promising to stay in touch and everybody knowing they never would.

Singing hymns, for Christ's sake. Dad really blasting it out.

Listening to a man you've never met sum up your brother's life. And doing a better job than you could have done yourself. Dad's speech.

He didn't say much: 'Grant was a well-loved son and brother. He was a good lad. He was good to his mother. He was making something of his life. He could have been somebody. Now he'll never have the chance. I'm gutted. We're all gutted. Whoever did this, they're going to pay.'

As he returned to his seat, she started clapping. Martin joined in. Before long, everybody was clapping.

Only the minister didn't seem too enthusiastic.

And then the burial. Not a cremation.

'No member of this family,' Dad said, 'is going to burn.'

Dad was something of an expert on burning, so she let him have his way. She wasn't looking forward to the burial, though.

At the graveside, sliding the coffin out of the back of the hearse, she had to concentrate.

Six pallbearers. Only just enough. The coffin was a fair weight, and the path was slippery. The graveside grass even more so. She imagined stumbling, falling to her knees. Imagined Dad laughing fondly at her clumsiness. Imagined laughing along with him.

Mum in the small crowd. Moira, the nurse from McCracken's nursing home, looking after her for the moment. She was okay, Moira. She'd brought Mrs H along and Mrs H had hugged Mum and said, '*Gesundheit.*'

Effie managed to stay on her feet. Laid the coffin to the side of the grave, grabbed hold of a cord. The hole was deeper than she'd thought. Narrower too.

Just the right size. Snug.

Moved into position and the funeral attendant said, 'Take the strain.'

They did, and there was a surprising amount to take. The cord unravelled and her brother dropped into the ground.

SHE LOOKED AT the hacksaw. Across at Martin. He'd picked up his, too. 'You want to . . . ?' she said.

'No way.' He shook his head and blood flicked off his hair like paint off a brush. 'Fraser's yours. I'm going to have a fag.' He held up a hand. 'I'll be careful, not leave any stubs lying around. Make a cup of tea while I'm at it. You want one?'

She gave him a nod.

He disappeared into the kitchen, and returned seconds later. She looked at him. 'Problem?'

'Effie, babe,' he said. 'You'll think I'm losing it.'

She carried on looking at him.

'I swear Phil Savage is staring at me,' he said. 'Through the bag.'

She said nothing.

After a bit, he nodded and went back into the kitchen.

EFFIE PAUSED TO take a sip of her tea, even though it was cold now. Wasn't that nice to begin with. Martin hadn't put sugar in it, but that was deliberate. He had a thing about sugar, how it was poisonous and all. He'd read about it in a magazine, done some research of his own and decided the article had been right. So, no more sugar. At least, not till the next article came along stating that sugar was good for you.

Truth was – and it was admittedly a little odd given what they were doing at the moment – Martin didn't have much of a sense of adventure. But she wasn't convinced she liked too much excitement either. She much preferred to live life – what was the word? – vicariously. That's why she liked listening to Richie's stories.

God, she missed him. Spent years missing her dad, then Richie got locked up too. Pair of bastards. Christ knew what Richie'd been thinking, helping some stupid loanshark prick set up a guy for the murder of his wife. Then Effie's mum got brain-damaged. And to cap it all, her little brother decided to run into a plate glass door.

Effie's life: one almighty fucking laugh after another.

She put the cup down, carried on hacking away.

'Hand sore?' Martin said.

She was getting back into the rhythm, and grunted in reply. A constant flow of blood dribbled into the tub. At least there was no arterial spray. Just what was in Fraser's veins.

'Probably not something you'd want to do every time,' Martin said. 'Cutting them up. If it was a regular job, you know.'

She grunted again. He didn't realise how right he was. It was cutting up Martin's dad that almost got Richie caught.

Martin looked towards her cup of tea. 'Going to have to cut out the milk, too,' he said. 'Cows get pumped full of antibiotics. Can't be good for you. Unless it's organic.'

If he wasn't naked, she might have found him annoying. But she couldn't. Not when he looked like *that*. He really did have a fucking gorgeous arse. In fact, he had a gorgeous body, not conventionally gorgeous, but it worked for her. Shame he was so uncomfortable with his clothes off. All because of that rope burn on his neck.

Another case of her having to protect him.

She glanced at the mantelpiece, trying to spot her dad's handiwork. But there was no sign of anything unusual.

Still, she had to concentrate on sawing to keep the guilt at bay.

The head was nearly off. In fact – *there*. A slap as it dropped into the tub. Blood splashed up the side, threatening to spill over onto the dropcloth. 'You got another carrier bag?' she asked.

She'd take a moment before starting on the hands.

That's what you did if you wanted bodies 'vanished'. They were going to do it properly. Impress Richie. Lose the heads and hands, burn the torsos. Had to knock out the teeth at some point, which wouldn't be much fun, but they'd have time to do that later.

Martin returned from the kitchen with an empty carrier bag. Knelt beside her and opened it.

Effie picked Fraser's head out of the tub. Held it at arm's length. 'He doesn't look his best,' she said.

Martin moved to the side, fidgeted with the bag.

'What's the matter?' she asked.

'Put it in the bag.'

She lowered the head inside. 'Okay now?'

He nodded. His hands were a little shaky.

THEY TOOK THE tub to the bathroom, upended it, poured the contents into the bath. Turned on the taps, flushed the muck away. Some bits got stuck in the plughole, so she picked them out and stuck them down the toilet. She rinsed the tub quickly – didn't need to bother about sterilising it; they'd be dumping it, anyway – and took it back downstairs.

She placed it by the front door, next to the bodies, both of which were now wrapped tightly in Fraser's sheets – one white, one pale blue, neither smelling spring fresh any longer.

While Martin ran a bath upstairs, she bagged the dropcloth in the sitting room, dumped it in the metal tub and fetched the carrier bags from the kitchen. The heads and hands were divided between three carriers. She added them to the tub.

Now she was exhausted, sweating, covered in blood, badly in need of a bath. The sound of the water running reminded her of Mum in the kitchen, in happier times, humming along to the radio, rinsing the dishes. Couldn't abide washing-up liquid. Made everything taste of lemon, she said. So the tap ran until everything was spotless and sud-free.

Fraser's house was very different from the one Effie had grown up in. Fraser had money. A lot of money for someone so young. Had a nice office job, but Effie guessed that Daddy had helped him out. Took a shitpile of money to afford to live in a modern villa, detached, with its own driveway. Effie could have guessed, even before she'd set foot in the bathroom, that the taps on the bath would be gold-plated. And she was right.

Martin must have turned them off. The thrum of running water had stopped. He was calling her.

He flung open the bathroom door. 'I said, bath's ready.'

She started up the stairs, each step a strange, sticky sensation as her plastic booties creased under her weight. They'd been Martin's contribution. Put these on and if you did happen to spread any blood around, at least you wouldn't leave footprints.

Martin ran towards her, the bathroom door open, steam lazing around inside.

At the top of the stairs, they met. He wrapped his arms round her, buried his face in her neck.

She said, 'You okay? Martin, baby?' She cradled the back of his head in her hand.

'Not really,' he said.

His breath tickled her neck. She stroked his hair. 'We'll be gone soon enough.'

'Something's wrong.'

'Everything's fine. It's all going to schedule. We're good.'

He lifted his head, stared over her shoulder. She turned, followed his gaze. He was looking at the carrier bags in the tub by the door. He said, 'They're watching us.'

And Effie experienced a moment of terror. Or panic. Or something similar. For just a split second, she believed him. She became acutely aware she was naked, which she thought she'd forgotten about. Hell, no she *had* forgotten about it.

But what did it matter? She knew the last thing on anyone's mind was her scrawny body. She still felt uneasy, though.

Martin stepped back. 'You feel it? Eyes on us?'

She looked at him, realised she'd put her hand to the back of her neck. She rubbed it. How could he know about the camera? It was tiny. No way he could have spotted it. She knew where it was hidden, and even she hadn't managed to pick it out. This was freaky.

'Shhh,' he said.

She listened. Now that the taps were off all she could hear was the low buzz of the central heating.

'What is it?' she said.

'I don't know,' he said.

Over his shoulder, down the hall, light spilled out from the bathroom. Ghostly shapes swirled inside. Steam. Nothing but steam. There was nothing there. Not even a shadow.

But there was something. A smell. A smell of roses.

Her muscles locked. She couldn't move. Couldn't speak. Couldn't even blink.

Eight years old. Waking up one morning, sunk into the mattress as if a fat man was sitting on each of her limbs, another couple weighing down on her stomach and chest. There was a smell like somebody had emptied a bottle of Mum's most expensive perfume on the pillow. Took a little while to realise what had happened.

Then she understood. She was paralysed.

She tried to cry out for help, but the sound stayed inside her. Knew she'd just have to lie there and wait until her mother came to wake her up for school. Hoped she'd be able to carry on breathing till then. Her throat felt tight, the walls of her windpipe thickening.

She lay in the dark, dizzy, occasionally willing a leg or an arm to move, trying to dislodge the invisible fat men. But nothing happened. Not so much as a twitch.

Got so that she was convinced she'd never move again. She must have broken her spine during the night. Yeah, that was it. Rolled over in her sleep, snapped something, and it didn't hurt cause she was paralysed. She'd live the rest of her life being shunted between her bed, a wheelchair and the bath with one of those hoist things she'd seen them use on her grandfather after he got all weak and started to shrivel up like a walnut.

Eight-year-old Effie had cried. Soundlessly. She didn't want to be like her grandfather. Everybody felt sorry for him and secretly hated him cause he was a burden.

She lay still for a while, long enough to lose track of time, long enough to lose hope of ever being able to move again. But finally – after how long, she couldn't say – the feeling vanished, the numbness seeping away into the bedclothes, the smell of roses dissipating into the air, her voice leaking out of her in a quiet strangle.

And she could move again. A finger. A toe. A hand. A foot. An arm. A leg. She sat up. The fat men had gone.

It was as if the whole thing had never happened.

The next day, she tried to explain how she'd felt to Richie, who wasn't young enough to wander around with his hand down his shorts and get away with it, but that didn't stop him. 'Richie, it was like I was a question mark.'

Her brother said, 'What do you mean?'

She shook her head. She couldn't explain. She didn't have the words. 'Forget it,' she said.

And she had, until now.

That feeling, being immobilised. All you could do was think. And when you thought, you asked questions.

Martin was staring at her, eyes wide. He was saying something but she couldn't make out the words.

Why? Because of the heads in the bags? No. Because they were being watched? No. So, what then? She didn't know.

She couldn't stand here forever being a question mark.

Shit. It wasn't going to go away.

But it would. She knew it. Blame Martin. She'd been doing pretty well until he got her all jittery.

God, she was behaving like a fucking amateur. Richie would disown her. So would Dad.

Everybody was relying on her.

If you were an expurgator, it was to be expected that you'd behave oddly, now and then. Especially if you were just an apprentice. You suppressed your emotions to this degree, something fucked up had to trickle out somewhere. Even Richie had his moments. Wouldn't be normal otherwise.

She squeezed her hand into a fist. She was not going to cry. She was a hard-arsed fucking bitch. Martin was spooked, that was all. The heads in the bags were watching them. Yeah, right.

Martin, Martin, Martin.

She wanted to lean forward, kiss him. She tried and was surprised to find she could move again. But of course she could. She'd just clenched her fist.

She kissed his cheek. She said, 'Let's have that bath, eh? Then get on with the show.'

EFFIE WAS STANDING in the bathroom watching Martin dangle his foot in the water, testing the temperature with his toes.

'Still a bit warm for you,' he said. 'But I'll get in. You can join me in a minute.'

They had to be at Old Mrs Yardie's in a couple of hours to pick up Tommy Savage. It involved a short drive, so she needed to get cleaned up. And try to focus. Her head was still a mess.

She dipped her fingers into the water. Yeah, still too hot.

Unfortunately they couldn't clean up the house quite so easily as they could clean themselves. She'd asked Richie's advice. His best guess was that no one would be looking for signs of blood, but if they were, they'd find something no matter how thoroughly the place was scrubbed. Once reported missing, the police would be looking for Fraser and Phil and Tommy Savage, sure. And they'd come visit Fraser's house, as they'd visit the others, have a look around. But as long as Effie and Martin took reasonable care the police would find nothing out of the ordinary. With no bodies, no overt evidence of what they called foul play, the police wouldn't look very hard. They'd have no reason to be bringing in the forensic team to check for traces of blood.

That's what Richie thought. And, as he'd pointed out when he phoned, even if the police did look long and hard, and found a little blood, they wouldn't be able to tell much from it. For all they knew, maybe Fraser had cut his finger or had a nosebleed. And if it was Phil Savage's blood they found, well, it wasn't unlikely that Phil would have visited his nephew. And he too could have injured himself.

As long as the house wasn't swimming in the stuff, every-thing'd be fine. And since Martin and Effie had used the tub, and done the dirty work *post mortem*, the blood was kept to a minimum. The important thing was that there weren't any bodies. Leaving bodies lying around was asking for trouble.

If everything went according to plan tonight, the heads would get buried, and the bodies cremated. Practically a funeral when you thought about it. Which was more than the bastards deserved. And after that, everybody could rest easy, job done, Grant and Martin's dad avenged.

SHE GAZED DOWN at Martin as he splashed pink water over his chest. The water swept away a circle of bubbles. He ran his hand through his hair, picked at some muck that had caught there. 'Need some shampoo,' he said. 'See any?'

There was none on the side of the bath. She looked in the shower stall. Found a small bottle of dandruff shampoo. She placed it on the side of the bath. 'Want me to do it?'

'You're okay,' he said. He slid his buttocks forward, ducked his head under the water. Resurfaced moments later, his eyes squeezed shut, water dripping down his face. He squeezed the water out of his hair, opened his eyes. 'Temperature's about right for you now,' he said.

Effie eased herself into the water. Her knees clicked like an old man's when she went into a crouch. Dad's were the same. She sat down.

Martin lathered his hair. 'Strange being in someone else's bath,' he said, lifting his legs onto the sides to make room for Effie. 'Don't you think?'

Didn't seem that strange to her. It did seem strange to be lying in bath water that was this colour, though. 'I suppose,' she said.

He brushed her cheek with his foot, left her face wet. 'You need to wash your face.'

She turned her head to the side. 'When I get out. Not washing it in this filth.'

He wiggled his toes at her. He'd forgotten that nonsense about the decapitated heads watching them. That was good. She should try to relax too.

Hell, she *was* relaxed. She just wasn't feeling playful. Still thinking about that odd feeling of immobility earlier. She should tell Martin about it. Although maybe this wasn't a good time. When *was* a good time, though? Fuck, she *should* tell him. Maybe she'd be able to explain it better than she'd done all those years ago when she'd tried to tell Richie. 'Something a bit weird happened . . .' she started to say.

He stopped tapping her shoulder with his toes. Looked at her.

She couldn't go through with it, though. It sounded stupid. 'Nothing,' she said.

He frowned. Eyes crinkled. Something she usually found very sexy. He said nothing, though, even though he was no doubt aware that something was up. His foot slid into the water. He guided his toes across her thigh. She raised her hips, pressed her yoni against the sole of his foot.

Nothing.

He pulled his foot away. 'Should be getting out.'

'Richie said not to hurry.'

'I didn't say we should hurry. Just meant we should watch our time.'

She nodded.

'You okay?' he said.

'Fine,' she said. 'Rinse your hair.'

He sighed, then ducked his head under the water. It rose to a dangerously high level. She realised she was holding her breath with him, and let it out. How many couples were there who could bond like this?

He'd known all about her family when they first met. Knew her dad was inside. Knew what Richie did for a living. Martin had spent some time inside himself a couple of years back for thieving manhole covers. And in prison he said Richie had been spoken about in hushed tones.

Martin had confessed to Effie that he was terrified of going back to prison. Said it was full of testosterone. Which was something he didn't much like. Truth was, he was just a little bit camp. But she liked that. Inside, though, it meant he got a lot of grief from guys who thought they had balls and that he didn't. Wasn't much fun for Martin being on the defensive all the time.

Effie told him she had no intentions of letting them get caught, told him to trust her.

Jesus, the guilt was a bastard.

When they first starting going out, she'd wondered if Martin knew what Richie had done. But she'd sought Martin out, not the other way round. And it hadn't taken long to realise that he'd never thought beyond a member of Savage's crew having killed his dad.

At least now Effie was making amends.

She winked at him.

'You know what I want, babe?' he said. He'd replaced his foot on the side of the bath, and water dripped onto the floor.

More mess for Effie to clean up. No, that was unfair. Martin would clean up after himself. He always did more around the house than her.

'What do you want?' she said, closing her eyes, enjoying the warm water covering her skin, easing her tired muscles. For a second. Until she remembered where she was and what they'd just done and what they still had to do.

'Ice cream.'

He wanted ice cream.

'Now?' she said.

He nodded.

'Fuck it,' she said, 'I'm not fetching you ice cream.'

'Aw, go on.' He grabbed her foot. 'If you don't, I'll just have to lick your tocs.'

'Don't you fucking dare.' Her feet were very tickly.

'Up to you.' He looked at her, still holding her foot.

'Fraser didn't strike me as the kind of person who'd eat a lot of ice cream,' she said. 'Don't think he'll have any.'

'What does someone who eats ice cream look like?' He pouted. Exaggerated the pout. His lip trembled.

'Jesus,' she said. 'Let go and I'll take a fucking look.'

SHE TUCKED FRASER'S dressing gown tighter around her. Didn't matter how tight she pulled the belt, it still felt like she was flapping about inside a sack.

There was no ice cream. Not in the freezer compartment of the fridge. Or in the separate freezer. There wasn't much in the way of food at all. Pint of milk, sliced ham, cheese, that was it. Get snowed in around here, you'd starve in a couple of days.

Maybe Fraser could afford to eat out a lot. Or he lived on takeaways.

Effie remembered the days when she used to do that. Not any longer. Not now she was engaged, and had a fiancé who cooked for her.

She closed the fridge door and jumped.

Hadn't expected to hear the doorbell ring.

Shitty-fuck.

She crept through the kitchen. No need to creep, but she did, anyway. Felt light on her feet without the booties on, even though they weighed next to nothing. Through the sitting room. Stared at the tub in the hallway. The carrier bags. Then the bodies. A bloody halfmoon shape near the top of one where the sheet was knotted. Other patches of blood. Handprints. She wondered if it was possible to see the bodies from outside the house. They'd taken the precaution of drawing all the curtains, but she checked for a gap just in case. Nah. No way anybody could see in.

So who'd come visiting? Shit, she didn't care as long as they went away.

This wasn't part of the plan, so they had no contingency for it. All the time they'd watched Fraser, he'd not once had a visitor. His house wasn't exactly accessible. Way out on the edge of town, where you never saw a bus, only the occasional taxi and fast cars. Anybody came to visit late at night, they'd most likely be staying till morning. That had been Effie's unspoken promise to him when they'd returned earlier tonight.

All Effie could do was wait out whoever was at the door. Hell, everybody goes away eventually, even if the lights are on and the curtains drawn and the homeowner's car is parked outside.

There was no law that said you had to answer your door. And there was no law that said you had to be at home just because the lights were on or your curtains were drawn or your car was outside.

She wasn't convincing herself.

Martin had parked round the back. At least that was something to be grateful for. It was secluded round that side, overlooked a railway line.

Effie realised she was holding her breath. Let it out slowly. Fuck's sake. So what if there was somebody at the door? They'd probably ring the bell once more, get no reply, and wander off.

She felt like those invisible fat men were sitting on her again.

The doorbell rang again and she clenched her jaw, screwed her eyes shut. Didn't help of course but it showed her that at least she hadn't sunk into catatonia.

Was that how Mum felt? Like a bunch of fat men were sitting on her?

Effie just had to wait. Then it'd be safe to carry on. The uninvited guest would be gone, normal service could be resumed.

But then she heard the clank of keys. And then a scratching in the lock.

She looked up. Martin was standing at the top of the stairs, a towel wrapped round his waist. He was looking at the door.

Effie tiptoed forwards. Caught Martin's eye and motioned for him to get out of sight. He frowned, but when she persisted, he disappeared back along the corridor.

The door opened.

A boy walked in. Looked about ten years old, wearing a mini-backpack, pushing a bike. He looked at Effie and said, 'Who are you?'

'Who are you?' Effie said, although she knew exactly who he was. Fraser's little brother, Jordan. He should be tucked up in bed in his own home where he lived with his dad and his grandmother. Although his dad hadn't been home in a while.

The kid ignored her. Breezed in, leaned the bike against the wall just beyond the tub and the packaged torsos of Phil and Fraser. He pulled at the strap on his left shoulder and asked, 'Where's Fraser?'

'Ah,' Effie said. 'He's not here.'

The boy stared at her. 'What are you doing in his house?'

'Well,' Effie said. 'I'm a friend of his.'

'That's his dressing gown.'

Effie shrugged. 'I'm borrowing it.'

'Did he say you could?'

'Didn't say I couldn't.'

'It's too big for you. Who are you?'

'I told you. You should listen.'

'No, you didn't. Where's Dad? Where's Fraser?'

'Honey.' Martin's voice. He was padding down the stairs, still in his towel, a second now draped round his neck to cover his scar. The hair on his shins glistened. The boy turned to look at him, his eyes shrinking. Martin said to Effie, 'Aren't you going to introduce me?'

'Sure,' Effie said, happy to play along. 'This young man is . . .'

'Jordan,' Jordan said.

'Jordan,' Effie said. 'And Jordan, this is my husband . . . Clive.'

Martin looked at her. Held out his hand to Jordan.

Jordan took it. The kid's grip looked slack.

Martin bent down a little, looked into the boy's eyes. 'And how do you know Fraser?' he said. 'How come you have a key?'

Oh, Martin was good.

'He's my brother,' Jordan said. 'Where is he?'

'He's away on business.' Martin glanced at Effie. 'We're looking after the house for him.'

Jordan nodded, seemed to think that was okay. 'Have you seen Dad?' Then he added, 'I was supposed to meet him here.'

The centre of Effie's forehead went cold.

Martin held both the boy's wrists. 'There's no one here but us.'

'He must be coming later.'

'Maybe.'

'When's Fraser coming back?'

Martin looked at Effie, but Effie was having trouble breathing. Jordan was supposed to meet his dad here?

'Well,' Martin said. 'Your brother had to go away in a hurry. We're not sure when he'll be home.'

Jordan said, 'I'm going to phone him.' He put his hand in his pocket.

Effie found her voice. 'I don't think so,' she said.

Martin said, 'It's okay.'

'It is?' Effie asked him.

'If Jordan wants to talk to his brother, that's fine.'

Jordan dug out his phone and dialled. A faint pop tune started playing off to the right.

'That's Fraser's ringtone,' Jordan said. He walked past them, into the sitting room, heading towards the sound.

They followed him.

Fraser's phone was on the coffee table where Effie had left it after she'd stripped the body. Jordan picked up the phone and cut the call. Turned to face them. 'Why didn't he take his phone?'

'Had to leave in a hurry,' Effie said. 'We told you.'

'Why?'

'An important deal.'

'A deal?'

'In London.'

'What kind of deal? He doesn't do deals.'

'A grown-up kind of deal,' Martin said. 'That we can't tell you about, Jordan. I'm sorry.'

'You mean like drugs?' Jordan said. 'Oh.' He laid his brother's phone back on the table, returned his own to his pocket. 'You haven't seen my dad, then?'

Martin shook his head. Effie shook hers too.

'I'll wait,' Jordan said. 'Why do you have that bath thing there?'

Effie looked in the direction of Jordan's gaze. He was staring through the open door at the tub in the hallway next to his bike. 'Throwing it out,' she told him.

'What's in those bags?'

She swallowed. 'Odds and ends.'

'And what are those?'

Now he was staring at the two bloodstained body-shaped parcels rolled up against the wall. 'Just some rubbish,' she said.

'What kind of rubbish?'

'Just rubbish.'

'Doesn't look like rubbish. I've never heard of anybody wrapping up rubbish in sheets.'

'It's special rubbish,' Martin said. 'Needs to be recycled. In sheets.'

'They're bleeding.'

'Nah,' Effie said. 'That's just sauce. Tomato sauce. Cranberry juice. That kind of stuff.'

The kid stared at her. 'That's not special rubbish, then.'

'The rest of it is,' Martin said. 'The solid part. Not the liquid part.'

Jordan turned away, scanned the sitting room and said, 'I've never seen you before.'

'That's because we're not from around here.'

'Where are you from?'

'England.'

'I have cousins in England.'

'I'm sure you do.'

'You don't sound like them.'

'It's a big place, Jordan. People sound different. Depends which part of the country you come from.'

'You sound like me.'

'Well,' Effie said, 'I'm from here. Originally. But I've lived in England for a long time. Live there now. With my husband. With Clive.'

'My mum's boyfriend's from South Africa.'

'Is that right?'

'Russell. He talks funny. He stole her from my dad.'

'I'm sorry to hear that,' Effie said.

'What kind of rubbish is it?' The little fucker turned his head towards the bodies again.

Martin went on the attack. 'How come you're up so late, Jordan?'

Which stalled him. He looked away from the bodies of his brother and uncle, shrugged. 'It's not that late.'

'Does your grandma know where you are?'

Jordan looked at the floor. Dragged his foot across the carpet.

'I'm sure she does, Clive,' Effie said.

'She doesn't!' Jordan looked up, his eyes wide. 'Dad said not to tell her. I sneaked out.' He grinned.

'When did you speak to your dad?'

'Little while ago?'

'Tonight?'

'Yeah. Told me to come round here.'

Effie looked at Martin. He shrugged. Effie said, 'You actually spoke to him?'

'He texted me.'

'He couldn't have.'

'How do you know?'

Martin was staring at her. 'You want a glass of milk or something?' he said to Jordan, still looking at Effie. 'Sit down, watch a bit of TV?'

Jordan shrugged. 'Yeah, okay,' he said.

Martin said, 'When did your dad say he'd be here?'

'He didn't.'

'Think you could call him and find out?'

THERE WAS NO reply. Of course there wasn't. Jordan was lying.

Effie took the phone from him.

'Hey!' he said.

'I'm just going to borrow it. You can get it back later.'

'I want it.' The kid's face crumpled. 'You can't take it. It's mine.'

'I'm just going to make a few calls, that's all.'

'Use your own.'

'I can't get a signal.'

Jordan's eyes latched onto Fraser's phone. 'Use Fraser's.'

Effie picked it up, pocketed it. 'Good idea. I'll try it, too.' Then she switched on the TV. 'Shut the fuck up and watch this.'

Martin came back from the kitchen with some milk, looked at the pair of them. 'What's the matter?' he said.

'She took my phone.'

Effie said, 'Stop moaning.'

Martin handed Jordan his milk. 'Or you'll never get it back,' he said. 'Now drink that, watch TV and behave for two minutes.'

'She's got the remote.'

Effie tossed it into his lap. Martin grabbed her elbow, steered her out into the hallway.

He pulled the door towards them, didn't close it. He whispered: 'Keep calm.'

'I am,' she said. 'But what the fuck's going on?'

'I'm sure everything's fine.'

'How can it be? That little bastard's here.'

'I know. And his father texted him.'

'But you know he couldn't have.'

'You heard what Jordan said.'

'He's lying.'

'Has to be. But why?'

She couldn't think of a reason.

Martin said, 'Give me his phone.'

She handed it over.

He fumbled around on the keys for a bit, then said, 'Here it is.' He read out the last message. Just as Jordan had said. 'And it says it's from his dad.'

'Shit,' Effie said. 'We have to go. This means Dad's in trouble.'

'Not necessarily.'

'Course he is.'

'Think about it,' Martin said. 'Why would Jordan's father text him? If you were in his shoes, and you got to a phone, you'd call, wouldn't you? And why would his dad send him to the most dangerous place possible? Right into our arms? You think that's likely?'

She still didn't say anything.

'Want me to spell it out?' He shrugged. 'Okay.' Continued: 'Somebody else sent the message using his dad's phone.'

She felt her face flush. 'You mean *my* dad? Why would he . . . ?'

Martin nodded. 'Let me call him.'

'We can't do that.'

'We can't *not* do it.'

'It'll give the game away. They'll trace the call. It'll prove that we were here.'

'I'll use my mobile.'

'No good. They can tell where you were when you made the call.'

He peered through the crack into the sitting room. Jordan must have been behaving himself cause Martin turned to face her again. He said, 'Then I guess we won't know what's going on till we get to Old Mrs Yardie's.'

Effie said, 'You think Dad's been planning this all along?'

'Shhh,' Martin said. 'Jordan'll hear.'

She lowered her voice. 'Answer me.'

'I'm guessing,' Martin said. 'I have no evidence to back me up. But knowing your dad, I wouldn't be surprised.'

'Even though we were against it?'

Martin combed his damp hair with his fingers. 'Yeah.'

She thought for a minute. 'I don't think so.'

'You could be right.'

'I know my dad better than you.'

'Sure.'

'He wouldn't do that.'

'Probably not.'

Effie ran her tongue over her lips. The sickly sweet taste in her mouth wouldn't go away.

'Forget it,' he said. 'I'm sure there's another explanation.' He leaned across, kissed her on the cheek.

'Yeah,' she said.

'So what are we going to do about the kid?' Martin adjusted his towel. 'Doesn't seem right to . . .'

'What doesn't?'

'You know. I'm no Moral Morag but . . .'

'Who the fuck's she?'

'You know what I mean.'

She sighed. 'I know. He's seen us. He can identify us.' Her dad had wanted Jordan dead, too, but she had refused to consider it. Martin wasn't too keen either. And they'd won. Agreed to do just the three adult males – Phil, Fraser and Tommy. Or so she'd thought. But now things weren't looking so rosy for Jordan. Fuck, her dad was a right bastard sometimes.

'Shit,' she said. 'He's only a kid.'

'Doesn't stop his eyes from working. And the police'll believe him, won't they? If he fingers us, case closed.'

Jordan's voice hadn't broken yet. He was older than he looked, but even so, Effie knew he was only eleven. 'I fucked up,' she said to Martin.

'How the fuck did you fuck up?'

'Not getting out of here when we could have. Having that bath. Not making a contingency plan.'

'You'd have preferred to spend the rest of the night covered in gunge?'

'Could have had a shower.'

'And how were we to know the kid would get on his bike, cycle over here and let himself in with his own fucking key?'

She shrugged. 'We should have considered it.'

'Can't consider everything. Anyway, doesn't matter. What matters is what we do now.'

He was right. No point dwelling on the past. She should know. Maybe she'd been trying too hard to impress him. Didn't matter for the moment who'd sent the kid round to visit. She had to let go of the anger and think.

She must have spoken aloud, cause Martin said, 'Yeah, we have to deal with this, babe.'

She nodded. 'I'm just not sure if we should . . .'

He said, 'Things are different.' His face twisted. 'The kid's dangerous.'

Sounded like he wanted to do it. 'You mean you've changed your mind?'

'You got any other ideas?'

They could ask Jordan not to mention them, say this was all a big secret. But that'd hardly be a smart move. Maybe claim that Jordan's brother didn't want anyone to know he'd gone off on that fictitious drug deal, so Jordan had to keep his mouth shut. They could bribe him. Money probably wouldn't work, but they could try offering him a fancy mobile phone or a computer console or something. But his grandmother would want to know where the new equipment had come from, so that was no good.

What else, then? Well, if Jordan was an adult, threats might work. Break something? Nah, if he went home with a busted arm, Grandma was going to wonder how that'd happened and word would get out about the bad couple at Fraser's house.

Effie looked up. Martin was watching her, arms by his sides, one foot planted on top of the other.

'Give me time,' she said. 'There's got to be a way out of this.'

'You think we have time?' Martin said. 'We have to leave. We need to decide what we're going to do with the kid.'

'*You* decide.'

'You saying you want me to do it?' Martin said.

'I'm not saying that at all.'

'Yes, you are. If you can't decide, then I'll have to. And because I make the decision, I'll have to do . . . it, too.'

'Look,' Effie said, 'I'm just saying, I don't think I can do it. That's all.'

Martin folded his arms. 'Well, I'm not doing it. You'll have to. You're the Apprentice, after all.'

She stared at him. She shouldn't have told him Richie'd called her that. 'What if we just leave the kid?'

'So he can tell the police we were here? Give them our descriptions? Identify us in a line up? If we don't sign his death warrant, we're signing our own. He knows what's wrapped up over there.'

Effie looked at what remained of Phil and Fraser Savage. 'No, he doesn't.'

'He said as much.'

'If he seriously thought those were the remains of his uncle and his brother, he'd be shitting himself, not drinking milk and watching TV. Anyway, we're taking the bodies with us.'

'Yeah, okay, but that's not going to make him forget we were here or that he saw a pair of corpses in the hallway.'

Effie paused. 'There is another option.'

Martin raised his eyebrows.

'Take him with us,' she said.

'Take him home?'

'Obviously we can't do that —'

'Well, where?'

'I don't know. I was just thinking aloud. If we take him along with us for now, at least it gives us more time to decide what to do with him later.'

'Let's clear up, get dressed.' Martin looked into the sitting room again. 'Jordan's not going anywhere. And I can think more clearly with my trousers on.'

THEY CLEANED UP as best they could, keeping an eye on the kid. If you didn't know any different, the place looked okay. Far from meticulous, but it would do.

Apart from the interfering little bastard it had been a pretty neat couple of expurgations.

Effie liked that word. She'd had no idea what it meant the first time she'd heard Richie say it and neither did he. But they'd looked it up in a dictionary and discovered it referred to the removal of obscene or offensive material from books. It was only a slight stretch to apply it to the removal of obscene or offensive people from society.

She stood to the side of Jordan's chair, looking at his profile. He was an ugly kid. Pale and too freckly for this time of year. If Richie was here, he'd expurgate him, no qualms at all. She caught movement out of the corner of her eye. Martin appeared in the kitchen doorway, testing the blade of a steak knife with his thumb.

Jordan hadn't seen him. He was staring at the TV, watching a car ad. He said, 'They look like bodies, eh?'

The car didn't look like a body. He had to mean what Effie thought he meant. Effie looked at Martin and Martin looked at Jordan, lips pressed together. Jordan turned his head.

Effie said, 'What are you talking about?'

'Out in the hallway. In the sheets.' He turned back to the TV. 'The rubbish.'

Martin said, 'Don't be silly.'

'But that's what they look like.' He sipped his milk.

Effie said nothing.

Jordan said, 'With the heads cut off.'

Holy shit. Was the little fucker taunting them?

Jordan gulped down the rest of his milk, left a frothy white moustache. He got to his feet. 'Fraser always drives when he goes away, and his car's out front. And he wouldn't leave his phone. So I don't think he's gone far. Can I have my phone back now?'

Effie'd done everything she could to save the wee shite's life. There didn't seem to be any way round it now. He'd have to go. 'You're wrong,' she said. 'They're not bodies.' Denial. The last resort of the coward.

'I'm not stupid.'

'You fucking are.'

'My dad says Uncle Phil's stupid. I'm not like Uncle Phil. If they're not bodies, let me see inside.'

'Your fucking brother went away,' Effie said. 'With your fucking stupid Uncle Phil. Left us in charge of his house. Now shut up and watch TV. Stop talking nonsense.'

Jordan wasn't looking at Effie. He was looking at Martin. 'Not till I see the rubbish. I want to see what it looks like. Inside.'

Martin looked at Effie, handle of the knife gripped tight. He stepped forward. 'We can't do that, Jordan. It took a long time for us to wrap up the rubbish all nice and tight like that and we wouldn't want to have to do it all again. Do you understand?'

Jordan turned his head away from Martin, fixed his gaze on the TV. An ad for processed cheese, one of Effie's secret pleasures. Martin couldn't stand the stuff and wouldn't have it in the house. 'Can I have my phone?'

Either Jordan was incredibly cold, or despite what he claimed, he'd inherited some of his uncle's genes.

Effie said, 'No.'

'I already told you I'm not stupid,' the little bastard said.

So he was incredibly cold. Good. She'd concentrate on that. Make it easier to do what had to be done.

Fuck you, Dad. Cause this was his doing, she had no doubt, whatever she'd said to Martin and however much she didn't want to believe it.

'You think they're bodies?' Martin said. 'Then you must think that we put them there. So if we did that, then why wouldn't we do the same to you?'

Jordan glanced at the knife in Martin's hand. Didn't seem so sure of himself any more. He sat down.

'You see?' Martin smiled. 'It's a ridiculous idea. Isn't it?'

Jordan nodded. Then, as if he couldn't help himself, he said, 'I'll tell my dad. When he gets here, he'll phone the police. They'll make you unwrap them.'

Martin lowered his head, tapped the flat of the knife against his knee.

Effie put her hand in her pocket, fumbled for the clothes-line.

Martin looked up at her. She knew what he was thinking: *You or me, babe?*

Jesus Christ. How could it have come to this?

PRELUDE TO A CERTAIN THURSDAY: ALMONDELL COUNTRY PARK

TOMMY WAS KNEELING in a clearing doing his best not to throw up.

Smith dragged the sword along the ground, splitting earth and parting leaves as he marched in a circle. He stopped right in front of Tommy and said, 'Is this close to the spot?'

Tommy licked his lips. His tongue felt as sharp as paper. 'I don't know,' he said.

'I asked you a question.' Smith's voice was loud.

Loud enough to attract attention, maybe. But it was late and they were in the middle of nowhere. Tommy wasn't about to get rescued.

'I wish I could help you.' Tommy's bicep throbbed, the object stuck in it still from when he'd made his fucking dumb attempt at rolling to freedom. 'Honestly,' he said, 'I've never been here before.'

'But you arranged for someone else to be here, right?'

Tommy said, 'I've never seen this place.'

'That's not what I asked.' Smith made a guttural noise and swung the *katana* in an arc, narrowly missing Tommy's shoulder.

'Okay,' Tommy said, his voice quivering. He'd have to lie to calm Smith down. 'I've been here before, yes. It's coming back to me. I remember.'

'No, you haven't.' Smith disappeared behind him. Bent over. 'This is the woods where Martin Milne's father was murdered.'

Jesus fucking Christ.

'On your orders.'

Tommy was afraid to speak. But he was more afraid not to. 'It wasn't me. I had nothing to do with it.'

'One more lie and I'll slice your head down the middle.'

Tommy closed his eyes. Fuck's sake, he'd just admit it. If he didn't, Smith was going to carry out his threat. The guy was beyond insane. 'Okay, it was me,' Tommy said. Opened his eyes. 'Yes, I arranged it.'

Smith leaned closer. 'That's better.'

Tommy waited, shoulders shaking.

Smith said, 'Are you even a tiny bit sorry?'

And Tommy said, 'Yes. Very. Completely.'

'Nice to hear you say so.' Smith stood up, his knees clicking. 'But Milne isn't important any longer. We're here because of Grant. You need to pay for that. What're we going to do, Tommy?'

'You can have everything,' Tommy said. 'All my money. My house. My properties.'

Smith said, 'You think Grant has a price tag? Sums you up.' He disappeared behind Tommy. 'Say your prayers.'

The wind moaned in the trees. Tommy could smell the sweet earth he was kneeling on. He wondered how the steel would feel biting into his neck.

He closed his eyes and muttered, 'Oh, Christ, oh, God, oh, fucking hell, oh, fuck.' He waited for the blow, muscles tensed in the back of his neck, eyes squeezed so tight his forehead hurt. He wondered how it would sound. Nothing. Still nothing. His neck muscles burned like they'd been stretched and twisted into a series of complicated knots.

Tommy said, 'Get on with it.' Behind him, he heard Smith's feet scuffing the ground.

'Not now,' Smith said. 'Get up.'

Tommy stood, tasted the air. Filled his lungs with it. He didn't dare speak.

After a while, Smith said, 'Back to the car,' and Tommy started to move.

Halfway along the path, Tommy said, a tremor still in his voice, 'Why did you change your mind?'

Smith said nothing.

'Thanks,' Tommy said.

OLD MRS YARDIE'S

THE BEDROOM WHERE Tommy was imprisoned contained an old-fashioned heavy iron-framed bed, a dark-wood wardrobe, matching chest of drawers and a bucket. Tommy was chained to the bed.

There was no clock in the room, and Smith had taken Tommy's watch. As he'd taken everything else. Stripped him bare. Literally. Given him just a ratty steel-grey blanket to wrap around himself.

This was Old Mrs Yardie's house, Smith had told him. What had happened to Old Mrs Yardie was anybody's guess. Tommy hadn't heard any signs of anyone else living here and he suspected that she wouldn't have willingly allowed someone to be held captive in her own home, so Tommy didn't rate Old Mrs Yardie's chances.

Must be about two weeks Tommy'd been here now.

He'd had time to think. Lots of it. It dragged, day and night. Time to think about Phil, Mum, Fraser, Jordan. Time to wonder how Hannah was coping with life in Johannesburg. Time to wonder how he might have saved their marriage. Time to wonder what he ever saw in her. Time to resolve to call Bella from Napoli just as soon as he was free to do so. But mainly, time to think about how he'd got himself into this mess and to wonder if he was ever going to get out of it.

Spikes of fear punched into his temples. Adrenalin flooded his bloodstream, mixed with the fever.

There was a constant burning in his stomach.

Each day, he grew sicker.

He lowered his eyelids. An image of torchlit blood on glass flashed into his head, vivid enough to make him shudder. If they'd called an ambulance right away, maybe the boy would have made it. Maybe that was Tommy's punishment. Left alone to think about what he'd done.

Tommy dug his nails into his hands. Forced the image to change. After a while, he was back home, sitting at the desk in his office, staring at his computer screen. Ah, yes, he remembered that day. He was checking out the website of a sash and case window specialist.

For one reason or another, half the windows in the house wouldn't open properly. And Mum was fed up with it. Told him he'd never treat one of his business properties the way he treated his own home. And she was right. So he'd been having a look at what was available. He'd thought about modernising, but wanted to keep the traditional look. And these guys came recommended.

He was thinking he should get a quote when there was a knock on the door and Jordan came in.

Tommy looked at his watch. He was surprised to see Jordan this early, then remembered it was the school holidays. And then remembered he was due for a conference call in just under two minutes. He said, 'What have you done?'

'Nothing.'

'What do you want, then?'

Jordan shrugged. He looked at the floor, scuffed the carpet with his shoe.

'Jordan. I'm busy.'

He muttered, 'Got to go to Fraser's.'

'Good. Be careful on the road.'

After a while: 'Dad, I think I'm too tired to take my bike. Been playing football all morning.'

'You want a lift? Is that it?'

'Suppose.'

Tommy nodded. Never liked the idea of Jordan riding a bike. Could have strangled his mother when she bought the damn thing. 'Give me twenty minutes?'

'Okay. Can my friend come too?'

'Sure, who's your –?'

Jordan pointed over Tommy's shoulder.

Tommy turned, saw something about the size of a well-fed dog just as it hurtled through the window. Tommy ducked, put his hands over his head.

A crash, a thump. Then silence. He stayed hunched over.

When he dared to look, shards of glass glinted on the floor, littered his desk, glistened like water on the keyboard. There were slivers of glass on the back of his hands. He wiped them off. Somehow, he wasn't cut.

He looked over to the door, asked Jordan, 'You okay?'

Jordan nodded.

There was no sign now of the dog, or whatever it was. But it couldn't have just disappeared. Tommy scanned the room, still couldn't see anything. He peered over the edge of his desk.

There was nothing there.

He brushed glass off his chair with his sleeve and sat back down. Jordan smiled again. Tommy smiled back, but realised that his son wasn't looking at him. Jordan was looking to his right.

Tommy snapped his head to the side just as something shoved him, sent him sprawling to the floor. He put out a hand, cut his palm, cried out. Twisted onto his side, gasping. And suddenly he was face to face with someone he never thought he'd see again.

He stared into the face, the white lips even whiter than the cheeks.

It couldn't be. Didn't make sense.

He looked down, along the pale throat, down the chest, past the stomach, to the waist. Where the torso stopped abruptly.

Grant said, 'Yeah, can I come too?'

TOMMY OPENED HIS eyes. Squinted at the sunlight streaming through the curtainless window, shivered as waves of cold rippled down his body. The fever was worse. He sat up on the bed, tried removing the cuff from his wrist again. He'd bruised his fingertips with repeated attempts. It was a waste of time, but that didn't stop him.

It was something to do.

Fear, fever and fucking boredom. Bastard of a combination.

The solid steel chain was about four feet long, if that. A closet chain, Smith had called it. One end was attached to a bedpost at the foot of the bed. The other was cuffed to his left wrist. The chain tightened well short of the door.

He had tried lifting the bed. He'd tried dragging it. Smith was prepared. Both legs at the foot of the bed were bracketed to the floor and the headboard was bolted into the wall.

For the first few days he'd spent a lot of time walking round the bed for exercise, but his arm hurt too much now.

The outside door slammed.

Smith was back. Popped out to get supplies again, no doubt. Hadn't left the house often, just a handful of occasions that Tommy knew about.

He came into the bedroom regularly. To bring food. To check on Tommy. To empty the bucket. Sometimes, they talked. Then he'd leave, and Tommy would hear the shower running or the low babble of voices from the TV along the hallway, or Smith's voice, quiet, talking to someone on the phone.

Footsteps pounded up the stairs. The door along the corridor opened.

Must be dinner time. Tommy wasn't hungry.

Clatter of floorboards in the corridor and the door to Tommy's room opened.

Smith, masked as always, had Tommy's *katana* in one hand, a laptop in the other.

Tommy wasn't stupid enough to think that he'd be allowed internet access, but he'd kill for a game of Minesweeper. Take his mind off things.

Without a word, Smith plugged in the laptop under the chest of drawers. It was a couple of feet beyond the reach of the chain. But the screen was big enough for Tommy to see from the bed.

Smith fiddled around with it for a bit, then stood back and said, 'What do you think?'

THE EVENING AFTER Smith kidnapped him, Tommy had been forced to make a call, the phone held away from his ear with the speaker volume turned up so Smith could hear.

Mum answered. When she realised it was Tommy, she said, 'What happened? Where are you?'

He was naked, wrapped in a blanket, sitting on a bed with a lumpy mattress in an old house somewhere in the country. 'I'm fine,' he said. 'Just that –' he looked at Smith, watched his eyes dart from side to side through the holes in his ski mask '– something came up.'

'What came up? How can something come up? Things don't just 'come up'. What do you mean?'

'Look, Mum,' Tommy said, 'I need you to trust me.' Smith had warned him what would happen to his mother if she suspected anything. 'It's just that I have to go away for a while.'

'What's wrong? What are you hiding? I spoke to Phil.'

He was alive. *Thank Christ.*

'He tried to cover for you,' Mum said. 'Pretended he knew where you were.'

Yes. Phil would come looking for him.

'Tommy?'

'Yeah?'

'If you don't tell me what's going on,' she said, 'I'm calling the police.'

Smith held up a warning finger.

'Don't worry about me,' Tommy said. 'Just take care of Jordan till I get back. And don't expect to hear from me for a while.'

'Tell me what's wrong, Tommy, please.'

'Look,' Tommy said, watching Smith's eyes through the ski mask, 'I just need to stay away for a while. Till things calm down.'

'What things? You said everything was fine.'

'You don't need to know. Just trust me.'

'I'm trying. Give me some help.'

'Please, Mum. I don't need the police looking for me, believe me.'

'You're in trouble with the police now?'

Smith nodded.

'Yeah,' Tommy said. 'Bit of bother. But it'll die down. Nothing major.'

Silence. 'But if you to have to go into hiding . . .'

'For a while.'

'And it's nothing major?'

'Not on the phone, Mum.'

'The tobacco again? Tommy, I thought —'

'It's not that.'

'Tell me,' she said. 'I can keep a secret.'

'I haven't . . . I can't say.'

A pause. 'Is there anything I can do?'

Smith leaned forward, whispered in his ear.

Tommy said, 'Tell the boys I've had to go abroad for a while. They won't be able to get in touch. Don't worry them.'

'Of course not.'

Smith whispered some more.

Tommy turned, looked at him. 'And Phil can't know either.'

'He doesn't know?'

'Not a word, Mum.'

'Okay.'

'Okay. 'Bye, Mum.'

Smith took the phone from him, gently, so Tommy didn't protest, and cut him off. 'Very good,' Smith said. 'You're a natural liar.' He fiddled about with the keys, dialled. After a few seconds he said, 'Phil, how's the head? Listen carefully. If I hear that you've been snooping around trying to find your brother, I'll kill him. You got that?'

Phil must have replied cause Smith said, 'Yes, that means he's alive. Worked that out all by yourself. Very clever. Now be quiet and listen. Someone will be in touch in due course. Just behave yourself till then and don't go poking around or breathe a word to a soul. Your family thinks Tommy's abroad. Let them think that or Tommy dies.'

That night Tommy hadn't slept at all. He was cold and scared and the chain kept getting in the way. Worse, something was stuck in his bicep from when he'd tried to escape the previous night back at the car. He'd have taken a look at the damage, but there was no lamp and he couldn't reach the lightswitch.

He waited till dawn. Saw that a piece of glass was embedded in his arm. Poked around tentatively, but couldn't get a grip on it.

Next morning, he threw the bucket at the window and broke a pane. He shouted for help.

Smith appeared in his mask, slippers, *katana*, said, 'There's no one for miles.' He left the room with the bucket, came back dressed, a gun tucked into his waistband and carrying a dustpan and brush, a roll of duct tape and a new bucket, a blue plastic one with a white handle. He taped a piece of cardboard over the hole.

Before he left, Tommy asked him, 'Can I have my clothes back?'

Smith said, 'No.'

Tommy said, 'Would you help me take this piece of glass out of my arm?'

Smith looked at him. 'Did you try to get any pieces of glass out of my son?'

TWO DAYS LATER and the wound didn't look too good. Tommy had managed to tease and pinch and tug the glass out yesterday but the wound needed more than sluicing with cold water. Ought to be properly cleaned, stitched, bandaged. But Smith wasn't about to take him to the nearest hospital, or play nursemaid. He'd made that clear before asking Tommy to hand over the piece of glass.

Yesterday seemed a long time ago.

Smith barged into the room. 'Morning,' he said. 'You want breakfast today?'

Tommy shucked off his blanket. 'My arm's agony,' he said. 'You have to let someone take a look at it.'

Smith said, 'No,' and turned his head away. 'Cover yourself up.'

Who'd have thought Smith would be such a prude?

Tommy pulled the blanket round him again. 'If the cut's infected, I could die of blood poisoning.'

'I don't give a fuck.'

'Your fun would be over.'

Tommy was relying on being worth more to Smith alive then dead. Smith had indicated to Phil that Tommy would be alive till somebody got in touch. It made sense that Smith would keep him alive till he'd screwed every last penny out of him.

'My fun,' Smith repeated. He kept his head turned away, poked the point of the *katana* into the floorboards. 'How about I cut your arm off at the shoulder? That'll be a sure way to get rid of any infection.'

'Won't help.' Play him at his own game, Tommy thought. 'Chances are I'll die of blood loss or shock. And if the blade's not sterile, there's the same risk of infection.'

'I'll get you some antiseptic cream,' Smith said. 'You can rub it on the stump.'

Tommy didn't know how far to push. He tried a little further. 'Cream would be good. Can I get some now?'

Smith said, 'I should really cut your *nnnngah* tongue off.' He left the room, walking awkwardly with his gun in his trousers and the sword in his hand. Came back ten minutes later with a plaster and a piece of cloth which he told Tommy to wrap round the cut and keep out of sight, it was ugly.

ANOTHER DAY.

Smith opened the door, stood there wearing a cheap dark suit and a black tie, studying Tommy through the eyeholes of his ski mask. 'Funeral,' he said. 'My son's funeral.'

Tommy held his gaze for as long as he could, then looked

away. When he looked back again, the door was closed and Smith had gone.

Pressure built behind Tommy's eyes until he cried, but it didn't help.

NEXT TIME SMITH let him call Mum she said, 'I've been worried sick. Why haven't you called?'

'Bit difficult.'

'Why? Where are you?'

'I can't say.'

'Don't you think you're being paranoid?'

'No. They can trace these things. Work out where I am.'

Smith flinched.

Had he not thought of that? For a moment, Tommy believed he'd got the better of him. But the sad truth was that nobody was going to trace his calls. Didn't matter if they could pinpoint their origin.

Tommy noticed he was playing with his chain, let it fall onto the bed.

'Jordan misses you,' Mum said.

'Can I speak to him?'

Smith shook his head.

'He's at Fraser's,' Mum said. 'You could try his mobile.'

'Okay.' He sighed. 'Got to go now.'

'Where are you? Tell me where you are.'

'I can't do that.'

'You don't trust me?'

'It's not a matter of trust, Mum. Just believe me that it's better you don't know.'

'Better for who?'

'For us all. For the family.'

'Tommy, are you in really bad trouble?'

He smiled, wished she could see him. 'Yes, I'm in some really deep shit.'

Smith dragged his finger across his throat.

Tommy went cold. Then he realised Smith only meant for him to end the call. 'In case I don't get through to Jordan,' he said to Mum, 'tell him I love him.'

A FEW DAYS later.

'Are you sick?'

When he'd looked at his arm half an hour ago, pus was weeping out of the cut. It hurt to touch. Painful even just to move his arm and there was a stiffness to it that was worrying.

He was weak and sweating. Even the phone in his hand felt like it was perspiring. He smelled sweet. His stomach ached. Last night Grant spoke to him again in a dream and this time both halves of the lad's body were there, the upper half hovering a few inches above the lower. The dead boy's eyes were unblinking black stones in a bone-white face. He told Tommy that there was no such thing as an accident. He told Tommy that a father had a duty to avenge his son or he was no father at all. Tommy said no, it didn't have to be that way. Grant told him he didn't know what he was talking about. As he spoke, blood dribbled from his mouth and then it started to pour from his nose and ears. Then those black eyes started to bleed. Tommy woke up drenched. He hadn't been able to go back to sleep.

'Tommy?'

'Just a bit of a cold, Mum,' Tommy said into the phone.

Smith stared at him, tongue flicking out of the mouthhole of the mask.

Mum said, 'You have to look after yourself.'

'I know.'

'Sure you're okay?'

He tried to inject some enthusiasm into his voice. 'Absolutely. Nothing to worry about.'

'How can I not worry?'

'I know.' Pause. 'I know.'

'You will come home?'

He glanced at Smith. 'When it's safe.'

'And when's that?'

He struggled to keep his voice from breaking. 'Soon.'

SMITH DUMPED THE food on Tommy's bed – snacks, as usual. Since his incarceration Tommy'd had nothing wholesome to eat apart from a couple of tins of soup and the occasional plate of baked beans. Smith tucked into a bag of crisps. Tommy knew he was about to say something, even though he couldn't read his face through the ski mask. Something to do with the way his body jerked to a halt.

'Not hungry?' Smith said. 'I'll have yours if you don't want it.'

Tommy stared at the junk pooled in a channel in the rumpled quilt, gathered his blanket round him. Actually, even the thought of a big juicy steak did nothing for him. Scarcely any flab bunched up round his stomach now when he sat forward. Not that he was ever fat like his brother, but there'd been a bit of excess. Changed days.

The blanket stank. Or maybe it was his arm. Or the bucket. Although he'd not had anything to deposit in it recently.

Tommy looked at the laptop screen. 'Can I call home?' he asked.

'Fuck off and eat something.'

'Let me call my mother. I want to speak to Jordan.'

'Eat.'

'If I eat something, will you let me make that call?'

'Okay.'

Tommy scooped up a bar of chocolate. Unwrapped it. His fingers were puffy and tender. He bit into the bar. Chewed twice, swallowed. Had a second bite. Finished it with his third. Licked his upper front teeth but couldn't stop them throbbing.

'Can I phone now?'

'No,' Smith said. 'I think you've spoken quite enough.'

NIGHTTIME. LIGHTS WERE out. The image on the computer was dark. He'd gone to bed too.

The quiet made Tommy's ears hum. His skin prickled all over, he felt lightheaded, his eyelids were solid weights, his eyeballs throbbed but he couldn't sleep. Didn't want to.

Asked himself the question he'd asked a hundred times since Smith had plugged in the laptop.

Why was there a live video feed into Fraser's sitting room?

'PINHOLE CAMERA,' SMITH had explained once the image was working. 'Set it up while he was out. On the mantelpiece peeking through the gap between a couple of picture frames. Hard to see, even if you know it's there. Bit worried about Fraser dusting, but luckily he doesn't seem to be that houseproud.'

The colour image was clear enough to make out the pattern of the carpet. Same as Fraser's.

The room was empty at the moment. A dead place.

'Like a nanny cam,' Smith said. 'Heard of them?'

Tommy said nothing.

'You'd think they cost a fortune.' Smith paused. 'Less than a grand, that one. Anyway, I've got a fortune, remember?'

Tommy didn't give a shit about the fifty grand Smith had stolen from him. He was welcome to it.

'Battery powered,' Smith carried on. 'They'll last much longer than needed. Wireless, of course. And some fancy software loads it to a website where I can play it in real time. Bit jerky. But it does the trick.'

'What's all this for?' Tommy said. 'What's it for? Tell me that.'

Smith said, 'Patience.'

UNTIL HE SAW Fraser, he hadn't believed the camera was in his son's home. Thought the image was a fake. But when Fraser walked into the frame, Tommy knew it was real. There was no sound, and Tommy watched as his son silently passed out of sight.

Tommy's hand moved towards the screen, clutched at the air, dropped to his side.

Fraser came back a few minutes later, wiping his nose like he'd just been snorting coke. Tommy smiled, couldn't help himself.

SMITH'S CRISP PACKET rustled.

Tommy dragged his gaze away from the screen. He blinked repeatedly, his eyes irritated as if they were full of grit. His forehead was hot and damp.

Smith had brought a chair in about ten minutes ago, and he sat there six feet away, eating his crisps, smug behind his ski mask, occasionally glancing at the screen, but mainly just sticking crisps in his mouth, salt dusting the mouthhole of his ski mask, watching Tommy watching the monitor.

'Let me see your face,' Tommy said. He'd never forgotten Smith telling the waiter that his face was horribly scarred. He was sure it was a lie, but it wasn't proof he was after. Just wanted to see what Smith looked like behind the mask.

'I don't think so,' Smith said.

'You're Grant's father,' Tommy said. 'I can identify you that way. Seeing your face won't make any difference.'

'I'm keeping the mask on,' Smith said. 'So fuck you.'

Tommy sipped some water from a plastic beaker. Wiped his brow. His forehead was slick with sweat but he was shivering.

'I need another blanket,' he said.

Smith crunched another crisp.

'I'm running a fever.'

'So you might die,' Smith said. 'I'll dig a grave for you in the garden. Dance on it afterwards.'

'That's your plan? Let my cut go septic and watch me die?'

'Stop fucking bleating about a fucking scratch.'

'Is it?' Tommy said. 'Is that the plan?'

'No, Savage. But the way you keep harping on, it would be a fucking bonus.'

Tommy swallowed the rest of his water. 'You want more money?'

'Don't piss me off.'

Course not. Tommy knew that now. This wasn't about money. For either of them. He shivered again. 'So what are you going to do?'

'You'll find out,' Smith said. 'Won't be long now.' He pointed to the screen. 'Keep watching.'

IT BEGAN IN the evening, a couple of days later.

Smith had brought his chair into the bedroom, but he couldn't sit still. Kept getting up, pacing around, swinging the *katana* – usually in Tommy's direction – and putting the sword away again. Then he'd sit down for five minutes, watch the screen, and fiddle with his gun.

And he kept checking his watch.

And back to the sword again.

Tommy couldn't see the screen very well, seated where he was, upright against the headboard. But if he sat farther forward, that would bring him closer to Smith's periodic lunges and swipes. Still, Tommy inched forward, peering at the screen all the while, keeping Smith in his vision, making sure he wasn't getting too close. He edged forward, until he was at the end of the bed, Smith just a couple of feet away.

Tommy crossed his arms over his blanket.

On screen, Fraser was eating his dinner on the settee, watching TV. All Tommy could see were his feet.

At first Tommy had refused to look at the screen. He didn't want to know what Fraser got up to in the privacy of his own home. But he'd found the temptation impossible to resist. And by now he'd grown used to watching his son. Truth was, Tommy now felt compelled to watch. He felt that Fraser would want him to watch. He'd appreciate the fact that his old man was looking out for him.

Or maybe Tommy was thinking like that to make himself feel better. His emotions were all shot to fuck. He wasn't sure what he felt any longer. It was hard to do the right thing when you'd no idea what that was.

The only thing he did have much of a clue about was that Smith was planning something unpleasant, and the only thing that mattered was stopping him.

Tommy said to Smith, 'Whatever you've got in mind, I'm begging you not to do it.'

Smith stood still, *katana* aloft. 'Did Greg Milne beg for his life?'

Tommy said, 'I don't know. Believe me. I didn't kill him.'

Smith sighed. 'But you arranged it.'

Tommy lowered his voice. 'I arranged nothing. Doesn't matter how many times you say I did.'

'You admitted it. Back in the woods.'

'I'd have admitted anything. For what it's worth, that bastard fucked everybody over.'

'You thought he was a bastard?'

'Yes. And not just me. There was a lot of pressure to make an example of him and I refused. I fucking refused. Whoever was responsible for his death had nothing to do with me. Or if they did, they acted in direct contradiction to my orders.'

'So you're saying maybe they did have something to do with you?'

Tommy shook his head. 'You're not listening.'

'I think it's you who isn't listening.'

'I had nothing to do with it.'

'It doesn't matter.' Smith stepped towards the bed. Tommy leaned away as Smith bent towards him. Smith said, 'Because what you're about to witness, what you're about to experience, is not for what you did to Milne. It's for what you did to Grant.'

That was different.

'Please,' Tommy said. He'd promised himself he wouldn't beg, yet here he was pleading with Smith yet again. It was all he had left. 'Don't.'

'What fucks me off most,' Smith said, 'isn't your lies about Milne.'

'It's the tr . . .'

'Shut up. What fucks me off is the way you won't take responsibility for my son's death.'

Tommy swallowed. Licked his lips. 'It was an accid . . . I won't say it again.'

'No, don't. Maybe it was an accident. But kidnapping him and torturing him, that was your fucking fault.'

'I didn't mean any harm.'

'I don't give a fuck what you meant. Only what you did. It was your fault.'

'I . . .' Tommy said. 'I don't know.'

'Your brother's fault, then? You saying he's solely to blame?'

Tommy said, 'It was nobody's fault.'

Smith raised the *katana*. 'Another word, I fucking dare you.'

Tommy held up his palms. 'Okay, I'm guilty. It was my fault. Is that what you want to hear?'

A moment passed. Then Smith lowered the sword. 'It's not about what I want to hear. It's about you accepting your role in Grant's death. Can you do that?'

'I didn't . . .' Tommy choked. 'I . . .' He looked at Smith, stared him in the eye and whispered, 'Yes.'

'I didn't catch that.'

'Yes,' Tommy said.

'Grant died because of you?'

Tommy nodded.

'Say it.'

'Grant died because of me.'

Smith said, 'Wasn't so hard now, was it?'

'I'm sorry.'

Smith pointed the sword at him. 'You think an apology makes everything okay?'

'I didn't say that.'

'Because it doesn't.'

'No,' Tommy said. 'I didn't think it would.'

Smith sat down, smiling.

Maybe because he knew he'd won.

Tommy had gone over and over that night in his head. Imagined different outcomes. Sometimes Grant survived. Sometimes he didn't try to bolt, just told them what they wanted to know. But the scenario Tommy kept returning to was the one where he arrived at the abandoned flat and immediately instructed Phil to let the boy go.

That's what he should have done.

What had happened to Grant *was* Tommy's fault. Looked at through a father's eyes, Smith was right. No way would he ever accept the blame himself and Tommy could understand that.

'Your boy's up to no good again,' Smith said.

On the monitor, Fraser was kneeling on the floor, a line of coke laid out on a magazine. He chopped up the coke with a razorblade, inhaled it with a sweeping motion and leaned back.

After a while, he rose, tossed the magazine away and checked his wallet for cash, then vanished from the picture in the direction of the hallway.

'You have about half an hour,' Smith said.

Tommy felt a pair of thumbs digging into his temples. He asked, 'Till what?'

Smith picked up his chair and left the room.

SAVAGE NIGHT
1 A.M.
A WHITE VAN

IN THE VAN, approaching a set of traffic lights, Martin said, 'There's no other way of making sure he'll keep his mouth shut.'

Effie said, 'He's listening.'

'So?'

'This is ludicrous.' Effie almost stalled the engine. The clutch took a bit of getting used to but she wasn't going to let Martin drive. Just because all vehicles were designed for men of average height, didn't mean a petite woman couldn't cope. A Transit might have been a slightly tougher prospect, but they'd bought a second-hand Escort, cheap and disposable, even if it was a bit crammed in the back. So no excuses. If she could strangle a bloke a head taller than her, she could drive a fucking van. She pulled on the handbrake, waited for the lights to change.

She could feel Martin's eyes on her.

He said, 'We should have . . . you know . . . back at the house.'

She shook her head, kept her voice low. 'Well, we couldn't.'

'I know. Fuck, though. Can't be that hard.'

'Go ahead,' she said. 'Try it.'

He said, 'What, right now?'

'Yeah. Climb into the back and do it.'

'I'm too big.'

'You could squeeze through.'

'Why don't you?'

'I don't want to.'

He stayed silent. He was working something out. Effie gave him peace to do so and after a while, he said, 'Why *can't* we do it, babe? Is it cause it's . . . unethical?'

'Big word.'

'Big situation.'

She chose not to respond.

He punched her lightly on the knee. 'Well?' he said.

She shrugged. 'Something like that. I dunno. He's a fucking kid. Course it's fucking unethical.'

'Grant was a kid too.'

She said, a vivid image of her brother's face in front of her, 'I've no intention of killing anybody I don't want to. And I don't want to kill the kid.'

'Fine.' He paused. 'Probably means we're all going to jail, Effie.'

'Cut the crap, Martin.'

'It's not –'

'Just shut up.'

It was one in the morning. She'd just killed someone. Cut up his body. And this kid was a whisker away from having to die. Most likely because of her fucking father. Not Martin. He wasn't to blame.

'Sorry,' she said. 'I'm tired.'

'Want me to drive?'

'I'll be fine.' She revved the engine. 'Why the fuck are these lights taking so long to change?'

She would have jumped them if she didn't have a couple of bodies in the back along with a kidnapped eleven-year-old, tied up and gagged. Hardly ideal circumstances in which to be taking risks just to get home to bed quicker. Anyway, bed was a way off yet. There was still a lot to do. Her head was fuzzy. She could have used a cup of coffee. Intended having one before they left Fraser's, but they'd had to leave in a hurry on account of her dad messing them around. He really was a fucking dickhead sometimes.

'You want to try Dad again?'

'Sure,' Martin said. 'Doubt we'll get a response this time either, though.'

There. At last. The lights changed. 'Just try.' Effie put her foot down. Kept just within the speed limit. 'Please. We have to know what we're walking into.'

Of course, there was no reply.

Martin put the phone away and Effie drove, awkwardly, Martin leaning against her. She didn't mind though. She liked the smell of him, fresh from the bath. She couldn't stay mad at him for long, especially after she'd realised it wasn't him she was mad at.

They headed out of town, west, along Dalry where straggles of drunk teenage girls stumbled along the pavements, through Gorgie, which was already much quieter. By the time they reached Saughton, the nighttime traffic had reduced to the occasional car, taxi, a coach. The new builds at Broomhouse passed on the right, and roundabout followed roundabout, causing Martin to sit up so Effie could change gear without banging his head off her arm or stalling. He yawned, dozed off again. They drove through Sighthill, then Calder.

They'd hit the Kilmarnock road and were out of the city when Jordan's phone rang. Muffled, but definitely a kid's song, fast and tuneful and chirpy. Effie felt the vibrations against her leg. Had three phones in there. Lucky she was wearing combats, so there was plenty of room.

She grabbed it, but it rang out before she could answer. She glanced at the keypad trying to figure out how to find out who'd called and was about to wake Martin and let him work it out when the phone rang again. This time it jolted him awake. He looked at her. She read the name on the display.

Fuck.

'Jordan's?' Martin asked, indicating the phone.

She nodded.

'Who is it?' he asked.

'It says: 'dad'.'

'I don't like this,' Martin said. 'What should we do?'

'We can't just ignore it.'

'No, we can't.'

She held it out to him. 'You want to?'

'You go on.'

'I'm driving.'

'Answer it, Effie. I wouldn't know what to say.'

'You expect me to?' Fuck's sake. She answered it: 'Who is this?'

'You fucking know, bitch.' Tommy Savage's voice.

She swallowed. Looked for somewhere to pull over. 'Where's my father?'

'What did you do to Jordan?'

'I want to speak to Dad.'

'I want to speak to my son.'

Her voice was weak. 'No,' she said. 'You can't.'

'I can't? If you've harmed him –'

'He's alive. He's here. In the van.'

'Put him on the phone.'

'I can't do that.'

'Savage? What does he want?' Martin said.

She shook her head at him.

'If you don't prove to me that Jordan's alive,' Savage said, 'your dad's dead.'

So Dad was still alive. Meant she'd be able to forgive him for landing Jordan on her.

Savage said, 'I know what you did to Phil and Fraser.'

Of course he did. He'd seen it in graphic detail.

'I don't know what you're talking about, Mr Savage,' she said.

'Want me to tell you about the tub? About the hacksaws? About you and loverboy all naked and covered in my family's fucking blood?'

Silence. She could hear him breathe, thought she heard him sniff. 'Where are you?' she said. 'Maybe we can arrange an exchange.'

'What about my brother and my other son? Who are you going to exchange for them?'

She'd already said too much. 'I don't know who you mean. But even if I did, there's nothing we can do about what's already done.' She waited. He said nothing. His breath rattled down the phone. 'Okay,' she said. 'Where do you want to meet?'

He told her. The parking lot at the East Calder entrance to Almondell Country Park. 'Bet you know where that is,' he said.

'I'll find it,' she said.

SAVAGE NIGHT
9.30 P.M.
OLD MRS
YARDIE'S

TOMMY WATCHED THE screen. A few minutes ago Martin Milne had wandered into Fraser's sitting room. Martin was much beefier than his dad. Then again, his dad was an alchy. Martin had looked around, then disappeared.

Now he was back again, staggering under the weight of a man thrown over his shoulder. For a minute, he turned his back to the camera and Tommy saw the back of the other guy's head. His hair was ginger. Was it Phil?

He asked Smith.

Smith cleared his throat, turned on his chair so he was facing Tommy, not the screen. 'It certainly is.'

White-hot balls of anger swelled in Tommy's stomach, heat rising into his chest, burning his gullet.

Phil dangled over Martin Milne's shoulder. Limp, as if he was . . . No, couldn't be. 'Is he . . . ?' Tommy asked.

'Is he what?'

'Doesn't matter.' Tommy shook his head. Sweat flicked onto his blanket. He pulled it tight around his shoulders.

'Go on. Is he . . . ?'

'Dead, you fuck,' Tommy said. 'Is he dead?'

'No,' Smith said. 'Not yet. But keep watching.'

Even through the mask, he looked smug.

Martin Milne dumped Phil on the couch, his leg trailing onto the floor. Milne stood for a minute getting his breath back. Then disappeared.

Nothing stirred for a few seconds. Then Phil's foot twitched. He was waking up. *Come on.* But there was no further movement. Maybe Tommy had imagined it.

He glanced at Smith. He was leaning in close. Absorbed. Staring at Tommy like he was some kind of exotic zoo creature.

Tommy'd never hit anyone in his life. But he couldn't just sit here and let Phil die. He had to do something. So he clenched his fist and swung it at the cunt.

PARK SAW IT coming.

He leaned back, and Savage's knuckles brushed past his cheek. Savage was weak and uncoordinated, and, anyway, couldn't punch for shit. Didn't help that he was trying to hold his blanket on with his other hand. Summed him up. Phil was about to die and all Tommy Savage cared about was that he might give Park an eyeful of scrawny cock.

And now he looked scared. Like he wished he hadn't just done that.

Park gauged where the festering cut was on Savage's arm. And punched him there. Put a lot of power into it.

Savage howled. Horrible racket.

He finally stopped, his attention grabbed by what was happening at Fraser's. Park sneaked a look. Martin had returned to the sitting room.

It was going to happen.

Savage had tears in his eyes and a runny nose.

Park could have cried too.

TOMMY BLINKED. HIS eyelashes were wet.

Martin Milne's back was to the camera, but he had a large navy blue bag out of which he was removing a rolled-up sheet. He turned to the side, so Tommy got a better view. Unrolled the sheet, laid it out on the floor. Left the room again and returned with a metal tub. He positioned the tub in the middle of the sheet, then moved towards Phil and bent over him. Tommy couldn't see what he was doing. Not till the trousers came off. And then the shoe and sock. Martin stuffed all the clothes into his bag. Then he hoisted Phil, naked, onto his shoulder and let him slump into the tub.

Tommy couldn't stay quiet any longer. 'What's going on? What's he doing? Why's he got a tub? What's happening? What's he doing to Phil?'

'Shhh,' Smith told him. 'Just watch.'

'Tell me what he's doing.'

'Fucking shut up and watch.'

Martin lit a cigarette, walked up and down, sucking the life out of it. He moved closer to the camera. Took his jacket off, folded it, laid it somewhere out of sight. He reappeared moments later, stripped to the waist. He had a long white mark on his neck, which made the rest of his face look dirty. A scar, maybe.

He moved away again. When he came back he was naked. He moved over to his bag, slipped on a pair of plastic gloves and a pair of plastic booties.

He stuck his hand back into the bag. Came out with a knife. Then a hacksaw.

Oh, Jesus. Oh, Jesus fucking Christ.

'He won't do it,' Tommy said. 'Martin Milne isn't a cold-blooded killer.'

Smith said nothing.

'You can stop this,' Tommy said. 'Call him. Tell him to stop.'

'And spoil the show?'

'JESUS CHRIST,' SAVAGE shouted.

About time Park looked away.

'Jesus fucking Christ, no.'

Savage's face was porcelain white. His quivering jaw told a story.

Park ought to be enjoying this but he felt squeamish. Took a strong character to do what he was doing. Maybe he'd be able to enjoy the next instalment, when Fraser returned with Effie. Savage would know what to expect by that point. A brother was one thing, but a son was an entirely different matter.

And then there'd be the surprise to follow. Park didn't feel good about dumping Effie in it, but she wouldn't agree to killing Jordan so it hadn't left him much of a choice.

Had to be done.

'You arranged this?' Savage said. 'You fucking sick bastard. You fucking sick fuck. What the fuck did he ever do to you?'

Savage really didn't get it, did he? Couldn't get his head round this *at all*. Maybe Park should try to explain once again. Or maybe he should leave Savage alone for a while.

'Oh, fuck. Oh, fuck me,' Savage said. 'He's killing him. He's cutting . . . oh, Christ. You've got to stop this.'

Yeah, Park was starting to feel a bit sick. Maybe he'd leave Tommy to it, see how Liz was doing. Or maybe go grab a sandwich or something, settle his stomach. Park got to his feet. 'Want something to eat?'

Savage gagged, made it to the bucket just before he spewed.

AT FRASER'S HOUSE, Martin was remembering that he had to stop Phil Savage's heart first. Effie'd said that he shouldn't cut him up while it was still pumping. It'd make a right fucking mess. And although Martin had the tub, and the dropcloth, he didn't want to make any more mess than necessary.

He'd thought it'd all be harder than it was. He'd psyched himself up and felt fine. Thought of Effie, what she'd think if he screwed this up. But he wouldn't. He stared at Phil Savage, just so much flab that looked dead already. Martin aimed the knife – holding it two-handed – over the heart. Counted to three and plunged it in.

The body jerked. The eyes opened. Fingers straightened. A foot kicked out.

Martin tugged the knife out and slammed it back in. Did that three times and then Savage was still. Wouldn't close his eyes though. Martin tried to force them shut, but they kept springing open. He gave up. Wrestled Savage over so he was face down in the tub.

Martin took a moment, remembered he was doing this for his dad, too. For Grant, for the Parks, of course. He wouldn't be here otherwise. But maybe he should have done this years ago.

He'd told himself there wasn't sufficient evidence. But everybody knew Tommy Savage had had Martin's dad killed. Everybody but his mum thought Phil Savage was involved.

Truth was, Martin hadn't had the balls. Not on his own. But with Effie, there wasn't a fucking thing he couldn't do.

He picked up the hacksaw.

Tommy Savage, your brother's dead. How does it feel?

Wished his mum was here to see this.

I'm about to carve up a corpse and I think of my mother.

He knew why.

Pictured it. Ten years old. Standing on the stool in the kitchen. Smelling Mum's clean gin-breath as she placed the noose round his neck. Pulling the rope tight. Her voice cracking as she said, 'I'll be with you soon, Martin.' Sound of chair legs scraping on the linoleum floor. Burning pain in his throat, neck jolted, legs lashing out, unable to breathe. And then Dad running into the room, grabbing him round the waist and yelling at his mum, 'You stupid fucking mental bitch.'

Dad had replaced the chair. Untied him. Held him. Martin was warm and in pain and safe.

Mum said, 'I'm sorry, Martin. I'm so sorry.'

'I won't say anything, Mum,' he'd said, a coil of pain searing his neck.

Dad had slapped her, told her to shut her fucking face.

An accident, they'd said when they arrived at the hospital. He'd been playing. Nobody suspected it was a lie. Why would they? What kind of mother would try to hang her son?

He hadn't told anybody that. Not even Effie.

Martin started cutting into the back of Phil Savage's neck. Revenge was much harder work than you could ever imagine.

PARK FLICKED ON the light in the kitchen and hurried over to the sink. Laid the sword on the worktop. Opened the window.

Better.

He'd done what any father would have done. The whole family had agreed. Well, apart from the business about Jordan. Richie had only wished he could have helped. Effie was all for it, too. Liz wouldn't have been keen on any of it, but she was always too soft-hearted. That was her downfall.

Somebody had to take responsibility.

That's all he'd done.

Park sat at the table. Brushed salt off Mrs Yardie's salt shaker. He'd wait a while. Give Martin time to finish the job. Sawing through a body. All that flesh and gristle and bone.

Blood rushed to his head. He tore off his ski mask. Lowered his head to his chest. Breathed deeply. Breathed till he felt better.

He sat for a while and thought about Grant and wished he could cry.

Then he got to his feet. Went back to the sink. Ran the cold water. Stuck his mouth under it. Drank.

Everything in small steps.

Turned off the tap, wiped his mouth with his sleeve.

He wanted to call Effie. See how things were going with Fraser. She'd befriended him easily enough. But was he going to invite her home again? Course he was. He was a bloke.

Anyway, Park had no doubt she'd be able to carry it off. She was tough. Maybe the toughest of them all, Richie included.

And what about Martin? He'd done it. Effie would be proud of him.

But Park couldn't call his daughter. No calls, they'd agreed. The police could trace these things. And they didn't want the police after them. Park had seen enough of the inside of a prison. A couple of prisons, in fact. He didn't fancy seeing any more.

Another drink of water.

Okay.

Park put his ski mask back on, picked up the sword, angled the gun so the handle didn't graze his hipbone.

Back to work.

As he passed his bedroom door, he thought about popping in on Liz, see if she needed to go to the bathroom. He'd been taking her every couple of hours since they moved out here, and she seemed to know what to do. Worked pretty effectively. With their new routine, he'd only had to change the occasional overnight nappy.

But, no, Liz would be fine. She wouldn't have to hold on much longer.

TOMMY SAVAGE SAT on the edge of his bed clutching his stomach. He had stopped puking, which was something. But he didn't look too good. Pale, sweaty, and his chin was quivering like an old woman singing a love song. He saw Park and said, 'You cunt.'

Just what Park needed. He switched the sword to his left hand, bitch-slapped Savage on the ear with his right.

Savage gave him a defiant look. 'You're still a cunt,' he said.

Park slapped him again, harder.

Savage screwed his eyes shut. Said, 'Cunt.'

Park slapped him. This was more like it.

Savage shook his head. Waited. Said, 'Cunt.'

Park slapped him.

Tears rolled down Savage's cheeks. Fucker. He said, quietly, 'Cunt.'

Park slapped him again.

Savage said nothing.

Park wondered if Martin had finished with Phil Savage yet. Park couldn't risk grabbing so much as a peek at the screen now. Frustrating as fuck.

Savage said, 'Cunt.'

Got Park back, focussed. Park slapped him. 'I can do this all night,' he said.

Savage whispered, 'Cunt.'

Park slapped him. His palm stung.

Savage stared at him.

Park slapped him before Savage could open his mouth. 'Huh,' Park said. 'Now who's the cunt?'

TOMMY'S EAR WAS ringing. His cheek was hot and smarting. Didn't matter.

Neither did the pain in his arm. He didn't give a shit. Together the anger and the fever seemed to be acting as some kind of analgesic. Smith could slap him all day and he wouldn't feel it.

Not like when Phil had slapped him when they were deciding what to do about Grant. That had stung.

Oh, Christ. Phil.

He couldn't think about that, he'd go mad.

Tommy licked his bottom lip, said to Smith, 'You're the cunt.'

'Hmmm,' Smith said, and slapped him again. Hard enough to knock him across the bed.

Okay. That one hurt. He wasn't going to achieve anything by keeping this up. Apart from making himself feel better. Mentally, of course. Wasn't doing him much good physically. He'd lie here for a minute. Give himself time to recover. He listened to the wash of noise in his ear. It was as if somebody was holding a shell over it.

Good God. That had really happened. *Was happening.* He glanced at the screen and there he was, the killer, Smith's daughter's fiancé, Greg Milne's son, bent over the tub, naked, making sawing motions.

Tommy moaned. He had to look away. But couldn't. Yet Smith wasn't watching. You'd think he'd have had his nose pressed right up against the screen, the equivalent of a ringside seat, the sadistic crazy fuck. But, no, he wasn't interested in the screen. He was watching Tommy instead. Maybe thought Tommy was going to attack him again.

'Stop it,' Tommy said, pushing himself upright with his good arm. 'Make him stop, for God's sake.'

Smith's tongue darted out from between his lips, and again. He said, 'You're boring me.'

Tommy pressed the back of his free hand to his cheek. 'Why does Milne have to do that?' He indicated the screen.

'What?' Smith said.

'Look and see.'

'I'm not falling for that one.' And he kept staring at Tommy. Tommy shook his head, asked him, 'So what's next?'

Smith grinned. 'Stay tuned.'

'Cunt,' Tommy said, lunged at him again. Missed.

Smith took his gun out from the waistband of his trousers, pointed it at Tommy and fired. The noise was much louder than Tommy expected. He heard the bullet whistle past his cheek. It slammed into the wall and plaster dropped onto the pillow. He started to shake.

'Look at the mess you've made,' Smith said. 'You're a thoughtless fuck. Broke the window with that metal bucket. Now there's a hole in the wall. You think I want to go round tidying up after you? I fucking hate DIY.'

Tommy kept his mouth shut.

PARK COULD TELL the exact moment Fraser Savage arrived home.

Firing that bullet had shut Tommy up. Shame about the wall, but a wee squeeze of Polyfilla and a slap of paint and Old Mrs Yardie'd never notice.

For a while, Savage had sat there shaking and whimpering, rocking and moaning, hugging that disgusting blanket round himself. But he was off on one again now. His mouth hung open, tears running down his cheeks. He was making a keening sound.

'Fraser home?' Park said.

Savage glanced at him. Shook like an electrocuted dog. Managed to stop moaning and shaking long enough to ask, 'What can I do to stop this?'

'Not a fucking thing,' Park said.

AFTER ALL THE bloodshed, Tommy had expected a knife. Maybe a sword.

Instead, Smith's daughter removed a length of clothesline from her pocket, and coiled the ends round her fists while she stood behind Fraser.

Tommy looked away. When he looked back at the screen, the cord was around Fraser's neck. He had his back to the camera so Tommy couldn't see his face. Tommy looked at Smith. He was staring at Tommy. Tommy couldn't look at him either. Not without wanting to charge at him, smash his head to a pulp, rip out his organs.

Felt like somebody'd shoved a couple of grenades in Tommy's ears.

Violence. Maybe Phil was right. Maybe it was the answer.

In any case, it was all there was. But Tommy had nowhere to go with it. He bowed his head. Whispered his son's name: 'Fraser.' And again. And again.

'Hey,' Tommy heard Smith say. 'Check on him. How's he doing?'

Tommy turned to face the screen. Fraser was slumped on the floor. Tommy willed him to move. He didn't.

Tommy said, 'I swear I'm going to kill you.'

'Feel free to have a go,' Smith said. 'I'm right here.'

Flay him alive, take a bite out of his heart, whatever it took. Tommy wasn't fussy, just so long as the bastard died.

Smith spoke again. Tommy couldn't hear him clearly. The buzzing in his ears was too loud. Not that Tommy was deaf. No, he could hear other sounds. He heard a baby crying.

'. . . and it's not as if you weren't warned in advance,' Smith was saying. 'You knew. I showed you. McCracken.'

There was no baby.

Tommy looked back at the screen just as the killers walked out of the kitchen, naked. The bitch now had a hacksaw. So Fraser was going to be carved up too.

Smith said, 'Your son's dead on account of you. Proud of yourself?'

Tommy lunged off the bed. But Smith was prepared once again. Jumped off his seat and stepped to the side. Still, Tommy kept after him, shouting, throwing wild punches with his good arm. Smith dodged them easily. Held out his gun.

'So shoot me,' Tommy said. 'Why are you waiting?'

Tommy swung at Smith again and Smith ducked inside, brought the butt of the gun down on Tommy's wound.

Tommy gasped, couldn't breathe. Dropped to one knee, his chain rattling as it tightened.

Smith placed the blade of his sword under Tommy's chin. Pushed it up, forcing Tommy to tilt his head backwards. 'If I can't control you,' Smith said, 'then I will kill you. Understand?'

Tommy gave the slightest of nods.

'Good,' Smith said. 'That's your last warning. Now stay there.' He stuck the gun in his belt, kept the sword where it was while he dug Tommy's mobile out from his pocket. 'Let's see,' he said. 'Text messages.' He spoke slowly as he typed the words into the phone. 'Jordan,' he said, his voice sounding cheery. 'Go,' he said, 'to,' he said, 'Fraser's.' Then he typed in, narrating along the way, 'Don't say a word to Granny. Our secret.'

'Oh, Christ,' Tommy said.

'And,' Smith said, 'send.' He pushed the button with an exaggerated gesture. 'What now, Tommy?' he said. Waited a minute. 'Run out of ideas? You could call me names again. And I could slap you. That was fun.'

Tommy said nothing. Something had pierced his heart and an unseen hand was squeezing it empty.

'No?' Smith said. 'Something else, then. You want to attack me again? That was fun too.'

'You killed my son,' Tommy said.

'Technically, no,' Smith said. 'I've been sitting right here.'

'You arranged it. You're responsible.'

'Oh, now, isn't that interesting? If somebody arranges a murder then they're responsible. Bit like you and Greg Milne.'

'I told you —'

'I know,' Smith said. 'Doesn't matter. Both our sons are dead.'

Tommy let his head drop, shook it. 'Let's leave it there. Please.'

'Now? When the fun's just beginning? You're not a party person, are you, Tommy? Let's wait and see what Jordan gets up to.'

Tommy didn't reply.

He'd been shot at and it wasn't so bad. Made him shake, but that couldn't be helped. Suicide for the sake of it was almost an attractive proposition. But he didn't want to die just yet. Because somewhere, somehow, he hoped Jordan would survive, no matter how heavily the odds were stacked against him and Tommy wanted to be there for him when it was over.

He had to get through this. Do whatever it took.

'WHAT'RE THEY DOING now?' Park asked Savage, some time later.

'Why don't you look for yourself?'

''Cause I don't trust you an inch. I'm not taking my eyes off you.'

'That's a shame.'

'Tell me what's happening.'

'Fuck you.'

You'd be forgiven for thinking Savage had grown some balls. Park said, 'Tell me.'

'I don't think so. You want to know what's happening, take a look yourself. I'm saying nothing.'

'Jordan arrived yet?'

Silence again.

Park couldn't help but wonder if Effie and Martin were screwing this up. All they had to do was make a decision about what to do with Jordan. And they didn't have much choice. The kid would have walked in when they were in the middle of disposing of a couple of bodies. What could they do?

They'd be fine.

Park watched Savage and waited. Savage wasn't giving anything away. But he couldn't keep it up forever. He was rocking to and fro. As if he was retarded. Maybe he'd lost it. 'Jordan dead yet?'

He just sat there. Eyes dull. Mumbling.

Park had seen this kind of thing before. One of the guys on his landing in jail had taken a beating. A blanket party, they called it, where a bunch of guys threw a blanket over their victim's head so he couldn't recognise them, then pounded the shit out of him. The guy had resisted for a while, then slumped into submission and took what they threw at him without complaining. He wasn't unconscious. You could tell by the way he jerked when a fist or a foot made contact with him. But he didn't move. Didn't say anything. Didn't cry out. If they'd whipped the blanket off him, Park bet his face would have looked like a *nnnnngah* bloodstained version of Savage's.

They sat in silence, Park trying to read Savage's face. Concentrating so hard that when the doorbell rang, he nearly fell off his seat.

PARK'S FIRST THOUGHT: leave it. Whoever was at the door would go away.

Savage had turned away from the screen and was watching Park. Park didn't like it. His face itched under the ski mask.

Still, wouldn't last for long. The fucker outside would go away and Savage would turn his attention back to the screen. Park just had to wait. Be patient. He'd been doing that all night. It wasn't a problem.

Who knew, maybe the fucker had gone already.

Wishful thinking.

The bastard bell went again. This time followed by a pounding.

And Savage was all wide-eyed and hyper now. No doubt thinking he was about to get rescued. Poor bastard.

Who the fuck was visiting Old Mrs Yardie at this time of night? It was midnight, near enough. Well, never mind what time of night it was. Point was, nobody visited old ladies this late at night and nobody knew Park was here, so there shouldn't be any fucking visitors.

He was wondering what he should do when Savage ran a few feet in the direction of the door, yelling like he was plugged into an amplifier. How the fuck someone in such a poor state of health managed to make such a din, Park didn't know. Park took out his gun, shouted at him to shut up. The fucker kept up his racket, though. Not so fucking sick or crazy after all. Malingering bastard.

Loose dust and crumbs of plaster fell onto the bed as Park grabbed Savage's pillow and stepped towards him. He'd reached the end of his chain, still a considerable distance from the open doorway, and was standing with his back to

Park, shouting his lungs inside out. Park dropped the pillow over the fucker's face, pulled it tight at the back. Muffled the sounds coming out of Savage's mouth.

'Shut up,' Park said. 'Or suffocate.'

Kept it up, the cunt. For a little while anyway. Then he started to panic when he realised he couldn't breathe. Hands flapped at Park. Having second thoughts now.

The doorbell rang again. The letterbox rattled. Then a voice called, distant but audible, 'Anyone in there? Open up.'

'Like fuck,' Park said, quietly. They'd heard Savage, and that's why they'd shouted through the letterbox.

Savage tried another shout but the sound was a pitiful squawk.

'Stop fucking struggling,' Park told him through clenched teeth.

The bell rang once more. A fist pounded on the door. Then a duller sound. Like maybe somebody was kicking it. Then silence.

Good. The fucker had had enough and was going home. At fucking last.

Savage stopped struggling.

Park waited a little longer, then eased the pressure on the pillow.

Savage gulped in air, said, 'Help,' in a weak voice.

And then nothing.

At first all Park heard was Savage wheezing as he fought for breath. Then he heard voices. Coming from below, inside the house. Jesus fucking Christ. There was more than one of the fuckers and they'd let themselves in the back door. Yes, he probably should have kept it locked but he'd had no reason to suspect company. Particularly the kind of company that invited itself in.

He dropped the pillow, letting Savage fall to his knees with a thump and a groan. Scuttled back to the bed, picked up the sword. Couldn't use it but he couldn't very well leave it there for Savage either. He'd take it with him. Make him look scarier than if he just had a gun.

Savage was croaking again. Got his breath back. 'Help,' he said. 'Help. Please.' Like some old crone who'd smoked unfiltered Woodbines all her life.

Park crouched beside him. Dug out the key for the closet chain. Unlocked it. Got an odd look and another, 'Help' from Savage. Shoved the gun against his temple. Whispered, 'Shut up or I swear I'll put a hole in you right this second.'

Savage shut up.

'Now stay quiet and move out onto the landing.' Savage crept towards the doorway, rubbing his wrist. Park tucked the pillow under an arm and followed him.

Park eased Savage onto the landing.

Below, someone said, 'Probably kids.'

And someone else said, 'We should call for back up.'

Shite. Police.

'And look like a pair of pricks who can't handle a couple of neds? Kids having some fun. Found an empty house, nobody home, door open. That's all it is. Probably skedaddled out the back while we were hammering away round the front.'

'Maybe,' the other one said. 'You want to check upstairs?'

The top of a black cap came into view. Another couple of feet and if they looked up they'd see Park and Savage. Park tucked the gun into his trousers. Didn't know where to put the sword. Looked at Savage. Offered the sword to him.

Savage took it in his good hand, no doubt wondering what the catch was.

Park had to move fast. He grabbed the pillow, pulled off his ski mask, threw it at Savage. Had to move *now*.

'Help,' Park said, running along the landing. 'Help.' Louder as he hit the stairs. 'He's got a sword, Officers.' Down a few steps. 'Up there.' Pointing.

The coppers looked very different. One was of retirement age. The other looked like he was about twelve.

'Hold on,' the old one said. 'Stop. Stop!'

Park stopped halfway down the stairs.

Savage said, 'Don't listen –'

'He's got a sword,' Park said. 'Look!'

The policemen moved forward and craned their necks to look up at the landing, where Savage stood with the sword in his hand, dirty blanket tied round his neck like a cape.

'It's not how it looks,' Savage said.

The cops glanced at each other, then the old cop said to Savage, 'Drop the weapon.'

'I'm not –'

'Drop it!'

'It's not –'

'Drop the weapon and move away! Now! Do it!'

The sword clattered onto the landing floor. Savage backed away, out of sight, into the bedroom. His voice carried through the open door. 'It's not mine. It's not me you should –'

Fucker had definitely got his voice back now. 'Thank God,' Park said, walking down the stairs, doing his best to look scared. 'I'm so fucking happy to see you, Officers.'

The young cop looked pretty scared himself, mind you. Bit of a fright seeing the madman up there with the sword, was it?

Park walked right up to the cops. No trouble at all.

Savage's voice came from upstairs: 'It's him you want to be arresting. He's a fucking murdering bastard. Killed my son. Strangled him. Cut his head off in a tub.'

Park smiled. 'He's crazy.'

'And my brother,' Savage shouted.

'Sounds it,' the older cop said. He looked at the pillow in Park's hand. 'You want to tell us what's going on?'

'I can do better than that.'

The younger cop looked at him.

'A demonstration.' Park whisked the gun out from his waistband, pillow held in front of him, fired. Moved the pillow to the side, fired again.

The policemen dropped. Bam, bam. From the floor, the young one said, 'Fucking hell. Fucking hell. You fucking psycho fuck.'

Of course Park couldn't look to tell for sure, but he thought he'd nailed them both pretty good. Aimed for the midriff so at worst they'd be incapacitated. Couldn't hear the older one at all. And the younger one might be mouthing off but he didn't appear to be moving. Good. Although it sounded like the younger one might be capable of radioing for assistance. Which meant that Park had to get out of here right now. Either that or scrabble about for the walkie-talkie with his eyes shut. They kept those things on their shoulders, didn't they? Or . . .

'Report in,' Park said. 'Tell them there's nothing here.'

'Fucking bastard cunt. You've killed –'

'And that you're going to go grab a cup of coffee.'

Pause. Gasping. Then: 'I don't drink coffee.'

'So tell them you're going for a glass of lemonade. But don't chat. Keep it short.'

The young cop did what he was told.

'Now throw the walkie-talkie away,' Park said.

He did.

'Now tell me you love me.'

'You what?'

Park aimed at the sound. Must have got it right cause after he pulled the trigger, the little fucker shut up.

Now what?

Savage.

Park took the stairs three at a time. Paused on the landing. Savage's bedroom door was closed, the sword nowhere to be seen. Presumably Savage was lurking behind the door, waiting to slice a chunk out of Park the moment he stepped inside. Park wondered if he could shoot him through the wall. It was only plaster. But tempting though it was, Park didn't want to kill him yet if he didn't have to. His punishment wasn't over.

So Park held his gun at the ready. Turned the door knob slowly. Pushed the door. Stayed where he was.

The door swung open, revealing an empty room, then started to close again.

No doubt at all where Savage was, then. Should Park shoot him? Hell, no. Park's only slight concern was the sword. But Savage was a useless fuck and he was exhausted and had a gammy arm. If Park couldn't handle him in that condition, he deserved what was coming to him.

Park kicked the door hard. Dived into the room. Rolled over twice. Spun around to face Savage behind the door, gun pointed at his forehead.

But Savage wasn't there.

Park heard a noise behind him, turned to see Savage, all dirt-streaked and skinny and naked under the flapped-open blanket, swinging at him with the sword. Rolled out of the way just in time.

Sneaky bastard had been under the bed.

The blade stuck in the floor. Savage tried to pull it out one-handed, getting some healthier pink in his otherwise grey cheeks as he watched Park point the gun at him.

Used up all his strength in the blow. But, no, there he was putting in an extra bit of effort.

Wrenched it free.

'Well fucking done,' Park said.

Savage was only a couple of feet away. Cock dangling practically in Park's face. Didn't seem to be so shy any more.

'Pull your blanket over it,' Park said.

Savage raised the sword.

Park said, 'Drop that or I'll shoot.'

'Why should I care?'

'Think about Jordan.'

'Nothing I can do.'

'There is. Get to Fraser's in time. Save him. Be a hero. Should be easy for a man like you.'

'You fucker.' You could tell he was struggling to keep from swinging the sword at Park again.

Park said, 'So much as twitch and I'll pull the trigger. So drop the fucking sword.'

'Did you kill those policemen?'

'What do you fucking think I was doing? Firing shots at the ceiling, hoping they'd run off and keep their mouths shut?'

'You won't get away with it.'

'That's for me to worry about. Now lose the fucking sword.'

'They'll send someone to look for them.'

'Yep. They'll take a while, though. I saw to that. Look, we can remain like this as long as you like. But every second you waste here is a second of what remains of Jordan's life.'

Sweat dripped off Savage's forehead. Ran down his nose. He looked like he'd collapse any second.

Park said, 'You don't have the strength to kill me, so put the sword down.'

'No?' Savage yelled and swung the blade.

Park swivelled out of the way. The blade hit the gun barrel. Almost smacked it out of his hand. Savage stumbled. Fell over. Bumped his face off Park's knee. Lucky he didn't skewer himself on the sword. Park stood on the flat of the blade and placed the muzzle of the gun against Savage's ear.

'Nearly took my fingers off,' Park said.

Savage didn't say anything. Just lay face down, making snuffling noises.

'You hear me? Nearly sliced my fucking fingers off.' Park pressed the gun harder against Savage's ear. And watched as a trickle of red appeared beneath Savage's face. 'Blood? Oh, you fucker.'

Yeah, the fucker was bleeding.

If ever there was a time when Park was desperate to overcome his fucking disability it was now. The nausea built rapidly and his limbs grew heavy and he thought of his mother lying with her head in a pool of blood in the kitchen. He lowered his head, tried to breathe. His vision was clouding. Fuck, no. Couldn't pass out. Not now. He couldn't. Had to stay . . .

TOMMY ASSUMED SMITH was playing games with him.

He'd banged his nose on the fucker's knee, hard enough to get a nosebleed for his trouble. Probably on account of him being weak and malnourished. But when Smith keeled over, Tommy had thought it was an act.

So Tommy got to his feet and started kicking him. And even considering he couldn't kick him all that enthusiastically with his bare feet, the fucker wasn't flinching.

Smith was out for the count.

Tommy grabbed the sword, was inches from going ahead, sticking it right through the fucker's belly, when he recalled what Smith had said. *Blood? Oh, you fucker.* Like that was a problem or something. The last thing he'd said before he toppled over.

And it clicked. Why Smith hadn't watched the screen. Why he'd had to get his daughter and her boyfriend to cut up Phil and Fraser. Why he'd asked if anyone was eating rare steak at the restaurant. Why he was lying unconscious because Tommy's nose was bleeding.

Jesus Christ. It made sense. At the same time as not making any sense at all. Whoever heard of a psychopath who was squeamish?

Tommy kicked him a few more times while he decided what to do. Then he wiped his nose with Smith's shirt. The flow reduced to a trickle.

He looked across at the laptop. Fraser's house was dark. Nothing moved. It was as if no one had ever been there.

He didn't know if Jordan was alive or dead. The cops' arrival had stopped him finding out.

Tommy stuck his hand in Smith's pocket. Got a phone. Wrong one, though. Tried the other pocket and found the one he was looking for: his own.

His nose was still bleeding a little but he sniffed the blood back. Spat it out. God, it tasted good.

He ignored the pain in his gut and dialled Jordan. No answer. Damn phone went to voicemail. Fuck. He hung up. Tried again.

Not Jordan, for Christ's sake.

Effie had Jordan's phone. Tommy had seen her take it from him.

Pick up, you fuck.

She answered, finally. 'Who is this?'

He waited. His teeth hurt. He was about to speak to the woman who'd killed his son. What could he say that would sum up how he felt?

'You fucking know, bitch.' It was the best he could do. He kicked her father again.

She swallowed. He could hear her. Not so fucking tough after all. 'Where's Dad?' she asked.

Good. Concern. He'd wondered if she was human. 'What did you do to Jordan?'

'I want to speak to Dad.'

'I want to speak to my son.' Oh, he was so fucking in control now. He'd beaten Smith. The daughter and her boyfriend were next. He felt the elation in his shoulders like balls of flame.

'No,' she said, voice cracking. 'You can't.'

'I can't? If you've harmed him –'

'He's alive. He's here. In the van.'

He wanted to believe her. Christ, he wanted to. 'Put him on the phone.'

'I can't do that.'

He heard a voice in the background. A man's voice. Martin Milne, no doubt. Tommy didn't want them talking. Didn't want them scheming. He said, 'If you don't prove to me that Jordan's alive, your dad's dead.' He meant it.

No reply. She didn't hang up, though. Must be thinking.

Tommy said, 'I know what you did to Phil and Fraser.' Just in case she didn't know he'd been watching.

'I don't know what you're talking about, Mr Savage,' she said.

But she knew his name. *Mister* fucking Savage, too. Why was she denying it? In case the call was being traced? Maybe it was. In which case, he ought to spell it out. 'Want me to tell you about the tub? About the hacksaws? About you and loverboy all naked and covered in my family's fucking blood?'

He thought he could hear her breathe, thought he heard her sniff. 'Where are you?' she said. 'Maybe we can do an exchange.'

'What about Phil and Fraser? Who are you going to exchange for them?'

Another pause. Then: 'I don't know who you mean. But even if I did, there's nothing we can do about what's already done.' He didn't know what to say to that. Maybe he should just play along. Take what he could get.

'Okay,' she said, interrupting his thoughts. 'Where do you want to meet?'

'Parking lot at the East Calder entrance to Almondell Country Park,' he said. It was close and it seemed appropriate. 'Bet you know where that is.'

'I'll find it.'

He hung up. He felt calm. Tasted blood on his lip, smelt the blood in his nose. It was all good. Meant he was alive.

He knew he should have called the police. He could still call them. But he'd have to explain what was going on and there wasn't time for that. He'd also have to explain why there were two dead policemen downstairs. And there definitely wasn't time for that.

Fuck, no, he felt great. He felt strong. He'd just taken out Smith, hadn't he? Shit, there was no messing with Tommy Savage. He wasn't going to sit around and let someone else do his dirty work for him. Anyway, Effie and Martin would have nothing to lose. The bastards wouldn't leave Jordan alive if they could avoid it. No, Tommy had to take care of his own. Hell, he wanted to take care of his own.

Grant's voice in his head: *A father's duty is to avenge his son or he's no father at all.*

Maybe it had to be that way right enough.

Tommy dug in Smith's pocket again and found a set of keys. Car keys, house keys, various other keys. He tried a couple before he found the one that fitted the closet chain.

He stripped Smith naked. See how *he* liked it. Hard work with only one good arm, but Tommy managed. Then he attached one end of the closet chain to the bed and clipped the other cuff on Smith's wrist. Tightened it, put the keys in Smith's pocket and tossed his clothes into the far corner of the room.

He left the sword by Smith's side, hoping the fucker woke up before the police arrived. If Smith had delayed them, as he claimed, so much the better. He'd have to figure out whether to cut his hand off or lie there and suffer the consequences. Of course, if he cut his hand off, he'd probably pass out from shock. Or if not, then he'd pass out at the sight of his own blood. Or maybe it was only other people's that set him off. Tommy kind of hoped the latter was the case. He'd really like Smith to have a good reason to cut off his hand.

Tommy picked up the gun. He was going to get his fingerprints all over a murder weapon, but he didn't care.

He took a last look at his prison cell, turned, and walked out. He scooped up Smith's ski mask off the floor on the landing and put it on. Probably wasn't a bad thing if he wasn't recognised.

But he was forgetting something. Apart from the ski mask, he was naked.

He guessed Smith's bedroom was the room next but one along the landing. He'd heard him in there listening to the TV and talking on the phone.

Tommy stopped in front of the door, turned the handle, eased it open.

And there she was. A small frail woman, salt-and-pepper hair thinning. She didn't deserve to be called Old Mrs Yardie. She only looked about sixty. She was staring at the wall and didn't acknowledge him when he stepped into the room.

She didn't look dangerous. But you never could tell. Some people looked harmless enough and then the next thing you knew they were chopping up bodies.

So maybe this was who Smith was talking to when Tommy had assumed he was on the phone. Although those conversations had all sounded one-sided.

Tommy was only a couple of feet away from her now and she hadn't turned to look at him yet. A naked man in her bedroom and it was as if he didn't exist. Maybe she was blind. Or deaf.

He stopped by the arm of the chair and poked Mrs Yardie's arm with the gun.

No reaction.

'Hey,' he said. 'Mrs Yardie.'

Still no reaction.

He poked her again, harder.

Same result.

Still staring ahead, unblinking, like she was transfixed by a movie playing on the wall.

'You okay?' he said.

Not the tiniest twitch of a muscle on her face.

He waved the gun in front of her. She didn't even blink.

Her expression reminded him of Smith's when he first heard about Grant's accident, sitting in the dark, unmoving, Tommy tied up next to him. A kind of catatonia.

So Smith had a girlfriend. One who really couldn't say no.

Tommy went over to the dresser. Bunch of crap on top of it. Combs and brushes, a jewellery box. No string or parcel tape or anything useful like that. He opened a drawer and found some of Smith's underwear. Put on a pair of socks and a pair of boxer's. Found a sweatshirt in another drawer. Put that on, too.

He tried the wardrobe. Shirts and trousers, couple of dresses, cardigans, some scarves. Put on the trousers. Tight enough round the middle not to need a belt.

The pair of men's trainers at the bottom were too small, but it felt good to be dressed again, even if he was wearing a stranger's clothes and didn't have any shoes.

Armed with a bundle of scarves, he returned to Old Mrs Yardie.

'Sorry about this,' he said.

He used one of the scarves to tie her left wrist to the arm of the chair. Didn't seem to bother her in the least, being tied up. He did the same with her other wrist. Even when it came to gagging her, she didn't react. Same indifference. Like she wasn't there. She'd gone. Left this body behind.

He tied both ankles to the legs of the chair.

Now, even if she was the best actress in the world and she'd fooled him into thinking she was catatonic, she'd still not be able to help Smith escape.

'You'll be safe,' he said. 'Just hang on.'

He left the room and hurried down the stairs.

Even from a distance, the mess that used to be the younger cop's face was tough to look at. How that hadn't set Smith fainting, Tommy didn't know. Maybe Tommy was wrong about the blood thing. Or maybe Smith had avoided looking at the cop somehow.

Anyway, there was no time to figure it out, and it didn't matter. Tommy had to get closer to the cop. He needed his car keys. He could probably use Smith's, but he'd get where he wanted more quickly in a police car. He'd try the older cop first. Maybe he'd been the driver, and he wasn't quite so full of holes.

Yep. Good guess. It was turning into Tommy's lucky day.

Even luckier was the size of the poor guy's feet. Slightly bigger than Tommy's, which was fine. He didn't mind shoes a size too big.

He grabbed some more weaponry while he was at it. CS spray canister, extendable baton, handcuffs. Never knew when they might come in useful. And he took one of the caps. At least that way he'd look the part from a distance.

He was going to get Jordan and no fucker was going to get in his way.

SAVAGE NIGHT
2 A.M.
ALMONDELL
COUNTRY PARK

'SHIT,' MARTIN SAID. 'This is just what we need.'

Effie followed his gaze. A police car was pulling into the parking area. Since the only other vehicle around was their van, there was no way they were going to avoid a confrontation. Fucking bumshite.

'Start the engine, babe,' Martin said.

'Don't you think that'll look suspicious?'

'Not half as suspicious as the two dead bodies and the trussed-up kid in the back.'

That was true. They hadn't been here long. Only about five minutes ago, Effie had overshot the entrance. Had to turn back, and spotted it easily enough second time. She'd driven past the gate house, where all the lights were out, and swung into the empty car park.

She'd tucked into the nearest parking spot, killed the engine.

While they waited for Savage to show up, they talked about what they were going to do once he arrived.

'Hard negotiating without weapons,' Martin had said.

'We have weapons,' she'd said.

He looked blank.

'Knives, saws, a hammer,' she said.

'I suppose. But if Savage has overpowered your dad then he's got a sword.'

'And a gun,' she reminded him. 'But we've got Jordan.' She put her hand on Martin's. 'Don't worry. We'll keep Jordan between Savage and us. First thing, we get Savage to lose his weapons.'

'If he says no?'

'Then no deal. We take Jordan and go.'

'What about your dad?'

'He'll be safe enough. Savage won't hurt him. If he does, he knows he won't get Jordan back.'

Tough to convince Martin when Effie wasn't entirely convinced herself but the argument seemed to console him. He'd been twitchy, waiting for Savage. But now that the police car had arrived, he was worse.

'Shit,' he said again. 'We going to make a run for it?'

'Let's sit tight,' she said. 'See what happens.'

'What's he doing?'

The moon was struggling to break through a bank of dense clouds. She turned on the lights. 'Better?'

The police car in the headlights was nosing into a spot directly opposite. Effie could make out a head over the top of the seat. There should be a second head sticking up over the passenger seat. But there wasn't. Unless the passenger was very small.

Police officers travelled in pairs. Corroboration was an essential part of the Scottish judicial system. Needed two versions of the same event before testimony stood up in court. Or something like that. Effie had had it explained to her before, by her dad, but he'd done so in his usual fashion. All she remembered was him saying: 'Cops are like balls. Always hanging around in pairs.'

The driver's door of the cop car opened. Stayed opened. Nobody stepped out.

'The fuck's going on?' Martin asked.

She shook her head.

Then an arm stretched out and the hand made a turning motion before disappearing back into the car.

'What's that mean?' Martin said.

She didn't know.

They waited. After a bit, the cop turned his headlights on and off. Then again. On, off. On, off. Left them off.

Finally Effie got the message. She turned off the van lights. It took a moment for her eyes to adjust to the darkness. The moon helped, shining through a tear in the clouds, casting a silvery light over everything, including the figure marching towards them across the gravel. He looked familiar. Skinny. Wearing a ski mask. Wearing Dad's clothes. About the same height.

But Dad would never wear a policeman's cap.

'Holy fuck,' Martin said. He flung open his door. 'Mr Park. *Andy.* We thought something'd happened to you.'

'Hang on,' she yelled.

But Martin was gone, leaving the door open. 'Savage is coming,' he said to the figure who was now jogging towards him. 'Got to get you out of here.'

Effie shouted, 'No.'

Martin glanced at her, narrowed his eyes, looked back at the figure in the ski mask. He still didn't get it. 'How did he escape?' Martin asked the man. 'And how did you end up in a police car?'

The figure drew a gun out of his waistband.

'What're you doing?' Martin said. 'Oh, sweet fuck.'

There was an explosion and Martin collapsed.

Effie grabbed the steering wheel. She let go. She grabbed it again. Fumbled for the keys. She wanted to get out of here. She wanted to stay, too. See if Martin was okay. She couldn't leave him. But she had to.

Her fingers shook. Oh, Christ. Martin's door was open. She couldn't see where he'd fallen. She listened but couldn't hear him cry out. Just heard the echo of the explosion. Faint, as if she was underwater.

She clutched the keys again.

'I don't think so.' Savage stood in the passenger doorway, pointing his gun at her.

She let her hands drift away from the dashboard.

'Where's Jordan?'

She didn't say anything.

'You better pray he's here and unharmed.'

She heard a scrabbling in the back of the van. So did Savage. He looked in the direction of the sound as his son wriggled into view above the partition behind the seats. Jordan squealed through the tape over his mouth.

Savage lowered his weapon and she knew she had a chance to start the engine and floor the accelerator. But she couldn't. Even if she made it, jolting Savage through the open door as she took off, she couldn't leave Martin. He'd been shot. He'd need her. She had to stay.

She stared at Savage as he raised his gun again.

'Untie him,' he said.

She turned round, knee on the seat, and thrust a hand towards Jordan. He yelped, moved his head back.

'Go on,' Savage said. 'It's okay, Jordan.'

But the kid wouldn't move any closer. So she leaned over the partition and grabbed his chin before he could get out of the way. 'Don't fucking move,' she whispered. She let go, and he didn't budge. She flicked at the top corner of his taped mouth and with her other hand, groped for the bag of tools in the hope her fingers might close on a weapon.

Suddenly Jordan dropped like a stone. Her fingers were crushed to the floor, forcing her to yell. The little bastard was kneeling on her hand. Judging by the look on his face, he was putting as much pressure on it as he could.

She tugged her hand, but it wouldn't move. Tried again and felt some give. Third time lucky. Her hand came free, throbbing, dead centre.

'Can't be trusted,' Savage said, inside the van now, pulling her backwards. 'I should have known that. Get out.'

She twisted round and opened the door, trying to control the shaking that rippled through her body. She stepped outside.

'Further,' he said. 'Move over a few feet.'

She did.

'Kneel down,' Savage said.

She didn't.

'I warn you,' he said, 'I don't have much patience. And we don't have much time. Somebody might have heard that shot. If we're really lucky, they'll think it's a poacher and leave it be. But they might call the police. You want them here even less than I do. So fucking move.'

She lowered herself to her knees. Felt tiny stones digging into her kneecaps.

'Hands behind your head,' Savage said.

She did as he asked.

'Don't fucking move.'

She turned her head, not trying to see him but trying to see where Martin lay, round the other side of the van.

Savage noticed, said, 'Eyes front.'

She'd spotted Martin's leg, the lower part, from shin to foot. No movement. Didn't mean she should fear the worst, though.

'Yeah,' Savage said. 'Your boyfriend's dead. And if you don't behave yourself, you'll be joining him soon.'

Martin was dead? She didn't think so. She didn't think she'd feel this empty if that was true. She'd seen him shot, seen him fall to the ground, but that didn't mean he hadn't survived. She'd once heard of a hostage shot in the head, point blank, by terrorists. The hostage had lived. Martin could have survived too. She didn't know where he'd been shot. But it was possible he was just lying there, playing dead. That's what she'd do if she were him.

She kept her eyes fixed in front of her. Didn't move a muscle. Apart from her stomach, which had developed a spasm she'd never experienced before. It was as if a rodent was crawling around inside her, stopping every now and then to gnaw at her belly.

'IT'S OKAY, JORDAN.' Tears streamed down Tommy's son's face. He was in danger of choking. Convulsing. 'This might hurt.' Tommy reached throught he gap between the seats, ripped the tape off Jordan's mouth.

'Dad?' Jordan said. 'Dad?'

'Shit, sorry, son.' He took off the policeman's cap, pulled the ski mask off. 'It's me, yeah. Keep an eye on that bitch out there while I untie you. Shout if she moves, okay?'

Jordan nodded.

Tommy pulled at the bindings.

'Dad?'

'Yeah?'

'I'm really scared.'

'It's okay now. You're safe. I'm here.'

'I'm still scared.'

'It's okay. We'll be fine. Is she doing anything?'

Jordan shook his head. 'Dad, you just killed somebody.'

Yeah, Tommy had just killed somebody. He'd killed Martin Milne, the fucker who'd stabbed Phil in the heart and chopped him up. And fucking hell, Tommy'd do it again in a heartbeat. 'To make you safe, son,' he said.

'They killed Uncle Phil. And Fraser. I didn't think they had, not really, I thought it was a joke but it's true they did and the bodies are —'

'Shush. I know.'

He cried some more.

But he was safe. Jordan was safe. Tommy started to cry too. Pair of them with faces like they'd been rained on. 'We have to hurry,' Tommy said, wiping his eyes, gently, swallowing to ease the pain in his belly.

He got Jordan's hands free and Jordan leaned over the partition and flung his arms round him. Tommy hugged him back, as hard as he could with one good arm. He wanted Jordan as close to him as possible.

'I'm keeping an eye on . . . *her* still,' Jordan said.

'Good lad.'

They remained like that, squeezing each other, till Jordan said, 'That hurts.'

Tommy eased off, kissed his son's forehead. 'Untie your legs and get in the front with me.'

Jordan said, 'Dad?'

'What, son?'

'You really stink.'

EFFIE SNEAKED A glance a couple of times. The kid was watching her. She couldn't risk it. He'd shout, Savage would turn, shoot her.

And Martin would be all on his own.

'WHAT'S IN THE back there?' Tommy asked Jordan.

'Uncle Phil and Fraser.'

Good God. Jordan had been trussed up in the back with his dead uncle and his dead brother. And no doubt he'd have been next. Tommy'd never felt rage like he felt now. Maybe because he was free of Smith, or because he'd killed someone, or because Jordan was safe, but whatever the reason, anger flamed in his gut, the pain excruciating.

Jordan said something and Tommy could only hold up a hand to tell him to wait.

Just when he thought he couldn't bear any more, the pain burst into his chest, fired through his windpipe and shot onto the dashboard. A solid thing that rattled around. He blinked, looked at Jordan who was still waiting for him to speak. He couldn't.

Back on the dashboard, the pain had rolled to a stop. It was a steel ball, red-hot. He reached out to pick it up, not caring if he got burned, but a fist burst through the windscreen and Tommy grabbed only a handful of air.

'Looking for this?' Grant lay on the bonnet, ball held between finger and thumb.

'Give that back,' Tommy said.

Grant placed the ball in his mouth. Tommy watched smoke seep through Grant's lips and then the lad swallowed and Tommy's anger started to build all over again. He could feel it, already a soft warm lump in his gut.

He closed his eyes and heard Grant laughing, but when he opened them the boy had gone.

Tommy turned to Jordan. 'Did you see that?'

'See what? Dad, you okay?'

'I'm okay,' Tommy said, slowly. 'Yeah, I'm okay.' He stared at the windscreen. It was intact. Not so much as a scratch. He listened to the silence.

'Dad?'

He had to focus. Forget what he'd seen. Or what he thought he'd seen. 'That's not what I meant, about Phil and Fraser,' he said to Jordan. He craned his neck, peered into the back of the van. 'I was wondering what that was.'

'The tub? That's where they —'

'No, the thing wedged in the corner. Looks like a petrol can.'

'That?' Jordan said. 'It's a petrol can.'

Tommy nodded, pushed the driver's door open as wide as it would go. Effie was kneeling on the ground, hands clasped behind the back of her neck. 'What's the petrol for?' he asked her.

She didn't turn around, said, 'We were going to torch the van when we'd finished.'

'Smart,' Tommy said. 'Whose idea was that?'

'Dad's.'

'Regular arsonist, eh?'

'Fireraiser.'

'Sorry?'

'Arson's English. It's fireraising under Scots Law.'

'Thanks for the lesson.'

'Just saying. I know about these things.'

'That right?' He still hadn't decided what to do with her. He knew what he *should* do. Grant would back him up. *Right, Grant?* Grant said nothing. Course, she was his sister and he wouldn't be able to make an impartial judgment. But, look, Effie was responsible for murdering Fraser. *Responsible.* There were consequences, for fuck's sake. Stupid fucking bitch. The whole family, whatever they were called, were fucking stupid.

'Watch who you're calling stupid,' Grant said. But Grant didn't scare him. Not any more.

'What's your name?' Tommy asked her.

'Effie. You've already used it.'

'No, your surname. Your *arsonist* daddy never told me.'

'Park,' she said.

'Park,' he said. 'Park. Such an insignificant name.'

'Unlike yours. A name like that, you were destined for a night like this.'

He wondered how she'd look without a head. He didn't think he could do that, though. Didn't have her constitution. He'd have to shoot her.

But he needed her help to tidy up first. And he was going to have to get Jordan involved too.

'No,' he said.

'No?'

'This is what I want to do. It's a choice.' He shrugged. 'Anyway, help me get your dead boyfriend in the van.'

EFFIE COULDN'T BELIEVE he'd handed the gun to the kid.

'Think you can handle it?' Savage had said.

And Jordan had nodded.

'Point it at her,' Savage said. 'If she makes a sudden movement, shoot her. If she doesn't do what she's told, shoot her. If she looks at you funny, shoot her.'

Surely Savage couldn't believe that Jordan was prepared to use the gun. Had to be a bluff. All she had to do was get the kid close, grab the gun off him. But Jordan's hand was shaking. And she realised all of a sudden that she didn't want to look at him funny. Maybe it wouldn't take much for him to pull the trigger after all. Certainly not if he was anything like his dad.

Her knees hurt as she got off the ground. She knew there were creases in them, ridges where stones had dug in. The pain felt good, though. She'd like to gouge deeper, see how much pain she could find.

'Come on,' Savage said.

'Yeah,' Jordan said. 'Get moving.'

Little bastard.

She limped towards the front of the car, Jordan trailing her, gun pointed at her.

Martin came into view bit by bit. First: part of his legs. Another step: up to his waist. Another step: his torso. But no sign of blood so far, which was promising. He was injured, but nothing too serious. Another step.

Looking good. Looking good. Looking . . .

To the side. The side of his head. A dark puddle, spread wide, balloon-shaped like a speech-bubble. His head . . . Jesus. She looked away but saw him still, a faded image but still enough to make her gag. Looked again. Forced herself to see the damage Tommy Savage had done to him.

Didn't want to see it. Didn't want to know about it. Didn't want to register it. Didn't want to accept it. But couldn't help herself. She *had* to see.

Look away. At what? At the blood on the ground? At the fucker who'd done this?

Had to look back.

Don't be fucking dead. No. Don't you fucking dare. Martin. Martin, baby.
It was obscene.

A dark, forked ribbon of blood draped down his cheek, dripped onto the ground.

But that wasn't what had made her retch.

She looked up at the jagged-boned eye socket and stared into the dark space in Martin's face where once there had been an eyeball.

'GRAB HIS FEET,' Tommy said. Effie Park wasn't listening. Caught up in the moment. Watching her dead boyfriend lying there. Very touching. Tommy almost felt sorry for her. He said, 'You can't will him alive, you know. Won't happen. I should know.'

She acknowledged him finally. 'Huh?'

'He's not coming back from the dead. They don't. Apart from dreams. In your head.'

'In my head?'

'Love to chat but we have to move. Grab him.'

She bent over, picked up his feet. 'Like this?'

Looked like she was in some kind of daze. That was okay. Made her easier to manipulate.

'That's fine,' he said. He couldn't use both hands himself, his bad arm was too sore, so he grabbed hold of a handful of jumper. 'After three,' he said. Counted. And lifted.

That's when she sprang for the gun.

'Shoot her,' he told Jordan.

Jordan glanced at him, then did what he'd been told. The shot went wide. But it stopped her in her tracks. 'Next time I won't miss,' Jordan said. 'You fucking bitch.'

'Language,' Tommy said.

SHE WASN'T GOING to cry. Fuck, no. She was stronger than that.

Savage closed the van doors. She wanted to ride in the back with Martin but they'd be jammed in pretty tight, the tub on its side, Martin resting on top of the headless Savages at an angle, so he'd fit. Anyway, Tommy Savage said no and he'd taken the gun back so she wasn't going to argue with him. She knew *he* could shoot straight.

She wasn't going to fucking cry.

Fuck off.

TOMMY SHEPHERDED EFFIE round to the front of the van.

He'd get her to drive. He needed to keep his eyes on her,

not the road, and anyway he'd found on the way here that driving was hard as fuck with his arm in such a poor state.

She had her hand on the door when the dog came at them out of the darkness and made her jump. Looked like a small Collie-Lab cross. It started barking, looked vicious, all teeth. Behind it stood its owner, a guy so pale he seemed to glow in the moonlight. He was wearing a flak jacket and a Che Guevarra cap. He held a shotgun in one hand and was tugging at the dog's leash with the other.

Tommy held his own gun by his side, behind his leg, out of sight and hoped the guy hadn't noticed it. Tommy said, 'Evening.'

The guy said, 'What's going on? What was that noise?'

At least, that's what Tommy thought the guy said. It was hard to hear him over the din the dog was making. Tommy squeezed the butt of his gun. He asked, 'Can you get your dog to be quiet?'

The guy nodded, then bent down to scold the dog. It had got into a rhythm, though, and seemed to be enjoying itself.

'We had a spot of engine trouble,' Tommy shouted. 'Fixed now.'

The guy stood, the dog calmed down a little, just growling now. 'Yeah. But what was that explosion?'

'Eh?' Tommy said, pretending not to hear him. 'Engine trouble. Nothing exploded.'

'I heard an explosion. Sounded like a gunshot.'

'Oh, explosion,' Tommy said. 'Came from back that way.' He had to use his bad arm to point behind him, into the woods, and only just managed. Hoped the guy didn't see him wince. 'The law are already off investigating.'

'They are?'

'See for yourself.' He nodded at the police car opposite. 'You didn't call them, then?'

'Not yet.'

'Well, somebody did.'

'Yeah,' the guy said. 'Yeah. Over that way, you say?' He pointed with the gun.

'Yeah.'

'Okay.' He didn't look convinced.

'Anyway, we have to be going. Engine seems fine now.'

The guy watched them all climb into the front of the van. Effie looked at Tommy.

'What's wrong?' he whispered. 'Get moving.'

'Won't it look odd, me driving?' she said.

'What's odd about that?'

'Women don't usually drive when men are around.'

'Yeah?' he said. 'And here's me thinking you'd be a feminist.'

As they pulled away, Effie driving, he watched the guy and his dog walk off along the path that led into the woods. Tommy wondered how long it would be before he realised there weren't any cops, that nobody was coming back to the cop car.

'WHERE WERE YOU going?' Savage asked her, his arm on the back of her seat, the gun dangling inches from her chin. His little bastard son was sitting on his knee, acting all hard now that Daddy was here.

Effie contemplated making another grab for the gun but decided to wait for a clearer attempt at it later. Anyway, her hands were still shaky from last time she'd tried. She gripped the wheel as hard as she could, didn't make any difference. She could feel the vibrations through the whole of her body. Next thing, her teeth would start chattering.

'Asked you a question,' Savage said.

She sucked her lips. They smacked apart. 'Heading towards town, like you said.'

'No, where were you going earlier, when I called you? Where were you taking Jordan?'

'To see Dad.'

'You mean to Old Mrs Yardie's?'

'He tell you that?'

'Mrs Yardie certainly didn't.'

Effie thought that was a strange thing to say.

'She his girlfriend?' he asked.

She glanced at him, see if he was taking the piss. Hard to tell. His pupils were tiny, eyes bloodshot and staring.

He nodded, as if she'd said yes. 'Poor woman,' he said. 'Taken advantage of like that. Can't even speak for herself.'

Now she got it. He'd found Mum, thought she was Old Mrs Yardie. 'You didn't hurt her, did you?'

'Now why would I do that?'

'I dunno. You shot Martin.'

'He killed my brother.'

'You killed Grant.'

'An accident,' he said. 'Like I told your dad. Many times. Old women and children aren't my style.' He cocked his head.

'Look,' she said. 'We weren't going to do anything to him.' She angled her chin towards Jordan.

Savage didn't say anything. She could feel the thump on the seat as his hand bounced up and down. With a gun in it. Not a good idea but she was hardly in a position to complain.

'I wasn't going to touch him.' She was looking at the road but she could feel his staring eyes on her.

'You said 'we'. Then you said 'I'.'

'Me and Martin didn't want anything to do with it. It was Dad,' she said. 'Dad wanted him dead. Fuck, if we'd wanted him dead, he'd be dead.'

'Like Phil?' Savage said. 'Like Fraser?'

'Dad's a psycho,' she said. 'The whole thing was his idea.'

Okay, that wasn't entirely true. But she didn't care that she was sinking her father deeper into the shit. It was his fucking fault, landing Jordan on them like that. Dad was already buried up to his neck in it. Maybe further. Nothing she did now would make it any worse. So she might as well do what she could to make the situation better for herself.

She was on her own now. On her own. Yeah. She heaved again, her stomach clenching, bile in her throat, that image of Martin's empty eyesocket flashing in front of her.

'Watch the road,' Savage said, and she realised she was veering into the wrong lane. She straightened up. Her eyes watered but she hadn't thrown up. Savage continued: 'You didn't want anything to do with it?'

She swallowed again. Better. For the moment, at least. She shook her head. 'All Dad's idea.'

'Interesting. So you strangled Fraser against your will? You cut him up?'

'She's lying, Dad!' Jordan said.

'Like fuck I am.' She looked at the little prick. His eyes were red like his dad's, puffy, cheeks smudged with dirt. Looked like a little boy who'd been out playing late with his friends and needed to get home to bed.

'She was going to kill me. Her and her boyfriend were going to kill me. They were going to drive off somewhere quiet with me in the back with the bodies and then they were going to cut me up and cut my head off and wrap me up like rubbish and put me in a hole in the garden or in the sea.'

'Lying little fucking prick.' She clenched her teeth. 'He's fucking making it up.'

'Don't swear in front of him,' Savage said.

'It's true,' Jordan said. 'She was going to kill me. She's a fucking bitch. And so was her poofy boyfriend.'

She gripped the wheel hard.

Jordan must have noticed. He said, 'Her *dead*, poofy boy-friend.'

The pleasure she'd get from hitting the little shit was almost worth the risk. She was going to die anyway.

Fuck it.

She backhanded Jordan across the mouth.

He yelled.

Savage said, 'Hey, what the fuck, what the *fuck*, did you do that for?'

Jordan was still yelling. Blood oozed from his bottom lip. It was swelling already. His teeth were stained red.

She said, 'I should have listened to my dad and killed the little cocksucker.'

Savage touched her neck with the gun. Pressed it into the skin under her chin. His mouth hung open like he was about to say something. But he didn't.

'Go on,' she said, pressing her foot on the accelerator. 'Do it.' Let the murdering bastard shoot her now. See if he dared.

What she didn't expect was Jordan to punch her in the mouth. She was still in shock when he punched her a second time.

His little kid fist had sharp knuckles. Her lip stung like a bastard.

'Stop it,' Savage said, grabbing Jordan's arm, in so doing moving the gun away from her neck. 'We don't want an accident. Not while she's driving.'

Jordan said, 'It hurt.'

'Good.' Effie sucked her lower lip. The skin was broken on the inside. Tasted raw. Didn't seem to be bleeding though. 'Why are you lying to your dad?'

'Why are *you* lying to him?'

'You know I never intended to kill you. I was trying to keep you alive. Why make up all that crap?'

'I'm not making it up.'

Savage was going to believe his son, whatever she said. She was dead. Or as good as. But she had to stay alive, somehow. She couldn't kill Savage if she was dead. And she had to kill him. He'd killed Grant, he'd killed Martin, and God alone knew what the crazy fuckwit had done to her bastard dad. She'd been wondering about that for some time. Maybe she should ask.

PARK WOKE UP with a start. Legacy of prison. He always woke up with a start. But he didn't usually wake up on the floor, bollock naked, with a pain in his ribcage that hurt like misery when he breathed. He tried to sit up. His ribcage told him not to. But he persevered. He had to get out of here before the police arrived. He'd delayed them, but sooner or later they'd come looking for their missing pals.

And he had to tell Effie and Martin not to come here as they'd planned. It wasn't safe any longer.

Yeah, time to go. Check on Liz first. Get some clothes on. Liz.

Fuck, was that why he was alive? Savage had found Liz, done something to her, something he wanted Park to see?

Had he taken the sword and . . . ?

No, the sword was lying right there next to him. Could have rolled on top of it, given himself a nasty cut.

Maybe Savage had shot her.

'Liz,' Park shouted. 'Liz?'

Something rattled as he pushed himself up. Then he realised why Savage hadn't killed him. The fucker had decided it'd be much more fun to leave him chained to the fucking bed.

This required some thought.

The closet chain was indestructible. No point trying to chew through it, or pull it apart, or cut it in two with the sword. Couldn't move the bed cause he'd screwed the legs to the floor with fucking L-brackets.

So there was no way he could get to Liz to find out if she was okay.

But Savage didn't know about Liz. He couldn't know about her.

Park looked at his watch. Effie and Martin should have been here by now. He just had to hope they'd arrive before the cops.

Sure. They would. Unless . . .

Oh, fuck.

Savage might have stopped them. Called them, let them know he'd got free, that the police were on their way. That's why the fucker had left him alive. That's why he'd left the sword. Because if Effie wasn't coming, there was only one way Park could escape.

Park couldn't do that. Never mind the pain, he'd pass out from the sight of his blood. He'd just have to sit here and wait.

Sit and wait. Get caught. Go back to prison. And stay there forever, no chance of parole, yet again. He'd killed a couple of cops. He was well fucked.

Meanwhile Savage would remain alive. And free.

That wasn't right. There had to be a way out.

But Park couldn't see it just now. He tried to figure out how Savage's mind was working. He was feverish and insane and no doubt simmering with rage, but chances were he'd gone looking for his kid. Left for Fraser's house. Maybe found Effie and Martin there. Park had faith in them. Savage had only got the better of him because of his blood phobia. And Savage was weak and . . .

The gun. Savage had taken it. No matter how weak he was, he could muster the strength to pull the trigger. He'd managed a half-decent strike with the sword, for fuck's sake. So if he'd found Effie, Park didn't fancy her chances. Fuck, yeah, she could look after herself and had Martin for backup but they'd be hard pushed to beat a crazy man with a gun and a good reason to use it.

Park looked at his watch again. Yeah, if they were coming, they'd surely have been here by now.

'Liz,' he shouted. 'Liz! Please, I need you. Liz!'

No answer. Of course.

He picked up the sword. When he sliced the air with it, his ribs felt like they'd been kicked all over again. Fuck that. He drove the blade deep into the floor. It was sharp. But was it sharp enough? He figured he'd only have one blow. One chance. He had to get it right. He wriggled the blade out.

Okay. Okay, okay, okay. He'd do it. He had to.

Effie needed him, if she wasn't dead already. And he had to believe she was still alive. And if she was, then he was going to be there for her.

Liz needed him even more.

He couldn't afford to be selfish.

Had to make sure he didn't see the arm, the blood spurting, the *nnnngah* blood on the floor or anywhere on the rest of his body. Essential if he was going to do this and get away with it. Didn't trust himself not to look at the damage.

He took off his watch, placed it on the floor. Then dragged Savage's discarded blanket over to him. It stank like a public toilet. He made a nick in it with the sword, then ripped it down a couple of feet. Tore that strip from the rest of the blanket. Did the same with a second strip. Looped it twice around his left arm, a couple of inches above his watch line. If he cut his hand off, he'd lose the tattoo. Fuck, who wanted to be decorated with a picture of barbed wire, anyway? Seemed like a good idea at the time. Different, you know. Everybody else with the barbed wire round their bicep, and Park with his round his wrist. Anyway, no loss. He tied the other strip over his eyes. An effective enough blindfold. Fumbled around for the ends of the strip wrapped round his wrist. Pulled them tight, stuck them in his mouth. Tasted something stale and sour. Started to salivate like he'd sucked a lemon. Clamped his jaws tight, felt the muscles in his cheeks dancing a frenzied jig.

He straightened his arm. The material round his wrist tightened. Squeezed his hand into a fist.

Groped for the sword. Grabbed the handle. Held the blade over his wrist. Lowered it so the metal touched his skin.

Lined up. Ready.

Didn't want to do this. He so didn't want to do this. But it happened all the time, every day. Some countries, you stole something, you got your hand cut off. He'd stolen plenty. He just had to pretend he was foreign. No big deal.

At least it was his left hand he was going to lose. Couldn't punch worth a damn with his left. He'd hardly notice it was gone.

In fact, he'd be glad to be rid of it. Fucking thing just got in the way.

Yeah. Okay.

O-fucking-kay.

Ready?

Fucking yeah.

He lifted the sword.

'YOU'RE SICK,' TOMMY said. 'That camera . . .' A minute, then he continued: 'What you did to Fraser.' No reaction. 'Your . . . bits hanging out.' Again, nothing. Fucking crazy bitch. He'd provoke a reaction. 'Your father was revelling in it.'

She looked at him. 'It was for you. Not for Dad.'

'His eyes were glued to the set. Ogling his own daughter like the sick animal he is.'

She smiled. 'That's impossible.'

'Oh, yeah? Were you there in the room with us?' Then he realised what she meant. Fuck the bastard and his fear of blood. 'You wanted to see what I've done with that piece of shit?' Tommy said. 'Okay. Let's take a drive back to Mrs Yardie's.'

Park had wanted Tommy to see his family murdered. No reason why Tommy shouldn't do the same. The cottage was only about half a mile away. Okay, there might be police there by now. More police. Ones that were still alive. But Park seemed confident the ones he'd shot wouldn't be missed for a while. Only one way to find out. If they saw any sign of a police presence, they could just head on by and leave them to get on with their work.

Jordan dabbed at his swollen lip with the back of his hand. Licked blood off it. 'Dad,' he said. 'I want to go home.'

Tommy ruffled his son's hair with his thumb. 'Me too,' he said. 'And we will. Just as soon as we're done with Effie and her dad.'

WHEN THEY ARRIVED, Effie nestled behind Old Mrs Yardie's car and turned off the engine. Savage stared straight ahead. She thought about making a grab for the gun, but despite the direction of his gaze, the gun was trained on her.

'You stay here,' Savage said, head still fixed to the front.

She thought he was talking to her. She was mistaken.

He looked at Jordan. 'Me and her will go inside.'

'I don't want to stay here.'

'You'll be safe.'

'Dad.'

'Please, Jordan.'

'I don't want to. There's dead bodies in here.'

'There're dead bodies everywhere, son.'

'But, dad . . .'

'You're staying right here. Do as you're told.'

'I'm scared.'

'Don't be silly.'

'I'm not being silly.'

'Look, they're corpses. They can't harm you. It's the people who are alive you should be scared of.'

Effie wondered why Savage didn't want the kid in the house.

'Jordan,' Savage said. 'I need your help.' Here was her answer. 'I need you to blast the horn if you see a police car coming this way. I can't do this without you.'

'Why not?'

'I don't have time to explain. You have to stay here.'

'And beep the horn?'

'Yeah. If you see a police car.'

'Won't it be too late by then?'

'Maybe,' Savage said. 'But at least I can finish up what I'm doing.'

'What're you going to do?'

Savage looked at Effie and she shivered. 'Not something you need to worry about,' he said to Jordan.

She'd stopped shaking for a while, hadn't noticed at the time, but noticed once it started again. The look on Savage's face was freaky as hell. The bastard was no doubt planning all sorts of evil shit. Not going to be content with shooting Martin. She still didn't believe he was dead. Somehow. Despite seeing the evidence. Still thought he'd get up and look at her and say her name.

Oh, God. There was that image again, the hole in his face, hitting her like a blow to the head. So much so that she flinched.

'What's wrong with you?' Savage said.

'Let's get this done,' she said.

He nodded.

'Dad,' Jordan said. 'I don't want to stay in the van.'

'Okay,' Savage said. 'We'll all go. If the police come, they come.'

TWO COPS. SHOT dead. One missing his shoes.

'You do this?' she said.

A pause. 'Your dad,' Savage replied.

Had they been alone, she was sure he'd have wanted to impress her, scare her, make her think he was ruthless and manly. But with the kid, he didn't want to seem like a bad daddy. He was a drunk trying to behave sober and fooling nobody.

Jordan put his hand over his mouth. He'd seen the bodies of his uncle and brother but they'd been all wrapped up. Now he was faced with the difference between butchering your own meat and buying it all neatly packaged in the supermarket. Far too much for an eleven-year-old.

Effie said, 'Where now?'

'Upstairs,' Savage said.

'Is he alive?' she asked.

'You might not believe me,' Savage said, 'but I really have no idea.'

FOR A FRACTION of a second Park thought it wasn't so bad. Then it hit him. And it *was* bad. Couldn't have predicted just how bad. He'd broken bones before but he'd never felt anything like this.

Deep pain sliced through his arm. Not just his wrist, but the entire arm, from fingertip to shoulderblade. He yelled, let go of the sword. It didn't fall to the ground. Either it was stuck in the ground, or still stuck in his arm. *Jesus. Jesus fuck.*

He breathed in. Yelled again. Legs kicked out. Toes curled. The fingers of his good hand squeezed into a fist, nails digging into his palm. Tendons tight enough to snap. Eyes watering. Moist breath against the cloth over his head. Gasps. Heartbeat going crazy. *Ba-boom ba-boom ba-boom.*

Every nerve in his body wrapped in a tiny parcel of boiling tar.

Had to tighten the ligature round his arm, stop the bleeding. But he'd dropped the ends when he'd opened his mouth to scream. Had to fumble around, try to find them. Couldn't concentrate on that now.

The pain. *Jesus fucking Christ.* Had to control that first. How he fucking wished he could take this back. He'd gladly sit here, wait for the police to arrive. Nothing wrong with that. The fuck had he been thinking?

Focus. Had he done the job? After all this, it'd be a shitter if he'd fucked it up. Needed to have cut all the way through. Couldn't tell, though, without being prepared to pull the sword out. Couldn't face that. Not yet. Just had to sit here. For a minute. Not pass out. Stay awake. *For Christ's sake, stay awake.*

Pulsing. The pain was pulsing now. Waves swelling. Floating on it. Getting carried along by it. Wondering if he was in shock. Probably.

Stuttered breaths. Sobbing. Eyes wet. Drooling. Something hot and warm trickling down his wrist, licking his fingers.

He could feel that, the warmth on his fingers. His fingers shouldn't be able to feel anything. Did that mean the blade hadn't gone clean through? Shit. Or was he imagining it? Tried to move his index finger. Thought he'd succeeded. But maybe he had a phantom hand. Always hearing about people getting limbs lopped off and their brains not accepting the loss. Maybe his brain wasn't accepting that his fingers were gone. Fuck. He needed to whip the blindfold off and see exactly what he'd done to himself. But of course he couldn't do that.

Shaking now like he had a vibrator up his arse. Moaning like a prison whore. Crying, for fuck's sake.

Okay. He could try to move his arm. If he'd cut clean through, he ought to be able to pull it away. Of course, if he hadn't, this was going to hurt much worse than it did already.

'Fuuuuuuuuuck.'

Nothing.

His brain was blocking any signals to his arm that might cause more pain. Couldn't fucking move.

Fuck his brain. He'd kick the shit out of it, bastard thing.

Well, his brain wasn't making any decisions for his other arm. Luckily, it was still thinking for itself. He reached for the sword handle. Palm cold and sticky with sweat. Pull the blade out now. Fucking had to. Then slip the cuff off and he'd be free.

Treat this like tearing off a plaster. Do it quickly. Short and sharp.

Yeah.

Held his breath and – *motherfuckingcuntbastard* – breathed out again.

No chance, then. Maybe he'd try it the other way. He lifted the handle slightly, testing the blade. Didn't feel any new pain, felt no resistance, no give. Moved it again, a little further, and liquid fire spewed through his veins.

He yelled until he was out of breath. Filled his lungs. Yelled again. Yelled until his throat hurt. Must be delirious cause he heard Effie say, 'Dad.' Yeah. He was losing it. Going to pass out. The blade was stuck in his wrist. He wasn't going to be able to shift it. So he was a dead man. Might as well just close his eyes, let the greyness take him.

Heard her voice again, closer: 'Dad. Dad?'

Couldn't help himself. He said, 'Effie?' Crazy, talking to her. But then he'd talked to her when he was in prison. At night. In his cell when he couldn't sleep. Sure, he'd talked to her. He'd talked to Grant, too. Some of the cons prayed to God. But Park was a family man. And he was head of the family. God didn't get a look in.

Savage's voice: 'Cover your eyes, Jordan.'

Park heard footsteps moving towards him. Urgent: 'Dad?'

'Effie?' Took a lot of effort to say her name. Wanted to let go. Just say fuck it to everything. Shut down.

'We have to get him to a doctor,' she said.

'Oh,' Savage said. 'Now that's funny.'

'He'll lose his hand if we –'

'And Phil and Fraser? What about their fucking hands?'

A pause.

'Jordan?'

'I'm going to throw up, Dad.'

'Well, I did tell you to stay in the van.'

JORDAN LEFT THE bedroom. Best thing for him, Tommy thought. Pretty horrible sight for a kid to see. Naked bloke, hacking his wrist off with a sword. Not much better out on the landing, mind you, where Jordan would be staring down at a pair of bullet-riddled cops. At least they had their clothes on and weren't spurting blood from any of their bodyparts.

There was no end to Park's sadism.

Tommy looked at the sorry fuck lying there, his daughter prodding around the cut, testing the blade, wondering no doubt if it was safe to pull it out. Wondering, too, no doubt, if she could attack Tommy with it. In her sweet little fucked-up head, going: *stop the bleeding or kill Savage?* Well, that was her dilemma and only she knew the answer. Tommy had his gun ready. He was prepared. If she attacked him, it'd be the last thing she ever did.

His finger was itching.

'You watching, Grant, you little prick?' Tommy asked, fire burning in his gut.

EFFIE HAD SEEN enough blood tonight to be able to examine the wound without feeling queasy. She spoke to her dad. 'Blade's gone about halfway through. Looks like the bone stopped it.'

He moaned at her.

'By the way, I'm fucking mad at you,' she said.

'For?'

'You know. Sending Jordan to Fraser's.'

'I didn't.'

'Don't start.' She grabbed the ends of the piece of cloth he'd wrapped round his wrist. 'I'm going to tie you off.' They were warm and wet. She didn't want to know where they'd been. She pulled them tight, ignoring his cry. Tied a knot. Ought to be enough to stop the bleeding. For now.

She didn't want to tell him what had happened to Martin. He could find out later. When he was well. But for that to happen, she first had to kill Savage.

TOMMY WONDERED WHAT she was waiting for. She'd applied the tourniquet. All she had to do was –

ALL IN ONE motion. The blade came out more easily then she'd thought. Her dad roared as she swung the sword towards Savage, rotating from the hips, putting everything into it.
  Something massive kicked her in the chest.

TOMMY EXPECTED THE shot to knock her back a couple of feet but she collapsed where she stood. Lay on the floor on her back next to her dad, a blossoming red stain above her left breast.

PARK GUESSED THE worst. 'Effie?'

'HOW DOES IT feel?' Tommy asked him.

PARK RIPPED THE blindfold off his head. Determined not to look anywhere else. Blinked at Savage. Fucker had a gun. Thought he was in charge.

Fuck him. He wasn't even wearing his own clothes.

Park swung at him with his good hand.

Missed by a couple of feet.

If only he'd managed to hack through the bone, he'd have been rid of the cuff, free to get in close and beat Savage to a pulp.

One thing he could do, though.

He scrambled around on the floor, trying to locate the sword. Effie had pulled it out. It had to be close. Had to be. If only he could take a glance. Enough to locate it. No more. If he didn't focus on the blood, he'd be okay.

He had no fucking choice. Take the chance or die. No fucking contest.

Okay.

He looked.

Effie lay still. Hair fallen over her face.

He looked down. Her hands lay palm up, fingers loosely curled around the sword.

He could get it. Awkward, but he could do it.

Oh, you stupid fucking bastard.

Couldn't help it.

He'd looked at his arm. Couldn't tear his eyes away. What a fucking mess.

Oh, shit.

He'd done it now.

IF TOMMY HAD known about Park's blood problem earlier, things would have been so much easier. Could have peeled the plaster off his infected arm, given the wound a squeeze, shown it to Park when he wasn't expecting it.

Knock yourself out, you cunt.

Maybe he should have worked it out from the way Park had

avoided looking at the laptop. But, really, who'd have guessed? Maybe if he'd spoken more to Grant the boy would have let slip. But, no, Tommy wasn't going to beat himself up about this. There wasn't a fucking thing he could have done to stop Phil and Fraser from being killed. Not a fucking thing.

He buckled at the stabbing pain in his belly. Shit, he'd thrown up something weird already. Wasn't going to happen again, was it? That wasn't real. He'd imagined it.

It wasn't fucking possible.

Then again, it wasn't fucking possible that Grant was dead, that Phil and Fraser were dead, that Tommy'd shot two people, that he was about to kill someone else.

He had to get on with it, stop wasting time. Stop fucking thinking about it and just do it.

'Dad?' Jordan was in the doorway. God knew how long he'd been there. Probably heard the shot. He was looking at the bodies. 'Is she dead?'

Tommy nodded. 'She can't hurt you now.'

'What about him?' He nodded at Park. 'Is he dead?'

'Not yet.'

'He's a mentalist.'

'He is. Complete psycho.'

'I want to go.'

'After I've killed him,' Tommy said. Only question was how. He ought to hack all his limbs off, leave him to bleed to death. That was all the subhuman piece of trash deserved. Tommy couldn't have done that to Effie, but Park was different. Tommy was tired, though. Really fucking tired. And he had hardly any strength left. The last couple of weeks were catching up with him.

And his stomach. Fuck, his stomach.

He swallowed hard and the pain eased, but he knew it'd be back soon enough. He just needed a moment or two to decide how to dispose of Park.

'Dad?' Jordan said. 'Do you think we're like them?'

'How can you say that?' Tommy said. 'They're sick.'

'I'LL COME WITH you,' Jordan said.

Tommy had said he'd go down to the van and back, he'd only be gone a minute. Jordan didn't want him to, even though Tommy pointed out that there was no danger in the bedroom now that Effie was dead and Park was chained up and unconscious. Then Tommy suggested that maybe Jordan could run down to the van and get the petrol, but Jordan wasn't any keener on that idea. The thought of the bodies in the back spooked him. Which was fair enough. Once upon a time Tommy would have felt the same way.

So in the end, they went together. Downstairs, hand in hand, past the dead policemen, and outside, where the chill in the air hit Tommy in the temples, soothed his tired eyes. He blinked away tears. He hadn't had the opportunity to enjoy any fresh air over the last couple of weeks. Wished he could lie down on the grass with Jordan, gaze at the stars, fill his lungs, sleep. Didn't ask for more than that.

But he couldn't. Not just yet.

'You okay?' he asked Jordan.

Jordan nodded.

When he thought about what these savages had put Jordan through, Tommy's stomach barrelled up into his throat and threatened to choke him. Yet another reason why he had to finish this.

They walked past Park's car towards the van, purple shadows bruising its pale body. No traffic noise from the road. No sound of police sirens. Peaceful.

Tommy opened the back door, climbed inside. There wasn't much space to get a foothold. Tommy slid on something and almost fell over. The floor was slick. Traced the wetness to Martin Milne. Seemed he was leaking. Tommy patted him down. He'd seen Milne smoking on the video. Sure enough, he had a lighter in his trouser pocket. Tommy stuck it in his own. Then located the petrol can. Illuminated, next to it, were three carrier bags. Tommy looked at the headless shrouds. Back at the carrier bags.

Three?

Had to check inside.

Two heads and a bag of hands. Tommy didn't need the hands.

BACK IN THE bedroom, Tommy screwed the cap off the petrol can. Went over to the bed, sloshed petrol all over the sheets. Moved round to Park. Doused him good and proper too.

Park spluttered, spat. Then realised where he was and what had happened to him. Maybe he even realised what was about to happen to him.

Tommy saved the last of the can for Effie.

'You'll be burning in Hell soon,' he said to Park. 'Might as well get you used to it.'

PARK STANK OF petrol. The fumes were making him lightheaded. Or maybe it was the blood loss. Both, probably. Could feel the weight of the chain on his arm. He was still attached to the bed. No way out.

Had to maintain eye contact with Savage. Couldn't risk looking away. Didn't know where his eyes would take him.

Stinging. The fumes making them water. Having trouble seeing.

Then again, did he want to see this?

The madman was taking something out of a carrier bag. Something hairy. Something . . . oh, fuck.

Park looked away, tried to stay conscious. Fought against his body shutting down, his mind deciding it didn't want to see this.

TOMMY SAID, 'YOU want to take Fraser out of your bag now, Jordan?'

'No.'

'Go on. He wants to watch.'

'He's dead, Dad.'

'Look, Phil's watching.' He was, too. His eyes were wide open.

'Dad?'

'Son?'

'Fraser doesn't want to watch.'

Tommy wasn't sure he believed that. 'Pass him to me,' he said.

Jordan looked at the bag by his feet.

'Come on. He won't bite.'

Jordan bent down slowly, picked it up. Scurried over to Tommy, dropped it at his feet, scurried away again.

'Thank you,' Tommy said. 'Wasn't so bad now, was it?' His arm felt numb. He didn't know if it could take the weight. He flexed his fingers. They seemed okay. Reached into the bag, grabbed a fistful of Fraser's hair. Eased him out. Fraser in one hand, Phil in the other. 'So,' he said to Fraser. 'Your brother says you don't want to watch. Is that true?'

Fraser shook his head.

'You do want to watch?'

Fraser nodded. Phil nodded too.

'See?' Tommy said to Jordan. Then bent towards the heads. 'What's that you say?' Paused. 'You want me to put on a video?' He straightened up. 'I know the very one.'

He turned to Park, whose head was lowered. Might have passed out again, for all Tommy knew.

'Just give me a second,' Tommy said to Fraser, placed him on the floor.

Tommy knelt in front of Park, lifted his head up. Park had his eyes shut, screwed tight, desperate not to see any of this. Tommy placed Phil in front of him, so their noses were inches apart.

'Hey,' Tommy said. 'Open your eyes.'

Park blew his cheeks out, kept his eyes shut.

'Come on, you fuck,' Tommy said. 'Phil wants to say something to you.'

Park's eyes stayed shut.

'If you don't open your eyes,' Tommy said, 'then Phil's going to have to give you a kiss.'

Park shuddered.

'And I don't think you'll like that.'

Park still wouldn't open his eyes.

'I don't think Phil would like that either, but you're not giving him much choice.'

Park said, 'Fuck you.'

'Fair enough,' Tommy said. 'Here we go then.'

'Cunt.' Park's eyes sprang open. He saw Phil and started to gag.

Tommy pushed Phil's face into Park's, angling it so their lips would touch.

Park yelled. Tried to get his face out of the way.

Tommy copied his movements so Phil's face remained right in front of Park's.

Park moaned, his eyes fluttered, his head lolled to the side.

Looked like a genuine faint, but Tommy slapped him hard on the cheek just to make sure.

No reaction.

Tommy picked Fraser up, crossed the room, set down Phil and Fraser next to the laptop and beckoned Jordan over.

'Right,' Tommy said to his family. 'It's about time we got this done, boys.'

'No,' Grant said.

'You shut your mouth,' Tommy said. 'You're fucking dead.'

AS MUCH AS Effie knew she had to lie here quietly, not moving a muscle, breathing as shallowly as possible, awaiting an opportunity, something inside her wanted to cry out that she was still alive. And she didn't quite trust herself not to.

Taste of petrol on her lips. Burning pain in her chest. Felt like her whole left side was swollen. Had to keep her eyes shut, her mouth shut. Couldn't cry out. Mustn't cry out. Breathed through her nose. Couldn't keep it up much longer, though. The fumes were getting to her.

She'd been awake long enough to hear Savage taunt Dad. Didn't dare open her eyes to see what he was doing. But she'd heard enough to know that he'd removed the heads from the van and was talking to them. Loony fucking tunes. The crazy fucking psycho had snapped.

Effie tightened her grip on the handle of the sword. She could do this. Dad was counting on her. Mum was counting on her.

'LOOK AWAY,' TOMMY said to Jordan.

Jordan looked away.

Tommy dug out Milne's lighter, moved over to the prostrate figures on the floor. Wondered if they'd go up with a whoosh. He'd light Park first.

As he was bending over, he noticed a movement out of the corner of his eye. Then, a punch in his gut.

A white-hot pain, all the way from his stomach to his back.

Effie was sitting up, panting, arm outstretched towards him.

He looked down, saw the handle of the *katana*. Most of the blade had disappeared. The fucking thing was inside him.

Steel. In his gut. Maybe he was imagining it. Maybe he'd throw up and the pain would go.

No, a fire raged in his belly like none before. And he couldn't cough this fucker out of him.

He couldn't speak, couldn't breathe. He could hardly think.

Grant was laughing again.

Tommy knew he couldn't let Effie get away. Had to take her out. Properly this time. Save Jordan.

Yeah, that's all he'd wanted to do and he was going to see it through.

He flicked on the lighter and fell on top of Park.

EFFIE ROLLED OUT of the way just in time. The flames moved quickly. Already flicking all over her dad, red and orange tongues, butterfly kissing him. Savage was yelling. The flames had found him too. At least Dad was unconscious.

She struggled to her feet, ran around the burning bodies,

ignoring the pain from her chest wound, thinking only that she had to find water to douse the flames. There was a bathroom downstairs. She'd have to get down there, find something to carry the water in. Fill it. Bring it back.

Savage screamed. Rolled onto his back, limbs jerking. Yellow flames spread across his sweatshirt.

She didn't have time to fetch water.

Blanket. She could wrap him in a blanket. But there was only one blanket and it was already on fire. All the time, the flames were getting bigger. Smoke now. Getting thicker by the second. The quilt on the bed had caught too.

She stepped back from the heat, coughing. Vicious smell of burning fabric, or maybe hair.

It was too late. She knew it was too late. It couldn't be too late.

It had happened so quickly.

Savage's cries made her bones vibrate.

There was nothing she could do. Not for him. Not for her dad.

Had to save Mum.

Effie looked away. The kid was there, couple of feet to the side. Pointing a gun at her. Struggling to hold it steady. Choking. Eyes streaming.

'Don't shoot me,' she said. 'Shoot him.'

The kid looked at her, eyes wide, uncomprehending.

'If you love your dad,' she said again, 'shoot him.'

Through the sound of the fire, Savage shouted. It sounded like he said, 'Grant.'

Jordan looked at her once more, turned the gun towards the flames.

And fired.

Savage carried on screaming.

'Again,' she said. 'Closer.'

Jordan moved towards the heat, free hand over his mouth. Fired again.

His dad stopped screaming.

A real bonfire going on now. The bodies burning, the whole bed ablaze.

'We have to get out of here,' she said. The kid didn't respond. Kept staring at what was left of his dad. Well, fuck the little bastard. She didn't have time to dawdle.

She staggered towards the door. The kid turned, pointing the gun at her, tears cleaning twin paths down his dirty cheeks.

She choked out the words: 'We need to leave.'

'You'll kill me.'

She didn't have time to argue. 'Suit yourself.' She left the room, lurched along the landing towards Mum's room. Grabbed the door handle.

'Hey.' The kid's voice.

She turned.

'You killed my brother,' Jordan said. Smoke puffed out of the doorway behind him. 'And you killed my Dad.'

She said, 'Actually, you killed him.'

'You stuck a sword through him.'

'True. But that didn't kill him.'

His gaze dropped to the floor. 'I had to do it.'

She turned the handle.

'You told me to,' he said. 'He was burning. I had to. Didn't I?'

'Yeah,' she said. She coughed. Spat blood. 'You did the right thing. He was in pain. You put him out of his misery.'

She pushed the door open, peered inside.

Mum was in a chair looking at the wall, something tied round her mouth. Her hands and legs were bound to the chair.

Effie stumbled over to her, said, 'We need to get out of here, Mum,' panting, fumbling at the scarf knotted round the back of her mother's head.

Jordan stood in the doorway. Raised the gun.

'You want us to end up like our dads?' she asked him. She pulled off the scarf. Started on the next one. 'Help me,' she said to Jordan.

As Jordan shuffled towards her, she freed her mother's wrist, started on the other one. 'Untie her ankle,' she said.

He stared at her.

And she knew what he was going to do.

'Come on then, you little bumshite,' she said.

Maybe the chamber was empty.

She saw his finger move, heard the explosion.

EFFIE WAS SITTING outside on the grass, having trouble breathing. She stared at the van, wondering how she was going to make it over there to Martin. She'd rested for a while, but she needed to get moving again soon. Jordan would help.

But she heard the sirens close in and knew it was too late. She raised her hands. Didn't know how long she could keep them there, though. She wondered if an ambulance was coming. Not for her – there was no point – but for Jordan. Smoke inhalation. He was coughing like a sixty-a-day-for-life man.

Behind her, the house burned. Effie hoped Old Mrs Yardie wasn't going to be too upset when she returned from her sister's.

'I'm sorry,' the kid said. He was sitting next to her. He'd put his hands up too.

A cop car nosed into the driveway, briefly lighting up the van as a figure leaned back in the passenger seat.

'What for?' she said.

'Telling Dad you were going to kill me.'

'That's okay,' she said, trying to make out who was in the van. Saw nothing but shadows, though. 'Come closer.'

He edged over till they were touching. He was warm and smelled of smoke.

'I didn't want to be on my own,' she said.

He nodded. 'I know how you feel.'

'Where's your mother?'

'South Africa. Went there with some dick called Russell.'

Effie thought of her own mother. Couldn't come to terms with the fact that her son was a hitman. Got too much for her, and she tried to drown herself. Nearly succeeded. Starved herself of oxygen for just long enough to leave her brain damaged, not long enough to do the job properly.

Effie said, 'Don't you have anybody, Jordan?'

'My nan.'

'I never knew mine.'

'Why not?'

'One died in an accident before I was born. The other died of cancer when I was a baby.'

'That's a shame,' Jordan said. 'I was thinking, maybe you could come visit. Afterwards.'

'I don't think so.' If she survived, it'd be a long time before she got out of prison. Maybe she wouldn't ever get out.

The door of the van opened and Martin shouted to her: 'I have to go. You coming with me or what?'

EFFIE OPENED HER eyes and she was back in Old Mrs Yardie's, on the floor in her mother's room, searing pain in her chest, between her shoulder blades. She slumped onto her side. Jordan stood above her, pointing the gun at her, pulling the trigger, again and again. Nothing happening, each time just a dry click. Buzzing in her ears. Stench of burnt toast in her nose. She could hear the roar of flames. Through the open doorway, she could see smoke billowing along the landing.

She couldn't move. Frozen again, as if those fat men were sitting on her limbs. The feeling would pass. It always did.

Jordan tossed the gun onto the floor. It slid across the floorboards, rattled to a stop against the back leg of Mum's chair.

Slowly, Mum reached down, untied the scarf round her ankle. Sighed. Picked the knot on the other one. Then eased herself out of her chair. Got to her feet.

Effie tried to speak.

Mum was staring at Jordan. 'Is that you, Richie?' she said. She held out her hand. 'Let's go, son.'

He stepped towards her, took her hand.

'Mum?' Effie managed to say.

Her mum looked down at her. 'Too much blood,' she said. 'I know,' Effie said. 'Go.'

Mum bent down, touched Effie's hair.

'Get out of here,' Effie said. 'Hurry.'

Nobody moved.

Effie closed her eyes again, a chill breeze caressing her face. Lights from police cars shone through her eyelids. 'I can't visit you, Jordan.'

'Well,' Jordan said. 'Maybe your Mum could.'

'Yeah,' Effie said. 'I think she'd like that. Wouldn't you, Mum?'